June 12, 2012

Scent of Double Deception

Thank you so much, Mr. Ethel — you're a wonderful delight to meet.

Jeannie Faulkner Barber

About the Authors:
Jeannie Faulkner Barber was born and raised in Marshall, Texas. Writing has been one of two passions in her life, the other being drag racing: she drives her own race car. She met her husband Monte at the track. She is an active member of the East Texas Writers Association. She currently lives in Kilgore, Texas with Monte. They have three sons and nine grandchildren.

Ann Alan attended college in Oklahoma before moving to Texas. She balances her work at a financial institution with her writing. She has two grown children and several grandchildren, and lives with her husband and dog.

Scent of Double Deception

**Jeannie Faulkner Barber
and
Ann Alan**

Desert Coyote Productions
Scotts Valley, California

Text other than quoted material © 2011 Jeannie Faulkner Barber
and Ann Alan.
Cover design © 2011 Stacey Martinez.
All rights reserved.

No part of this publication may be reproduced, stored in a retrieval system, or transmitted in any form or by any means, electronic, mechanical, photocopying, recording, or otherwise without the express written consent of the author.

Library of Congress Control Number: 2011938063

EAN-13: 978-1-463-70588-6
ISBN-10: 1-463-70588-3

Typeset in 11pt Book Antiqua
Printed in the U.S.A.
First edition 2011

For Natasha and Olivia—who carried us through an escapade of obscurity and mystery and inspired every written word.

Viva la France!

Acknowledgments

To our husbands…for your constant support and unconditional love.

Contents

ONE – THE GAME	1
TWO – HEIR APPARENT	13
THREE – RUSSELL'S APOLOGY	17
FOUR – AN EVIL PLAN UNVEILED	26
FIVE – THE INTRUDER	39
SIX – THE SEDUCTION	47
SEVEN – SABOTAGE DETECTED	59
EIGHT – UNWANTED ARRIVAL	66
NINE – AN UNEXPECTED ENCOUNTER	71
TEN – CLAIR'S BLUNDER	78
ELEVEN – UNDERCOVER BODYGUARD	87
TWELVE – THE CON	96
THIRTEEN – THE BLACK BOX	107
FOURTEEN – COMPROMISE REACHED	119

FIFTEEN – A MYSTERIOUS BOTTLE	125
SIXTEEN – A SUCCESSFUL INVITATION	129
SEVENTEEN – THE BLIND DATE	139
EIGHTEEN – A SECOND BOTTLE	143
NINETEEN – AN ENCHANTED DAY	149
TWENTY – ATTIC SECRETS	156
TWENTY-ONE – THE GREEN HORSE SALOON	161
TWENTY-TWO - DOUBLE DATES	165
TWENTY-THREE – A CLOSET RENDEZVOUS	170
TWENTY-FOUR – THE LONG GOOD-BYE	177
TWENTY-FIVE – VOICE OF FRUSTRATION	182
TWENTY-SIX – WEDDING DAY	188
TWENTY-SEVEN – THE DISCOVERY	194
TWENTY-EIGHT – A SILVER DAGGER	199
TWENTY-NINE – THE MOTIVE	205
THIRTY – HONORED ALLEGIANCE	210

THIRTY-ONE - REFLECTION	213
THIRTY-TWO – SEATTLE SOIREE	217
THIRTY-THREE – SECRETS REVEALED	223
THIRTY-FOUR – THE LOST ROOM	229
THIRTY-FIVE – A FAMILY DISCOVERY	232
THIRTY-SIX – THE CANINE PROPHECY	236
THIRTY-SEVEN – KELLEY'S DISBELIEF	239
THIRTY-EIGHT – A HIDDEN DOOR	242
THIRTY-NINE – THE JOURNAL	246
FORTY – THE OLD TRUNK	250
FORTY-ONE – THE NEXT ADVENTURE	255

Scent of Double Deception

One
The Game

Christmas Eve

The sleek, black limousine stopped in the circular entrance of Adams Rib Restaurant and Nightclub.

Kelley Malone noticed a tall, weather-tanned cowboy in black jeans and leather vest leaning against a white Grecian column. She nudged her colleague, Clair Matthews. "Looks like the perfect birthday present, if you ask me. Hope he's not waiting for someone."

"I'm not sure about this idea, Kel. Maybe forty is too old to play these little games. Anyway, he's gone back inside."

"Hey, you're the one who taught *me*, and if you mention your age one more time, I'll leave you here on the curb. I like the look of him, and there's probably more than enough for both of us inside. Let's go." She motioned the driver to open the door. The folds of her silky, red dress parted to reveal a sexy, bare leg. "Thanks, Russ. You will hang around to watch the fireworks, right? Never know when we'll need a quick escape."

"I'd never leave you two alone. It's a full moon, the alter egos are out, and your bodyguard awaits." The dapperly dressed chauffeur swept into a full bow, and grinned.

Clair's black sequined dress caught the moon's brightness, and shards of light frolicked in the cool night.

"Damn, Clair, you'll blind 'em into submission. Stunning dress. Ready, girls?" Russell Gibson offered each an arm.

The leather-vested wrangler sat in a corner of the restaurant, tipped his hat in their direction, and smiled.

"Game on, Clair. Happy Birthday," Kelley whispered.

Russell patted the maître d' on the shoulder. "Take care of my girls—I'm gonna see a man about a sandwich."

"Look Clair, we scored the center table, perfect vantage point for this evening's prey." Kelley shifted her attention as a young woman approached.

"Ladies, I'm your waitress, Wendy." She glanced over her shoulder. "The gentleman by the fountain sent this bottle of wine and a note."

Without any hesitation, Clair said, "Tell him no."

Wendy took a step back. Her voice wavered, "Uh, ma'am?"

"You heard me. Tell him we're not interested."

The waitress nodded and retreated to deliver the message.

"Mission accomplished, Clair. Here he comes."

"Ladies, forgive my lack of manners. I'd like to apologize for the bone-headed note. Not my best move. May I join you for dinner?" He placed a hand on the extra chair.

Clair pushed away from the table and stood. "We'll dine alone, thank you. Please leave."

"Wait a minute." Kelley took her cue, adjusted her strapless gown, and smiled at the brawny admirer. "Couldn't we make one tiny exception?"

Scent of Double Deception

Footsteps thundered as a blur burst through the kitchen doors. Russell landed a blow on the cowboy's jaw. The stranger hit the floor with a thud, shattered glass and silverware rained down.

"Russell, stop. What are you doing?" Clair shouted.

Two bouncers pinned Russell against the wall and addressed the fallen man. "Sir, want us to call the police?"

Recovered, he straightened his hat and rubbed a reddened jaw. "Well, before the interruption, I wanted to introduce myself. I'm Joe Paul Farrell. It appears you know this man, ladies. Should I press charges to get rid of him?"

"No, throw him out, he's totally out of line," Clair said.

Kelley pulled out the extra chair and patted the velvet cushion. "Mr. Farrell, please join us."

Russell fought his restrainers. "What?" They drug him toward the door. "Fine—you two are on your own. Who'll protect you now?" His shout carried over the din in the room.

****

"Let me reintroduce myself. Joe Paul Farrell, rancher and veterinarian, at your disposal." He took the seat between the two women and handed each a business card.

The blonde tumbled it in her palm and winked at her friend.

"May I ask your names?" He looked from one to the other. *A punch to the face should at least get me an introduction.*

The dark-haired one snapped open a linen napkin. "Natasha."

He caught a subtle exchange, curious at its meaning, but shrugged it off.

"I'm Olivia. Maybe you should order a steak to go on your chin." She touched the contusion on his cheek.

"I see Russell hasn't lost his touch, you've a doozy of a bruise," Natasha added.

"Nothing a little ice won't cure." He marveled at the night's treasure trove of beauty, two gorgeous women, every man's dream. Yet Olivia aroused him, stirred curiosity, and captivated his mind. He raised a wine glass. "A toast to new friends?"

The stemware clinked together, and their laughter made him relax. "Speaking of friends, are they all so rowdy?"

"Russell is a bit overprotective sometimes and reacts before he thinks," Natasha said.

"You need a protector?"

Olivia put her napkin on the table. "Only from big, bad cowboys. Do you like to dance?"

"Yes ma'am, I do. May I escort y'all into the club?" He motioned to the waitress and pressed a $50 bill in her hand. "Fresh wineglasses and a constant supply of the bubbly, please. We'll be next door."

Maneuvering between them, he started toward a table near the bandstand, visible to the entire room. He pulled out their chairs and made sure to sit next to Olivia.

The words *Steel Wool* flashed in red neon above the band. A shirtless, lead singer wore tight, tattered jeans and a long, purple scarf. Tattoos exploded over large biceps.

Joe Paul wasted no time. "Who'd like to dance first?" His eyes locked on Olivia, she accepted. An arm encircled her waist, and they melted into the crowd.

The glare of reality evaporated. Scars of his past vanished, and warm desire seeped into a once cold heart. Perfume engulfed him as she rested her head against his chest. A seamless beat heightened the primal rhythm. The band announced a break, but he hesitated, reluctant to release the embrace. The crowd cleared, yet they stood rooted in place, their gaze united.

"Hey cowboy, the music is over."

Shaken from the reverie, he took her hand and walked to the table. "Thank you Olivia, you're a great dancer. Do y'all do this often?"

"What do you mean?" The girls exchanged a sideways glance.

A husky voice interrupted, "JP, I haven't seen you in a while. Those mares got you busy on the farm?"

Joe Paul looked up, surprised. "How are you doing, O'Donald?"

"Not as good as you, it appears. So, you plan to share tonight?" The newcomer placed a hand on one chair.

"Ladies, let me introduce this rogue. Shade O'Donald, this is Olivia and Natasha. Would you like to join us?"

"Thanks, I can't. I need to line out my guys for the next set. My cameo singer didn't show tonight—second time this week."

"Cameo singer?" Natasha raised an eyebrow.

"Yeah, I have someone who does a couple of..."

"I know what a cameo singer is, you don't have to explain." She pointed across the table. "You've got the best little songbird right there."

"You sing?" Shade looked at the blonde.

"I can belt a tune or two."

"Well, if you sound as good as you look, I'm in luck. Would you do us the honors?"

"Only if I set it up."

Shade extended a hand toward the platform. "My band is all yours, my lady."

"Kill 'em girl," Natasha said."

She stepped onstage, her back to the patrons, hands at her sides.

The drummer slapped the drumsticks above his head. "One, two, three…"

On four, she whirled around to start a fiery rendition of Reba's newest hit. After the song ended, the crowd whistled and shouted for more.

Joe Paul joined the contagious enthusiasm. "Bravo, bravo."

A finger tapped him on the shoulder. "She's not through, my dear man."

The lights dimmed, and a spotlight haloed the singer's face. A bluesy R&B performance stimulated more applause. She blew a kiss and walked off the stage.

A heavyset man stumbled through the crowd, grabbing her arm. "Hey baby, wanna sing me a little song?"

In an instant, Joe Paul firmly seized the intruder's shoulder. "You need to leave, Mister. *Now*. She's not interested."

The drunken man jerked away. "Stuck up broad, never mind."

"To the rescue once more, Mr. Farrell?" Natasha smiled.

Joe Paul waved off the club bouncer. "I apologize for his rudeness, ladies."

"Thank you—again," Olivia said.

"My pleasure. Tell me, do you sing professionally?"

She raised a glass to her lips. "I might someday. Right now, Natasha and I stay too busy."

"You work together?"

"I need to find the powder room," Natasha interrupted. "Olivia, want to come along?"

Disappointed, he stood as they left. *Damn it, Natasha. Guess I'll have to get more resourceful because I am interested in Olivia.* He ordered a bottle of champagne, looked at his watch, and waited, impatient until he saw her coming toward him. "Sounds like another slow song, shall we?"

"I'd love one more dance."

"One more? You're not gonna leave, are you? It's early, there's so much to talk about. Please stay a little longer."

"Whether we stay or go is *not* your concern, Mr. Farrell. Enjoy the dance while you can, it's almost over," Natasha said.

They slipped into an embrace. His hand pressed against her bare back, she didn't resist. He noticed the sparkle in her blue eyes, and the visual connection ignited a flame in his heart. They whirled across the dance floor, the music soft and magical. In mid-step, her body stiffened. He slowed to follow her gaze.

Wonder who is at Natasha's side? Maybe he'll ask her to dance and buy me more time.

****

Clair focused on Kelley's conquest of the night. The only concern—could her friend walk away? Their conversation in the ladies room left her unsure. *Don't forget its make-believe, Kelley, our game, our rules.* Bright red fingernails tapped the table in rapid succession. *I've enjoyed several dances and a slew of admirers. Maybe the night should end before the cattleman gets any closer.* A slight chill settled over her. *What an odd sensation.* She tried to dismiss the distraction, but the hair on the back of her neck prickled. Someone stood beside her. "Pardon me?"

A baritone voice repeated, "May I have the pleasure of this dance?"

Mesmerized by russet eyes and curly black hair, she took his hand. Steel Wool played 'Every Time You Go Away'. She found herself in his embrace, breasts pressed against a crisp, white shirt. The light musk of cologne, the warmth of his breath, the close and tender way he held her, stirred buried emotions. *Déjà vu?* She tried to speak, ask his name. Words didn't form. Unconnected thoughts tumbled in her head, and too soon, the song ended. Silent, they returned to the table. He seated her, politely tapped a hand to his forehead, and walked away.

"Who is he, Natasha? What's his name? Where did he come from? I didn't see him earlier, and where the hell did he go?" Questions tumbled in rapid succession.

"Sit down, Olivia, I don't know. I have no idea."

Scent of Double Deception

"What? You don't know? You didn't ask? Not like you, girl. I watched you on the dance floor. You went into a virtual trance. What's going on?"

Joe Paul interrupted, "Olivia, let's go dance. Leave her to catch her breath."

Kelley leaned over Clair. "Sure you're okay?"

"Yes, go dance."

The couple disappeared into the crush of dancers.

Clair scanned each dim corner of the club. Distorted images from shadows made her blink. She needed answers. *Have I met him before? It isn't my imagination. Something seemed familiar.*

Once more, the music ended, and Kelley and Joe Paul returned.

"Do you want to leave?" Kelley whispered in her ear.

Joe Paul knelt on one knee. "Natasha, can I get you anything, a wet cloth, a drink of water? You look a little shaken."

"No, I'll be fine." *How ridiculous, I'm not prone to intimidation. Why didn't he say something or at least offer conversation?* Determined to regain her composure, she took a sip of champagne. The cool liquid trickled down her throat. She opened a compact to freshen her lipstick. The small mirror framed the same crisp shirt and handsome face. *He's back.*

A low, husky voice offered an invitation for another dance. Her body trembled as she grasped his outstretched palm. Determined to ask his name, she tried to speak. His hand moved up—up between her shoulder blades. Once more, her breasts pressed next to his powerful chest, the sensation explosive. Breathless, she fought to maintain control and searched for a clue. *Our paths crossed before, but where or when?*

The music ended before rational thought returned. No answer.

A hand settled at her waist, and he walked her to the table. "Thank you." Once again, he vanished into the crowd.

"Did you get a name this time? Where is he?" Kelley quizzed.

"Excuse me, I need air," Clair said.

"I'll go, too."

"No. Stay here." Clair elbowed through the dancers, exited the club, and entered the hallway. Ornate mirrors on the walls reflected bountiful Christmas arrangements of holly, mistletoe, ribbons, and silver bells. *Did he slip down the corridor? No mystery man, only the doorman at his post.* "Excuse me, please call my driver."

"Ma'am, I can't, he left. I heard about the little ruckus in the restaurant. Do you need a room at the hotel?"

"No." She rubbed her forehead. *How could I forget Russell's words? He warned we were on our own.*

"Do you need reservations somewhere else?" He stepped to her side.

She shook her head.

"I talked to him earlier, a decent guy, a little vague though. I asked if you and your friend were celebrities. He wouldn't say."

Clair didn't reply, only continued to watch the hallway.

"I say, are y'all movie stars, ma'am? Ma'am?"

"What?"

"I asked if you're a movie star or celebrity."

Scent of Double Deception

"No...will you please get me a taxi and make it quick." She whirled around, headed back inside, and confronted Kelley. "Let's go, Olivia."

****

Joe Paul stood, alarmed at the look on Natasha's face.

"We have to go. I called us a taxi," she snapped.

"I'm sorry, Joe Paul." The blonde smiled. "You made the night magical. Goodbye."

Arm in arm, the women rushed out the door.

I cannot let Olivia walk out of my life. What if we never meet again? Damn, the night can't end like this. She isn't Cinderella. I want to see her, hold her. "Wait, Olivia!" A knot formed in his stomach, and he bulldozed through the mass of couples. "Excuse me, sorry, excuse me, I need to get through."

Helpless, in the hallway, he glimpsed the hem of a red gown disappearing through the foyer. Panicked, he hurried outside in time to see a taxi pull to the curb. The doorman helped the brunette inside while the blonde rifled through her purse, slow to follow. His heart pounded like a jackhammer, an earlier confident air, now only a façade. *I haven't allowed myself this sentiment since...* "Stop!" He grabbed Olivia's arm. "Please, can I call you? I don't even know your last name. Give me a few more minutes, don't leave like this."

She hurried forward, threw her arms around his neck, and brushed soft lips against his cheek. The hug lasted only seconds. She stepped back, took his left hand, and folded the fingers shut. "Goodnight."

Powerless to stop her, the cab whisked the women into the night, and red taillights faded in the noisy traffic.

What is this? He opened one finger at a time to reveal a crumpled piece of paper.

Two
Heir-Apparent

Paris, France

The force of Linford Thurlow's gnarled fist struck like a bolt of lightning against the cherry wood desk. "Get out." He narrowed his eyes at the mousy secretary, Miss Violet Gregory, and waved a free hand toward the door. "I will wait no longer, Highgrove," his voice boomed into the phone. "My brother, Lyle, is dead, and there *is* no more time. Tell her immediately, or I will do it myself." Twisted fingers drummed on his favorite Milano humidor full of expensive cigars.

Linford listened to Edgar Highgrove, his minister of administrative affairs, plead for more time. "Celeste will tell her, Mr. Thurlow. Clair's wedding business takes her to Shreveport, Louisiana, and Celeste plans to join her for the extravagant event. A promise is a promise, and she knows she needs to keep it. She would like to do it herself. We have waited this long, a few more days shouldn't matter, and Spencer is close. Clair is not going anywhere."

"I let my niece dictate the matter all these years, and Lyle always took her side. Well, he is gone, and I will not tolerate it. If you cannot get her to agree, I will board a plane and fly to Seattle myself. Understand?"

"Yes sir. I will tell Celeste."

The business mogul banged the phone into its cradle, lifted the wire-framed spectacles from his long nose, and threw them on the desk. He pushed away from the

Scent of Double Deception

console, stood up, and paced the room. "I should have handled this long ago. Why did I listen to my weasel of a brother? This industry needs new blood, and by God, it is *my* way this time."

He flung the office door shut and stomped past the secretary while she tapped out a rhythmic cadence on the typewriter. She didn't look up. *Years of experience taught her well, the wrinkled old prune. Wonder why she stayed all this time? Well, I will not let her off easy today.* "I am going out, Miss Gregory. Do you think you can manage things while I am gone, or is it too much to ask of a woman your age?"

"Yes, of course, Mr. Thurlow."

The bare office chamber resounded with his loud snort, and he thumped a wooden cane each step on the way out of the building. *No backbone, I cannot stand spineless women. No wonder she never married.*

Not sure of a destination, his gait slowed. Anger, a constant companion since the death of his brother, simmered in his brain. Between the twists and turns of the sidewalk, a strange emotion emerged around the rage and took him by surprise. Linford never got along with his brother, but the death brought loneliness for the first time in his life. "Stupid Lyle. Dead. Now I assume the total burden of this company. I let him talk me out of my plan to install the heir apparent, to groom her for the position she must assume. Too late now, I am the one to fix the mess he left. Incompetent fool." He stopped in front of a familiar cottage. "Ah, my feet led me to a place of solace." Hesitant no longer, he ascended the stairs and lifted the brass knocker.

The stained glass door swung open. "Monsieur Thurlow, what brings you here this time of day?" A shapely manageress stood adorned in a glorious royal blue, satin gown framed by a splendid feather boa. Long, dark wavy hair caressed a generous bosom.

He plucked the hat from his head and bowed in formal acknowledgement. "Ms. LaChance, have you company today? I know it is not my regular appointment."

****

Marguerite LaChance opened the door to find a tall, lanky seventy-eight year old autocrat with stooped shoulders in an oversized, wool greatcoat. His spindly legs and bird-like features resembled an old balding crane. "Tsk, tsk. I am never too busy for *you*, Linford. Please come in." She swept her hand to invite in her most generous paying customer and led him into a small, comfortable parlor off the foyer. "May I take your coat and derby?"

"Thank you," his gravel-like voice melted like warm butter, and he sank into the tan overstuffed sofa. "Looks like you need a cup of my special tea." She rang a small brass bell. He nodded at the offer, and she settled beside him. "What brings you here, Linford? Do you need my attention?" Head tilted, she pushed her hair away to expose abundant cleavage.

"No, no, not today, Marguerite. I need someone to listen, to understand."

The tea arrived, and she poured a cup of the steaming brew. "Of course, cherié, I am a good listener."

His gaze remained on her breasts. "It is my business. My father migrated from England and built the perfumery, his dream. I am older now, and Lyle is gone. I must think about a replacement. The person I have in mind knows nothing about this proposal. She built a life in the States. We wanted to educate her for the position, although Lyle talked me out of it each time I brought it up. Now, I need to put the plan in motion. There is no other choice."

"What is the problem, Linford? You have decided. Fetch this woman, and begin the process. She should be grateful for an opportunity such as this."

"The problem is—I do not even know her. They have sent pictures, of course. I had her followed since childhood, but never laid eyes on her. Foul play is afoot, a mutiny I fear. I am a hard man, difficult to please, as you well know."

She rubbed his shoulders, ran cool fingers through his sparse gray hair, and clucked her tongue. He yielded to the practiced touch. "No worries, cherié. It will work out. After all, you are Linford Thurlow. People jump at your command. We are humble servants of the man who single-handedly dictates business in Paris. No one would dare undermine your decisions. If they do, you will show them no mercy."

The light faded in the cozy parlor, and she waited for him to drift off while her fingers performed their magic.

"It is the right thing to do. Highgrove and Celeste Vandergriff cannot persuade me otherwise," he mumbled, eyes closed. "Clair Matthews will bend to my authority whether by her own volition or by force."

Marguerite smiled wickedly. *Yes, in your own mind you are the most powerful man in France, you old bastard. Sounds like your brother might finally get some revenge.*

Three
Russell's Apology

Christmas dawned cold, and frost blanketed the treacherous sidewalks. Early morning walkers breathed into gloved hands, huddled against the frigid air. Bowed beneath frozen sleet, tree branches glistened to perpetuate the wonderland illusion.

Russell Gibson stood at the window, blind to the icy beauty before him. He shook himself from the daydream. *I must get back into the girls' good graces. My rare lapse in judgment cannot destroy a cherished friendship. The Riley wedding is too big of an event. They will need my help.* Ribbons, tissue paper, and empty boxes covered the bed and half the floor of the hotel room. Satisfied, he stuffed the peace offering into a large, colorful holiday bag and hurried to catch Clair and Kelley before they left for the day.

His fist pounded the door. Down the corridor, doors opened, heads poked out, and guests grumbled at the incessant racket. He stood in a long overcoat, fur-lined cap, arm raised to strike the inflexible barrier until it swung open.

"Russell, what are *you* doing here, and why are you dressed like a Russian spy? Never mind. I don't want to know. We are still mad at you," Kelley said.

"A hearty ho, ho, ho, and Merry Christmas," he said.

"We are not interested in lame presents." Kelley moved to shut the door.

Clair shouted from inside the room. "What, he has gifts? Let him in, after all, it is Christmas."

Kelley stepped back to let him pass.

"So, what's up?"

"You cannot buy our forgiveness, you know," Clair said.

"I only wanted to say I am sorry. Here, Merry Christmas." He shoved the bag into Kelley's hand and turned to leave.

"Wait, don't go. You came to apologize?" Clair's voice rose.

Kelley retied her pink and white striped, satin robe and sat down in the armchair next to the large holiday tree. Tiny, white lights, and garlands of colorful beads, festooned the branches while clusters of small, crystal doves twinkled.

Clair remained on the bed in a red and green plaid, silk robe and waited.

Kelley grabbed a plump berry from the breakfast cart. "Strawberry, Russell?"

He shuffled from one foot to the other. "No thanks."

Clair stood and took the gift. "Sit there, Russell. Now, let's see what is in here." Through the ton of tissue paper and ribbons, she found two identical boxes wrapped in red foil, bright green bows perched on top. Kelley looked at Clair—Clair looked at Russell.

"My token of apology, one stipulation attached." He crossed his arms.

"Continue," Clair said.

"Wear it every time you go out, no exceptions."

"*Wear* it?" Kelley raised an eyebrow.

Both girls tore into the packages. Each produced delicate, gold bangle bracelets. The letter 'M' hung from a short, gold chain with a blue topaz encrusted in the center.

Scent of Double Deception

"Our birthstone, oh Russ, how beautiful," Clair said.

"Not only beautiful, the stone disguises a transmitter inside. After last night, I need to make sure you two stay safe. I don't like the alter egos you invented, its trouble."

They stared at him.

Kelley spoke first, "What happened is our business, Russell. You had no right to interfere."

Clair interjected, "But . . . we understand why. Right, Kelley?"

"We will wear them if you promise to act more professional next time," Kelley said.

Relieved, he said, "Hey, what is under the tree?"

The somber atmosphere disappeared, and the rest of the morning went by in a flutter of gifts and laughter.

He decided to spring the next surprise on his pals. "Time to put these Christmas presents to good use, I have something else in mind. Clair, put on the new, blue cashmere sweater from Kelley."

"What about me?" Kelley poked out her bottom lip.

"I want to see you in those black, European boots Clair gave you." The scramble to the bedroom for the quick change made Russell chuckle. He wondered who would appear first. Clair returned with Kelley right behind. "You look so festive."

"I love this sweater, it compliments my white, leather slacks. Kelley, those boots look great with your red blouse and black pants.

"I know, a perfect fit," Kelley said.

"Girls?" Russell placed both hands on his hips.

They lifted their wrists to expose the new bracelets.

"Good," he said. "Let's go."

Fragile, white snowflakes stuck to the windshield of the Chevy dually on its way to the barn. The heater failed to thaw Joe Paul's ice-cold feet, and he cursed under his breath as the large iron gate appeared. The phone call at 5:30 AM evaporated his erotic dream.

Damn! The urgency in Duffy's voice alarmed him. *The old cowboy delivers many foals on the ranch — this time he needs help. Three weeks is too soon.* He grabbed his black bag and sprinted to the barn to escape the fury of the storm. *Great. Snow and ice. How did I get so lucky?*

A gravelly voice called out, "I'm over here, Doc."

The ranch foreman, Lester McDuff, knelt in the last stall, sleeves rolled up past his elbows, hair disheveled — his look grim. Perspiration yellowed the armpits of his rumpled shirt.

"Looks like you have worked up a real sweat."

Before Duffy could respond, the chestnut thoroughbred let out a horrible whinny, and her little bundle of joy slid onto the warm bed of straw. The foal's awkward position made the delivery difficult. Wet and worn out from the struggle, his coat glistened, ears twitched, and his sides heaved from the effort of the birth.

Duffy wiped beads of moisture from his forehead. "Sorry Joe Paul, I guess Asparagus Tips and I have things going our way now."

"Looks like ya do. Where is ol' Bulldog? Does he know he is a granddaddy yet?"

"No, he hurried back to the big house after I called you this morning. Said he needed to get Isabella. If something happened to her prize mare, and he didn't tell her, there would be hell to pay."

Scent of Double Deception

Bulldog and his daughter burst into the barn, Isabella two strides ahead of her rotund father.

"Oh Tips, is she all right? Is the foal okay? Please, Joe Paul, tell me they are not gonna die."

"Whoa, slow down, darling, I just got here myself in time to see Duffy pronounce Asparagus Tips Mother of the Year."

She smiled, and he knew his big brother act calmed her down. He watched her fall onto the damp hay beside the horse to soothe its brow while Duffy cleaned the foal.

"Thanks so much for coming, Doc. Sorry to bother you on the holidays," Bulldog said.

"Well, Miss Tips, and her fine, new baby, don't care if it is Christmas Day, much less that it's gonna be a *white* one," Joe Paul said.

"You are right. Can you come up to the house? We need to talk about the wedding."

He knew it was not an invitation—but a command.

"Sure, let me look over the new addition, and I will join you." He dropped to his knees and did a routine check. His professional mode of a licensed veterinarian kicked in, all business. "Mother and newborn pass my inspection, satisfied? Wanna ride to the house?" he offered.

Isabella did not hesitate to snuggle over to his side of the truck. "Thanks so much for always being there for me."

"Yeah, well I still say the reason you are marrying this Troy fella is because you cannot have me. After all he is a real doctor."

"You cad, I guess he is the next best thing to a *Joe Paul Farrell*. Sometimes, I see qualities in him like my daddy, too, so who could turn down such a combination?"

The truck stopped in front of the large house. The rolling acres of Silks and Saddles bordered Joe Paul's property. The Riley's and Farrell's had been neighbors a long time. Isabella grew up before his eyes, from a foal to a filly.

Bulldog sat at his desk in the enormous family room amid holiday decorations, a ten-foot pine tree the focal point. A broad smile crossed Joe Paul's face in appreciation of the first glimpse of the magnificent tree. This year proved true to tradition. White, flocked branches held tiny multi-colored lights and ornaments in all shapes and sizes. Little, wooden hand-carved horses set off the theme of the ranch. The place of honor at the top of the tree held a luminous antique star, a memento of Bulldog's beloved wife, gone now twenty-seven years.

Straight to the point, Bulldog wasted no time. "Son, we have a special request. It comes from Troy. He got a page from the hospital, so I am elected."

Joe Paul stood silent.

Bulldog continued, "You mean so much to me and Isabella, and Troy knows you are the son I never had. He wants you to be his best man."

Still silent, Joe Paul lowered his head and took a deep breath. His voice choked as he looked up at Isabella, a small tear trickled down her cheek. "I am honored."

"He will ask you in person if you will come to dinner tonight. How about eight o'clock?" Isabella pleaded.

"You got it, girl."

****

Right on time, he parked his truck in the circular driveway at the Riley's palatial manor. Reluctant to enter, he sat quiet for a moment. Something about Troy Maxwell did not sit right the first time he met him — two days ago. For a city guy, he asked too many questions about the new foal. His excuse was an idea to buy Isabella a spectacular species of a horse as a wedding gift. *Lame*. However, for Isabella's sake he would keep the promise.

He stared into space and wondered what it would be like to find *that* special woman. There had been relationships in his life, yet no one made his heart do cartwheels except . . . his reverie carried him to an extraordinary night at Adams Rib.

"Olivia," he spoke her name aloud and closed his eyes. He could almost feel her soft hand in his again, the small of her back silky to his touch. Her fragrance flooded his mind. He recalled how she nuzzled his chest, the tenderness in her smile as she squeezed his hand before she slipped away into the night. The words on the crumpled piece of paper danced in his head. 'Thank you for your phone number'.

His eyes flew open. "Earth to Joe Paul, get over it. She never called."

****

Spencer Walker watched Russell stop at the casino entrance. The front door opened, and a valet extended his hand for Kelley to step out. In another instant, Clair stood beside her friend. Russell flipped the keys to the attendant, positioned himself between his friends, and seized their elbows. "Time for a little fun, ladies."

From his vantage point, in the gray Nissan behind them, Spencer made sure they did not notice him. Once they were inside, he gave his keys to the valet, pulled his Seahawks cap low over his eyes, and entered the casino. Camouflaged in the crowd, he saw them move from slot machine to slot machine. Their laughter carried over the musical clinking sounds of the gambling devices and the murmur of the patrons. *Wait a minute? Where is Russell?* He slid between machines and customers, caution uppermost in his mind. Around the next corner, he spotted the bodyguard at the roulette table. *Good. I can do my job without his interference.* Spencer maneuvered until his view of Clair Matthews became unobstructed. She had grown into a beautiful woman. To observe from afar became a privilege as he watched the transition over the years. *I am not sure how much longer I can remain an invisible part of her life.* He allowed himself the luxury of a deep sigh. *I am falling in love with her.* Deep in thought, he did not notice the shadow fall across his vision, a hand on his forearm.

"Hey man, don't I know you? What do you think you are doing?"

Crap. That is why I don't need to do this anymore. I am slipping. "Butt out mister. This is a free country. I'm leaving anyway," Spencer said.

"No wait. I know you. I have seen you before. What's your name?"

Spencer saw Clair look up and make her way toward the two men. He shook off Russell's hand and ducked around the corner, sure Gibson would follow. He guessed right, but didn't care. He just did not want Clair to see him up close. Russell followed him into a jewelry store and out the back door. Too late, Spencer braced as the stout bodyguard landed on his back and knocked the breath out of him. He recovered and landed a blow to his assailant's eye. The surprise punch caused Russell to fall backward. Spencer took the opportunity to escape. He looked over his shoulder in time to see Clair in the doorway. The familiar glint of steel caught his attention. *A gun? Aimed at my head?*

Four
An Evil Plan Unveiled

Faint shadows danced across the hotel wall like a silent movie. *Reminds me of my life lately.* Clair relaxed, content to watch Kelley sleep. *The dawn is so quiet, so peaceful. I could lie here forever if it meant I would not have another bizarre episode. Things are complicated enough. I saw him. The hair on my neck stood up. Dread hit the pit of my stomach, and still, I ignored it, like all the other times. I cannot believe Aunt CeeCee tried to wave it off, said everyone feels that way once in a while, but this is different.* She flung the covers off, sat up, and dangled bare feet off the side of the bed to shake the dark mood.

Kelley moaned. "Are you awake already? I can't stand morning people."

"Go back to sleep, Kel. I didn't mean to disturb you."

Kelley sat up and faced her roommate. "What's wrong? You look bothered about something. Is it the guy in the casino? The gun?"

"Look, someone stalks me, I can tell. It has happened before, every time more intense. I *saw* him and chose to ignore the obvious. The tingle on the back of my neck put fear in my heart, not annoyance, real fear. A person is attached to the sensation this time."

"You think he is after you? Oh Clair, how scary. Maybe he is the focus of one of Russell's cases. Being a private investigator keeps his radar on high alert. Did you ask him?"

"No, and he didn't say anything. The gun shocked me. He drew it out of the holster in front of us. Didn't you notice his silence on the way back to the hotel? I think we were all numb." She hopped off the bed. "Enough, we have a full day ahead, and I need a shower."

"But if you want to talk about it…"

"No, it's over. I am fine. Russell would tell me if something was wrong. Let's drop it."

****

The sound of Clair's fingernails tapped the keyboard like a woodpecker, all business. Thoughts of the mystery man and gun evaporated.

Kelley rustled through papers near the portable file cabinet. "We need to finish the details on the Riley-Maxwell wedding before we can take on any more clientele. Our overzealous secretary booked two new appointments yesterday; we cannot put them off forever. Wait—the phone, let me get it. Hi, Rita, we were just talking about you. Well, let us confer. I will send an e-mail, and by the way, no more new appointments," Kelley said. The phone rattled into the cradle, and a chuckle escaped her lips.

"Problem?"

"Nothing we can't handle. Rita was unable to find the desired fabric for the Kimbrough-Hunter nuptials. We special ordered the design from a quaint shop in Maui. Remember, DeLinda Kimbrough's mother saw it while on vacation? The company no longer manufactures the original dye for that particular cloth. Now, the elder Ms. Kimbrough is in a panic. DeLinda told Rita she is satisfied, but her mother wants to make waves. Darn…looks like we may have to fly to Hawaii for a consultation." Kelley grinned. "Plans are at a point where we could leave for a couple days to take care of this little fire, don't you think?"

"What about the new customers in Dallas?"

"Rita can . . ." Once more, the phone interrupted, and Kelley reached across the desk to answer.

Clair watched a frown crease Kelley's forehead. "What's the matter? You look unhappy."

"Forget those white, sandy beaches. Bulldog Riley's secretary, Nora, said a water main broke. It supplies the sprinkler system for the racetrack oval. The whole area is flooded, and the texture of the grass is compromised, too soft, and muddy for the reception. One of us needs to survey the damage to decide on an alternate plan."

"Sounds like a real mess, Kelley, but here's an idea. I will go to the ranch, and you pack your bikini, agreed? You have all the details on the Kimbrough problem. I will handle this one," Clair said.

"Are you sure? Don't you need a break, too?"

Clair shook her head. "No, you go to Hawaii, and we will knock out both problems. Take Russell to make sure the handsome, dark-tanned surfers let you come back to Cajun country. Otherwise, I will be forced to board a plane, rescue you from the white beaches on some secluded island, browned from the tropical sun, your hair ruffled from the sea breeze, a Piña Colada in your . . ."

"Stop, enough already, I get it. I will *owe* you, right?"

"You got it," Clair said.

****

The Last Drop Coffee Shop smelled of bacon and eggs, waffles, melted butter, and the wake-up aroma of strong coffee. Russell slid into his favorite booth.

Scent of Double Deception

Scenes from the night before tormented him as he waited for someone to take his order. *Why did I draw my gun? The guy didn't do anything. I lost my touch and alarmed Clair and Kelley. So unprofessional.*

"Sir, would you like to order? Sir?" The petite waitress held a coffeepot, tilted to pour.

"Yes, sorry, my mind wandered I guess. How are you, Candy? Give me the usual and plenty of black coffee."

"They keep me busy Mr. G—tips are good though." She winked. "I'll get your order right out."

Any other day, his gaze might have lingered on the tight, little wiggle of the young waitress as she sashayed toward the kitchen. Today, he did not notice. He leaned back in the booth, lost in thought. A muffled argument behind him caught his attention.

"Helms, I told you not to worry. I've already got a plan in action."

"Listen man, you've got a long way to go to prove I can trust you and your plan, Jess."

"I understand, but I can take care of the job. My twin sister is already on the inside. It'll start soon."

"What about a background check? I know that dame over the office is tough and smart."

"Relax, relax. We are way ahead of you. The person in charge of the coin for this caper has plenty to spare. It's all paid for, understand?"

Russell turned halfway in the booth and saw a man about fifty. A younger man sat across the table, a cap squashed low on his head.

The older man smacked his lips, wiped the crumbs from his mouth on the back of one hand, and pointed a fork at his partner. "Your person better pass out the payoff fast after this goes down. My bags are packed for Mexico. I'm gonna find me a big busted senorita and disappear."

"Don't worry so much, be patient. My grandma always said good things come to those who wait. So what if we have to hang loose a while, Lee? Up to now, we have gone undetected."

"Well, I thought for sure ol' man Duffy screwed everything up the day he called his prick of a neighbor, who claims he's a vet."

Russell leaned closer. *What did he just say?*

"Hey, it worked out, and Bulldog *will* play the game."

"Shut up, Jess. How many times I gotta tell you not to say his name?"

"Okay, it's cool. Let's blow this place."

The men tossed some change on the table and walked out.

"More coffee, Mr. G?"

"Sure thing, Candy. Say, do you know those two men who sat behind me?"

"Uh, those two? No. They always come in here together, at least for the last week or so. Lousy tippers though, not like you, Mr. G." She grinned and popped her gum.

"Thanks for the info and the good service." While he finished his meal, he ticked off the men's description in his mind, a habit developed as a former cop. The older man, about 5' 10", 180 pounds, looked like a ranch hand by his clothes. The other one was much younger, maybe 25, short and slender, dark brown hair. They called each other Jess and Helms, the kicker — the name

Bulldog. *I took Clair and Kelley to Bulldog Riley's home earlier this week, too much of a coincidence for my taste.*

He left a generous tip, exited the shop, and spotted the two men next to a red pick-up. The cab door sported a logo of some kind. Able to read the license plate from where he stood, he pulled out a cell phone and called in a favor. The information confirmed his suspicions. Preston Riley, of Silks and Saddles, owned the vehicle. Alarmed, he said, "Check for a Lester McDuff in Shreveport." *If I am right, the Duffy they mentioned is my old buddy from years ago.* The answer turned his blood cold.

****

Russell maneuvered around the crowded parking lot of The Laughing Gator until he found a space. *Wonder if I will know the old coot after 20 years.*

The attractive brunette hostess led him through the bar to a table in the back of the restaurant.

McDuff stood and smiled. "You haven't changed a bit, Gibson. How do you do it?"

The two friends grasped hands.

"Can't say the same for you, old man, you're working too hard," he said.

They took their seats.

"We're ready to order, miss. Please send a waitress right away."

She nodded and left.

He snorted a laugh as Duffy followed the sway of her backside. "Still have an eye for the ladies, Duff?"

Red-faced McDuff said, "Knock it off, Gibson. I may be old, but I am not dead. Now, from the sound of your voice, this ain't no social call. What's up? You on a mission?"

Scent of Double Deception

"I don't do missions anymore, not since you left the force. I am in private business now. By the way, this is my treat today." He looked up at the waitress. "We'll have the jumbo shrimp with remoulade sauce. Thanks, miss. Drop the surprised look, Duff. I still remember your favorite food." He slipped off his jacket. "Let me get right to the point. You work for Bulldog Riley, correct?"

"Yeah, you've done your homework. So?"

"I'm security for Memory Makers, and their specialty is high profile events. Bulldog hired them for his daughter's wedding. Isabella, you know her?"

"Know her? I practically raised her from a baby. What is wrong? Spill it."

Russell described the chance encounter in the coffee shop.

Duffy's eyes narrowed. "Did you get names?"

"Helms and Jess is all I heard. Recognize them?"

"Sure do. Lee Helms is my racing manager. He hired a young kid named Jess Owens as an apprentice. We needed a new jockey."

"Does anything I overheard worry you?"

"You know, it might be a long shot, but we have a new foal, and I don't like the way it acts. The mama is Isabella's pride and joy, Asparagus Tips. I thought the breech birth caused all the difficulty, now I wonder."

"What difficulty?"

"He can't stand up long, doesn't want to wake up. I called our resident vet, Joe Paul Farrell. He did blood work, and a saliva test, and promised to do a rush on it. Maybe we'll know something this afternoon."

What? Joe Paul? That's the name of the man I punched at Adams Rib.

Scent of Double Deception

The pop and sizzle of seafood, hot off the grill, stopped their conversation. Duffy speared a shrimp and continued, "Let me explain the lineage of this foal. See, his daddy is Fire and Ice from a champion and classic sire, Partners in Crime, and a Triple Crown winner mare, Roxy's Folly. The mother is Asparagus Tips, a mare out of a three-parts-relative to the famous Houston Night, a stakes winning, sprinter stallion, and the famous French Derby winner, Lola's Prophecy." Duffy paused for the waitress to refill his tea glass.

Russell motioned for him to continue.

"The cross makes Tip of the Ice, or Tipper as Isabella likes to call him, a breed-shaping influence with international classifications. This little fella owns a reliable pedigree of speed and talent."

"You could've said he's worth a lot of money, Duff. Sounds like this new career suits you. So, how does Helms and Owens fit into the picture?"

"New career? I've done this for two decades. Anyway, I don't know how they fit in, but I'm sure gonna keep my eye on them. Can I call you about those test results?"

He handed Duffy a business card. "Definitely, call if you get any news. I want to protect my employers. Looks like we are working together again, ol' buddy."

They finished the meal over small talk and promised to keep each other informed.

Russell slid into the SUV, grabbed his laptop, and searched the name *Joe Paul Farrell*. He ran down the list of information—a resident of Caddo Parish, retired Air Force Lieutenant, an accredited pilot, stationed in Turkey and France, and headquartered at Barksdale Air Force Base. "I see he received a registered vet license in the military." The laptop slapped shut. "I know people, Farrell. If you have a secret, pal, you can't hide it. Trust me, I will dig it up."

****

Clair surveyed the grass oval and wrote a few notes on a pad.

"What's the verdict?" Isabella called from the golf cart.

Here goes my new manicure. Clair tiptoed onto the mushy turf, bent down, and pressed two fingers into the wet lawn. "Miss Riley, I think it's a good thing your wedding isn't next weekend. However, I checked the local Doppler, the weather looks clear for the next couple of weeks. It is awful, but overall the damage is minimal."

"I can have industrial fans brought in to help dry the area," Bulldog offered.

"Excellent idea," Clair replied.

"I'll arrange it now." He walked toward the field house.

"Let's go over a few other items, Isabella. You want large tents to provide a pavilion effect, correct?"

"Oh yes."

"It will also provide shelter and shade for the guests. Even though there is grass, I suggest a carpet of artificial turf secured so everyone can mingle and dance."

"I love it," Isabella agreed.

"Now, for the sit-down dinner, you want the band on a platform?"

"Yes."

"All right." Clair continued to write. "The horse-drawn carriage will bring you and Troy to the oval after the ceremony, and I suggest we provide canvas-topped shuttles for everyone. They could walk, but give them an option. Your thoughts?"

"Marvelous suggestion." Isabella clapped her hands.

"Great. I will take care of the details, put together a report, and make a follow-up call. Don't worry. Day after tomorrow soon enough?"

"Perfect."

Things are under control here, I hope it goes good for Kelley, too.

****

Clair scanned the hotel lobby and waited for the elevator. *Alone again. It would be nice to see a familiar face. Someone to share dinner, but I guess its room service for me.* The elevator opened, and something on the floor caught her eye, a business card. She reached down and picked it up. The front said Bud's Tavern. She flipped it over and caught her breath. Scrawled on the back ... **RILEY**. *A coincidence? No need to panic. It's a common name.*

Clair glanced over her shoulder, hurried to the room, and turned the lock. The notebook dropped on the bed, and she kicked off both high heels. A quick study of the card only brought confusion; she tossed it on the nightstand. A low stomach rumble diverted her attention. *Gosh, I haven't eaten since breakfast. I refuse to be a prisoner of fear. I'll go to the hotel restaurant and eat a good meal, maybe later check out Bud's.* She ran a brush through tousled hair, touched up her lipstick, and picked up the notebook. *Angel hair pasta and a good sauce, comfort food is all I need.*

The elevator stopped at several floors. As people entered, she wondered if one of them dropped the card. A teenage boy in torn jeans, with a pierced lip, and Mohawk style-hair, and a young, uniformed woman, maybe a nanny, held the hand of a small girl. Three other couples crowded inside. *Goodness, I have started to think like Russell.*

She made her way through the crowd to the restaurant.

The maître d' motioned for a waitress. "Good evening, madam."

"Somewhere in the back, please," Clair said.

The waitress placed a menu on the table. "What can I get you to drink?"

"A glass of white wine." She spread the portfolio open and made some notes.

The waitress returned, mixed drink in hand.

"No, dear, I ordered wine, remember?"

"I know, ma'am, this drink is from the gentleman at the bar. It's a Fuzzy Up. He said it's your favorite."

Clair turned to look. "Which one is he?"

"Uh, he's gone."

"Describe him."

"Handsome, black hair, a muscular body, long-sleeved white shirt. That's all I really noticed."

"His voice, what about the voice?"

"Soft, kinda deep and pleasant. Shall I take the drink back?"

"Leave it, but I still want the white wine."

"Of course."

Clair stared at the bar as the hair prickled on the back of her neck. *The voice, she described the same voice, or is it my imagination? How could a stranger know what I like? Well, I refuse to drink it.* While she tried to concentrate on paperwork, the drink taunted her. After the third glance, she raised the glass to her lips. The cool, effervescent liquid trickled down her throat, and she tried to visualize the man. *Could it be the same person? The one who rendered me speechless the night Kelley and I let Olivia and Natasha out to play?*

She savored the comfort food, took her time, and focused on work. Frustrated, she threw a tip on the table and returned to the suite.

Thoughts of the man in the restaurant receded while she typed the Riley wedding report. The phone rang. "Hello?"

"Honey, its Aunt Celeste. Did I call at a bad time?"

"No, Aunt CeeCee, you're the voice I need to hear. How are things in Seattle? Do you have a cup of your famous hot chocolate on the table in front of you?" The laughter on the other end of the phone confirmed her intuition.

"You know me too well, darling. Old habits die hard."

"It's an age-old tradition you and your two sisters enjoyed, Aunt CeeCee. I remember the stories. You took me in, into your heart, and your home. Those midnight chats, and the tales you told, are still cherished memories."

"Me too, and I miss them so much. Something told me you needed a chat tonight. Is anything wrong?"

"You never cease to amaze me. I swear you know things I don't." Clair grabbed a tissue as a tear ran down her cheek, nerves unsettled. "I had another episode, I don't understand. What do you make of it?"

Celeste Vandergriff replied, "Oh my sweet, you sound like Russell. Don't start to act like him as well. Everyone experiences a little déjà vu, its natural. Now,

Scent of Double Deception

let's change the subject. Is it possible you can come for a visit?"

"I can fly up after the Riley wedding and stay a week. How's that?"

"Wonderful, and bring Kelley and Russell, too. I would love to see them."

"I'll see what I can do, but you need to plan one of your soirees for Kelley. She loves for you to invite the eligible millionaires to meet your debutantes."

"Done, and I bet my famous Black Forest cake will be enough to entice Russell's sweet tooth. Let me know when I can expect you, dear. Better go now."

"I love you, Aunt CeeCee. Thanks so much for the call." Clair sat on the bed for several minutes, the phone cradled in her lap. *Unbelievable. Something in her voice, cautious, anxious to change the subject, she calls every time there is an incident. Is my aunt clairvoyant? I'm too tired to think about this tonight. Maybe in Seattle I can get to the bottom of it.*

Five
The Intruder

Russell tossed Kelley's baggage into the SUV.

"Hey, you'll mix up my bikinis," she scolded.

"Yeah, yeah," he replied.

"You're sure in a mood today. Aren't you happy to fly off to beautiful Hawaii, a gorgeous blonde on your arm, or would you prefer Clair?"

Russell shook his head as he opened the car door. "Got a few worrisome business details I need to handle before we leave. You ready to go?"

"I think so. No, wait. I forgot my bracelet." She ran toward the hotel.

"The one I gave you for Christmas?" He followed.

Clair stood in the lobby; arm outstretched, and flashed the bracelet at her friend. "Forget something?"

"Thanks, *Mom*. Got yours?"

"Never leave home without it."

"It's good to know I have my women trained so well." Russell grinned.

"Oh puh-lease." Clair gave each a hug. "Be careful and keep in touch."

****

On the magic isle of Maui, hot pink, bright red, and exotic yellow flowers lined the walkway of the Westin Resort. *Oh Clair, wish you could see the view. It's postcard perfect.*

Kelley took a deep breath. The briny smell of saltwater floated in the air. In the breeze, huge palm trees swayed against a royal blue sky like native dancers.

The hotel employee guided the baggage carrier. Russell tipped him and gave Kelley a key card. "Here, I am right next door. Give me a call after you unpack."

"My appointment at the Kalona Import/Export Warehouse is at ten in the morning so, let's sightsee this afternoon."

He saluted and clicked his heels together. "Yes, boss. I'm your escort, at your service."

A large basket of fresh pineapple, mango, and kiwi rested in the middle of the coffee table. She kicked off her shoes and walked out on the balcony. White-capped waves lapped the shore like a lover's gentle kiss. Multi-colored umbrellas dotted the blanched sand, refuge from the sun's golden rays. She changed into shorts and sandals, and called Russell. "I'm ready to hit the town."

"Let me make a couple more calls, and we'll go."

"Fine, I'll call Clair." She stretched out on the chaise and dialed the number. "Clair, we're here. Maui is gorgeous, and the scene from my balcony is spectacular. Too bad you aren't here, too. You can't imagine how white the sand is…" A hard rap on the door interrupted. "Wait, I think Russell's here." She opened the door and motioned the burly friend inside. "How did the crisis at the track go today, and how is Isabella? Great, good work, as always. I hope my appointment tomorrow goes well, also. What? Let me check." She placed a hand over the receiver. "Hey Russ, do you know of a place called Bud's?"

Red-faced, he grabbed the phone and started to pace. "Clair, what are you up to?"

Scent of Double Deception

A pang of alarm shot through Kelley.

"Look, Bud's isn't somewhere you should go alone. No. Why don't you wait, and we'll all go together? I'm sorry you're not here." He sighed. "Promise me you won't go to Bud's. Thanks."

Kelley took the phone and returned to the balcony, voice lowered, "What's the deal? You will stay in, right? Good, talk to you soon." She snatched her purse from the nightstand. "Let's go."

"Clair's not going to that club is she? What did she say? Don't keep something from me," Russell's voice raised.

"No, and besides, she has on the bracelet. Don't be such a worry wart."

Roadside stands displayed a bounty of fresh produce, souvenirs, and surf ware along the beachfront. At the Hilo Hattie, Kelley found a unique wooden item.

"Do you like the Shaker Monkey?" The salesclerk smiled. "Island legend says if given to someone you love, or a friend, they'll receive great fortune and good luck, as well as the giver."

Kelley held the carved souvenir up like a treasured piece of art. "This is perfect for Clair. I'll carry it on the plane to keep it safe."

Russell shook his head. "Whatever. Right now, I am hungry. Let's find a place to eat." He parked the red Mustang in front of the Banyan Tree Restaurant and Club.

"Aren't you glad I talked you into this convertible? I noticed a few honey-tanned admirers back there," she teased.

"Think I've still got it?" Russell grinned.

The marquee boasted of eclectic, pacific cuisine, and a feature band, the Surf Dogs. Inside, impressions of the beach at dusk decorated the walls. Superimposed clouds floated, and stars twinkled in the ceiling. Brilliant colored birds nested in paper Mache greenery. Dressed in traditional surfer attire, the band encouraged the crowd to karaoke.

"Why don't you give these folks a real treat?" Russell said.

"No, tonight let's show them how we do it in Texas."

Kelley left the table and headed toward the main guitarist. He nodded. She grabbed Russell by the arm, and the two friends ruled the dance floor while the Surf Dogs hammered out vigorous rock and roll. Russell dipped her low, and her long, blonde hair brushed the floor.

The small crowd burst into applause.

Russell wiped the sweat from his forehead. "What a rush."

"To answer your earlier question, my dear friend, yes, you've still got it." She popped him on the butt.

"Excuse me, excuse me." A woman from the next table broke in. Her short, black hair matched ebony eyes. The lady leaned toward Russell, a hand on his shoulder, the other on the table. The jacket of her white, silk suit flapped open and plump, tanned breasts threatened to tumble out.

"Uh, yes?"

"Pardon me, but I loved your performance. I'm curious, are you a dance instructor?"

"Well, no ma'am, but thank you for the compliment."

"What a shame, so you don't give lessons. Oh well, I apologize if I bothered you."

Scent of Double Deception

"No, no problem," Russell stuttered.

She patted him on the shoulder and left through the main corridor.

He leaned forward, eyes riveted on her tight, white skirt.

"Russell, oh Russell, you can float back down now." Kelley snapped her fingers.

"What?"

"Shame on you, I saw you ogle every movement she made. Oh no, look." She pointed to the woman's table. "In the chair...her clutch purse. Quick, try and catch her!"

He grabbed the wallet, and they hurried to the front entrance in time to see a white limo pull away.

"Do you know the name of the woman who left in the limo?" Kelley asked the thin, young valet.

"No ma'am. She's a looker, though." He winked.

"We have no other choice, Russell. Open the pocketbook."

He read from a driver's license, "Katherine R. Forche."

"Let me see." Kelley took the purse. "Here's an ID card and a cell number. Why not call? Put your phone on speaker so I can hear, too."

He punched in the numbers. "Ms. Forche?"

"Yes?"

"Ma'am, I'm sorry to bother you. Did you leave The Banyan Tree in a white limo?"

"Yes I did, and just who *is* this?"

"Ma'am, I'm Russell Gibson. You came to our table and asked if we were dance instructors. You forgot your purse. I looked inside for some identification and found this number."

After a brief silence, she replied, "I'm grateful for your chivalry, Mr. Gibson."

"No problem, we'll wait here for you to return."

"I have plans for the rest of the night. Can you be a dear and bring it to me tomorrow?"

"We have an appointment at 10:00 AM, afterwards, we're free."

"Good, let me give you directions to my condo."

****

"It's another beautiful day in Hawaii, I love this." Kelley climbed into the convertible. The brisk wind fondled her hair as they sped along. She reclined the seat, relaxed. The vibrant sun tingled her skin, pinked her cheeks. A method of approach to handle Mr. Kalona whirled in her mind. "I plan to make quick work of this little problem. I can't wait to wear my new bikini on those pearl-colored beaches." She peeked over the top of tortoise-shell sunglasses at Russell and nestled back into the leather seat.

"Yes ma'am," he said.

The hum of tires on asphalt, the sway of curvy roads, rocked her like a cradlesong.

"We're here, babe." He eased the car into an open spot in the Visitors Only section.

She jerked the sunglasses off. "This isn't the place. You took a wrong turn."

"Sorry my sweet, the big sign says it is." He pointed.

The words, Kalona Import/Export Warehouse, sprawled across a large billboard. On one side of the commercial building, a steady stream of 18-wheelers waited in line like a row of schoolchildren, while forklifts and front loaders whizzed to and from the docks.

Scent of Double Deception

"It isn't at all the quaint little shop Delinda's mother implied. This better not turn out to be a headache," she warned.

Inside, the native receptionist greeted them, "Aloha."

"Yes, hello, I'm Kelley Malone. We have a ten o'clock appointment to see Mr. Kalona."

"One moment please." She disappeared down a hallway.

Tropical plants in an array of colors decorated the atrium foyer.

"I expected a small, crowded shop in the mainstream of town—bolts of fabric stacked high, not a spa atmosphere."

"This way please." The young girl gestured.

Behind a pile of folders and scattered papers, a slender, gray-haired man sat, hands folded. Large angled windows, flanked by floral, overstuffed chairs, hosted a panoramic view of the island. After introductions, he said, "Ms. Malone, I'd like to apologize for this unfortunate predicament, but irresponsible suppliers, and our heavy workload, as well as…"

Kelley butted in, "Mr. Kalona, I'm a business owner, too. Unpredictable circumstances happen, however, we need the exact day the fabric will arrive. Our client isn't concerned about your dilemma."

"Ms. Malone, I'll try my best to correct the problem even though your demands are a bit harsh."

She cocked an eyebrow. "You have one more day to handle this quandary. Expect my phone call tomorrow by 5:00 PM. Let's go, Russell." Kelley marched out of the office to the parking lot. She slapped his hand away from the door handle, slid in, and slammed it shut.

Scent of Double Deception

"Hey, take it easy on the ride," Russell said.

"Guess he thought since I'm blonde he would win the battle."

"Kelley, I don't think he…"

"I don't want to talk. I'm mad." She crossed her arms. Thoughts of the firestorm created blazed in her head.

"Yes ma'am. I always say you're the boss."

****

Silence shrouded the drive to Katherine Forche's condo. A rainbow landscape of lush, tropical forests, busy workers in pineapple groves, and botanical gardens led them to 703 Imi Estates. At the gated entrance, the guard waved them through.

"Look at the size of this place," Kelley said.

"Impressive," Russell replied.

"Well, I hope our good deed to return the wallet is worth our time. I'd rather shop."

At the house, a valet took the car.

A maid welcomed them inside. "Ms. Forche waits for you on the beach. Please follow."

"Are those paintings and sculptures real?" Kelley tugged on Russell's arm as they passed through the spacious house. "It looks like an art museum in here."

A long, wooden deck led downward to the beach. Under an oversized, blue umbrella, a lady sat at a table, a newspaper across her lap. As they approached, she stood and waved. A hot pink bikini glowed against bronze skin. Draped on a nearby chair lay a thin sarong. The woman bent over to retrieve the filmy wrap, tied it around her waist, and left a bountiful cleavage exposed.

"Try to keep your eyes in your head, Russ."

"Kelley hush, she'll hear you.

Six
The Seduction

Katherine Forche slammed the cell phone shut, frustrated because her dolt of a son didn't seem to grasp the urgency of her plan. Footsteps on the wooden deck diverted her concentration. A wicked smile formed, the tip of her tongue wet eager lips, her gaze hot on the muscled gentleman. On the dance floor, Russell's boyish good looks, and ripped physique, titillated her attention like a moth in a spider's web. His jeans fit in all the right places, and each sensuous move eased any prior annoyance. Thoughts of her son's stupidity vanished.

"Thank you so much for coming." She smiled at Kelley, but extended a hand to Russell. Her thumb rubbed the crest of his rough knuckle in a slow circular motion, the other hand rested on his left bicep. A muscle flexed beneath her touch. *Buff, the way I enjoy my men. I have not allowed myself to dabble in romance for a while. Do I dare?* "And you must be Mrs. Gibson."

"No, I'm Kelley Malone—we only work together, and we're here on business."

"Last night, I thought you were a couple. Please sit down. Let's chat."

"Ms. Forche, here's your pocketbook," Russell said.

"Please...call me Kitty." She reveled in his thick hair, sculpted arms, and broad shoulders.

The housemaid appeared and offered glasses of lemonade.

Kitty set her glass aside and leaned toward him. "May I ask a blunt question, Mr. Gibson?"

"You can call me Russell."

"Okay, *Russell*. Were you a scoundrel? Did you look inside the money compartment?"

"No ma'am, I did not."

She jerked the wallet open and handed him a folded piece of paper. "Here." She leaned back and took a sip of the tart juice.

"Oh my God!"

"What?" Kelley snatched the paper from Russell.

"It's a check written to Katherine Forche for a million dollars. Why didn't you have us return this last night?" Russell stood up, retrieved the check from Kelley, and waggled it in the air.

"Sit down, mon trésor." Kitty flipped the checkbook open, pen poised. "My intuition never fails me. Please, let me reward your integrity."

Kelley shook her head. "No, we couldn't."

"She's right," he added.

Kitty crossed her legs, and the sarong fell open. "At least allow me to show you the island from my yacht. Agreed?"

"If things go as planned, we need to return to Louisiana tomorrow," Kelley said.

"I see, and tell me, how did your business appointment go?"

Kelley's eyes narrowed. "Since you asked, we intended to pick up the correct materials for one of our client's nuptials. I'm co-owner of Memory Makers."

"Are you wedding planners?"

"Yes, however, I'm on hold for the rest of the day until I hear from my vendor."

Scent of Double Deception

"You sound upset. Might I ask the vendor's name?"

"Mr. Kalona at Kalona Import/Export."

"I believe I can help. I am indebted to you and Russell. I could make a couple of calls, so where would you want the goods shipped?"

"Thank you, Kitty, but that's not necessary," Russell interjected.

"Russell, I need the material, so yes, Ms. Forche, we'll take you up on the offer. I prefer to see it for myself. We are working a wedding in Shreveport; I'll give you the hotel address."

"Shreveport?" Kitty pointed to the newspaper on the table. "I read a wedding announcement in USA Today. Is Riley one of the couples?"

"Yes, it's the Riley/Maxwell nuptials."

"I traveled through Shreveport before on my way to my home in New Orleans. You should come for a visit sometime. I need to make those phone calls I promised. Let's walk up to the house." Kitty stretched long, brown legs across Russell's lap. "Sandals, please?"

A quick blush spread across his face, and he obliged.

She hooked her arm in his. "Now tell me, my love, what is your job at Memory Makers?"

****

The sunlight slanted through the balcony window, a gentle draft of air tickled the sheers. The sweet fragrance of tropical flowers filled the room. Kelley opened her eyes and tossed back the sheet. "The plumeria is in bloom." The neon, digital numbers glared 7:00 AM. "It's already noon in Louisiana. Clair should have gotten my message." *Did you defy Russell and go to Bud's alone? You told me you would wait. So why haven't you called? Never mind, I don't have time.* She

Scent of Double Deception

opened the closet and grabbed a blue sundress. "Wouldn't want to be late for our island expedition."

Luxury boats in the harbor lined the dock like racehorses at a starting gate.

"Goodness." Kelley adjusted her sunglasses. "They're so similar, Russell. How do we know which one is Kitty's?"

"Follow me, I know the slip number," he replied.

As they neared a beautiful 70-foot cruiser, a voice called, "Ahoy mates." Kitty waved. "Come aboard. Let me give you a tour. It's large enough to sleep eight and all the comforts of home." Kitty grabbed Russell's hand.

Kelley followed the twosome inside the cabin. China and crystal goblets graced the table of the dining room. Lotus green, oversized recliners, and a large bamboo settee, encircled a tiki wood entertainment center. Vibrant aqua and saffron gold artwork enhanced the tropical scene.

"Beautiful," she said.

"Thanks. Here's the master bedroom, a marble hot tub in one corner, and a glass-bottom viewing port in the other."

Kelley caught the quick wink Kitty gave Russell.

"Change into swimwear, and I will meet you on the upper deck," Kitty said. "You'll find the proper attire in your rooms."

Topside, Kelley relaxed in the warm sun while the yacht slid out to sea. The prim, black one-piece swimsuit Kitty supplied made her feel outdated. In the next chaise, Russell stretched out in navy floral, surfer shorts. She watched his jaw drop at Kitty's runway entrance in a skimpy, yellow-striped bikini.

Scent of Double Deception

A uniformed deckhand served cups of fresh fruit, shrimp cocktails, and Mai Tais.

"We need to eat light, dinner plans are a surprise," Kitty said.

Kelley leaned over and whispered to Russell, "Is this an all-day affair?"

"I hope so." He flashed a smile.

Kitty wiggled into Russell's lounge and nuzzled his ear.

"Well hello," he said.

Kitty used the thin cover-up to blot droplets of sweat on his bare, broad chest.

Kelley pretended to nap. *Oh God, she makes me nauseous.*

The deckhand returned and announced, "Madam, we dock in twenty minutes, the luau is in thirty."

"Time to go freshen up." Kitty disappeared into the lower deck.

Kelley wrapped a loose curl around her finger. "Are *you* on the menu?"

Russell's nose wrinkled as he stuck out his tongue.

"Can't fool me, you're excited," she said and left.

Inside Kelley's spacious cabin, a long red and white, Hawaiian print dress lay across a king-sized canopy bed. "Well, she thought of everything, even what I'll wear tonight." She slipped into the garment, twisted her curls on top of her head, and spritzed on a favorite perfume.

On the sundeck, Kelley found Russell next to Kitty propped against the rail, one arm wrapped around her waist. She noticed the sultry slit up the side of Kitty's blue and orange dress, a peach flower perched over her left ear. *In the glare of the afternoon sun, how can Russell miss those crow's feet around your eyes? Just how old are you, anyway?*

"You look very nice. Here honey, put this white Hibiscus behind your right ear," Kitty said.

Don't call me honey, or I'll stuff this precious white Posy down your obnoxious throat. "Why is yours on the left? What's the difference?"

"Tradition says if you're single place the flower behind your right ear, but if taken, it belongs on the left, the side closest to the heart."

Kelley crammed the flower behind her ear and crossed her arms.

Russell slapped his hands together. "I'm hungry. What's on the menu?"

It's a fishing trip, Russell, and you're the fish de jour, you idiot.

"We're invited to the Royal Luau, an authentic hula, feast, and fire dance," Kitty said.

After they docked, natives presented colorful flower leis and escorted them to a private beach area. Muted light from mystic lanterns and torches surrounded an open fiery pit. Tourists sat cross-legged on woven straw mats in a semi-circle. They dined on roasted pork, salmon wrapped in Ti leaves, fresh wedges of pineapple and coconut. Several young girls gyrated in sync to Hawaiian folk music, the beat rumbled in the ambience of the night.

Kitty leaned across Russell's lap and tapped Kelley on the arm. "This particular dance originated to pay homage to ancestral gods."

"Look at the graceful sway of their hips and hands," Kelley said.

"Yeah, I kinda like those hip movements," Russell added.

"I love perfect rhythm," Kitty purred.

The island sunset created a watercolor canvas across the ocean waves. Fire dancers' batons blazed and spiraled in the air to the tribal cadence from ceremonial drums.

Russell and Kitty held hands, their silhouettes danced on the beach from the glow of the flames.

Restless, Kelley's fingertips traced the silky petals of the Hibiscus and sparked a twinge of melancholy. "I'll be back." She kicked off her sandals and headed down the beach.

At the crest of the seawall, she sat on a large rock. The orange moon evolved to a butter yellow orb, its reflection rippled on the water like braids of ribbon. *What is my problem? Russell deserves to find a little happiness.* The moonlight reminded her of the night before Christmas, a handsome cowboy, his firm hold, and undaunted attention to her every word. *I meant to call him, but the wedding, the details. . .*

Cool waves slid in, and white foam covered her bare feet. The grainy sand squished between her toes, something caught her eye. *Oh, a sand dollar, a sign of good luck. I do want to talk to you, Joe Paul. I would like to call right now.* She traced the outline of the crustacean. *What would I say? I can't ask you to come to Hawaii. You only know Olivia, the masquerade of my alter ego.*

She beat her fist against the rock. *The truth is — my heart races each time I think of those moss green eyes, your muscular body molded next to me. I can still feel your breath on my cheek. Why didn't I let you kiss me, so the taste of your wet lips would stay safe in my memory?* Her grasp on

Scent of Double Deception

the sea treasure tightened. *Would Kelley Malone enchant you like Olivia?* The laughter of people close by halted her mind's diary of the magical encounter. *I am going to call you when we get back to Louisiana. I must see you again.*

****

Portentous gray clouds eclipsed the California sun as the plane landed in Los Angeles. Inside the airport, Russell read the display board to Kelley, "Hydrologic conditions exist. A strong squall line and intense wind off the coast makes conditions right for thunderstorms to develop. We may be in for some bumpy weather."

She pouted. "Oh great."

They boarded their next flight. The airplane taxied down the runway, but stalled on the tarmac.

"What's the deal?"

"Calm down darlin', this big bird will get her turn," Russell answered.

Kelley pointed to her watch. "It's been over half an hour."

"Sweetheart, they won't take off under unsafe conditions."

"If we left now, we'd beat the bad weather. Why wait until it gets worse?" her voice amplified.

"Excuse me, ma'am?" Russell waved to the attendant.

"Yes sir, can I help you?"

"We need something to drink, please."

"Of course sir, what would you like?"

He ordered a glass of tea and a mixed drink. "Here, Kelley."

"I don't want anything; I want this plane to leave right..."

"Hey, take a few sips, relax. Before long, we'll be airborne." He patted her arm.

She downed the drink in one gulp, handed him the glass, and laid back. The hours slipped by, and soon, the roar of the engines' descent woke her. She blinked. "Where are we?"

"In the clouds, high above Texas."

"Did I drift off?"

"Uh, for a little while."

He grabbed the overhead and nudged Kelley toward the exit. They followed a long line of people to the next gate for the last leg of the trip.

"They've beefed up security," Russell said.

"Not another delay." She shook her head. *I'll be glad to see Shreveport again.*

He emptied his pockets and walked through the security equipment to the other side.

Kelley put the Shaker Monkey, and her purse, on the conveyor to walk through the scanner.

As the souvenir passed through the x-ray, buzzers started to scream, red lights flashed, everything halted. Security personnel flooded the area, ready to draw their weapons.

"Russell, what's wrong? This didn't happen in Maui or Los Angeles."

"Ma'am, please step to the side," a security officer instructed.

She tapped a foot. "Are you kidding me?"

"Please cooperate, you'll only make things worse," Russell whispered.

"I want to get back to Clair."

"Ma'am, please follow me. We need to screen this item again, shouldn't take long. Anything you'd like to declare?"

"It's only a monkey, for Pete's sake!"

Russell intervened, "Sir, it's a gift. We bought it for our mother while we were in Hawaii. She collects monkeys. You have our permission to check it out. Go right ahead."

"Our *mother* — who collects *monkeys*?" she said under her breath. "I'm gonna tell."

Russell grabbed her elbow. "Please play along so we can get out of here."

A few minutes later, the officer returned. "A nail in the bottom of your mother's gift is made of unusual metals. Our equipment is sensitive."

"I'm so sorry." She batted her eyes. "Bad monkey. You're supposed to bring good luck."

Russell escorted her through the air terminal at a quick pace. "Hurry, we'll miss our next flight. You can talk to Mr. Monkey once we're in the air."

Breathless, they arrived at the next gate too late.

She sunk onto one of the hard thin-padded chairs. "I can't believe we missed it, Russell." Tears filled her eyes.

"Stay here, and call Clair. I will go exchange our tickets. I don't want her to worry about us."

"Thanks." Weary, she dialed Clair's mobile. She watched until Russell emerged from the crowd.

"Got the tickets, did you talk to Clair?"

"No, it said the customer is out of the area, I called three times. Where is she?"

"Hey, let's go to the sports bar and play a few games of pool, unwind. Unless, you think I'd kick your ass...never mind."

Energized, she stood, hands on hips. "What? I'll whip your butt, boy. Come on."

Neon light advertisements illuminated the walls of the Airborne Sports Bar. She leaned over the billiard table toward the colored target, steadied the cue stick, and took the shot. The white ball curved around the eight ball. *Bull's eye.* It landed in the corner pocket with a thud.

"And that, my dear man, is what they call a Masse' shot."

Russell shook his head. "Where in the world did you ever learn to play pool, woman?"

"Clair and I taught our boys, cheap and fun entertainment. Don't take it so hard, they hated to get beat, too."

He placed an arm around her shoulder. "At least it calmed you down a little."

"Yeah, I can't believe we're stuck at DFW. I could have taken a taxi to the house, picked up my corvette, and *drove* us to Shreveport." She glanced at her watch. "Oh Russell, its 7:00 PM. Clair will be frantic, she expected us around 6:00. Damn it, my cell battery is low. I can't get a signal."

"Don't worry, she's at the hotel," Russell said.

"Did you forget? This is the night we are going to Bud's."

"Bud's? Good grief, it slipped my mind. Come on, it's time to board."

Between the businessman on his computer in the center seat, and a crying baby in front of them, she couldn't continue the conversation. The tires scraped the rough pavement on the runway, and she breathed a sigh of relief.

Three chatty women inched up the incline in front of them in the jet away.

"Let's push our way through," she mumbled.

"Patience, sweetheart."

In the airport lobby, she headed toward a row of pay phones. "I need change, Russell, please."

He handed her his cell instead. "Calm down, Kelley. The hotel is number seven in speed dial." Russell cradled the Shaker Monkey in the crook of his arm.

Her hands trembled. *Four rings, five, six. Clair, answer the phone! Are you in the shower? Have you dozed off?* "No answer, Russell."

He grabbed the GPS from his pocket. Nausea swelled as she saw the color drain from his face.

Seven
Sabotage Detected

Files, registration forms, a half-eaten donut, and a mug of cold coffee littered Duffy's desk. Nervous fingers tapped a steady rhythm until a rapid knock disrupted the automatic tempo. "Come in," he grunted.

"Hey old man, got a minute?"

"Sure Doc. Did you get the test results?"

"Mind if I lock the door before we talk? This is confidential." Joe Paul dragged a chair close to the desk.

Duffy winced. "Geesh, JP, go easy on an old man. That sounded like a cat caught in a combine."

"Sorry, I don't want anyone to hear. Neither Bulldog nor Isabella can know any of this. Understand?" Joe Paul's eyes narrowed.

"Well, sure — if you say so. What's up?"

"The reason Tipper acts lethargic is because I found drugs in his system," Joe Paul said.

"What? Drugs? I, I can't imagine."

"Think hard, before I got here to help, did anyone else come around?"

Duffy took off the soiled cowboy hat and scratched the bald spot. "Several ranch hands and staff wandered in and out. A few expressed concern, others only curious. Why?"

"Think through the entire day's events. Did you notice any new faces? How long did the mare's labor last? Did you leave her alone? Anything unusual?"

Scent of Double Deception

Duffy pointed to the wall calendar. "First, because of the holidays, I didn't ask anybody to work; some live in the bunkhouses. Second, the first contraction came around 11:00 PM, Christmas Eve. The pain increased, saw it in her eyes, so I left to get more chloral hydrate from the medicine cabinet."

"How much did you administer?"

"Just standard procedure, Doc, five grams per hundred pounds for a slower reaction time. I thought I'd have to tranquilizer her, though."

"Did you?"

"Did I what?"

"Use any tranquilizers?"

"No, you got here, the foal got here, and everything settled down."

Joe Paul thumbed through a folder. "The tests show traces of methadone hydrochloride, or Dolophine, in Ms. Tip's blood."

"Doc, I don't even stock that stuff. What's it for?"

"The horse is less responsive to painful stimuli—add tranquilizers, and it's lethal. A chain reaction starts and puts extra stress on vital organs until it's too late."

"Oh my God." Duffy shook his head.

Joe Paul stood up. "You said Tipper acts drowsy, doesn't want to nurse. I thought it might be CSNF."

"What?"

"Convulsive Syndrome of Newborn Foals, a nervous disorder. The foal doesn't want to eat, only sleep or lie still. Sometimes you have to insert a tube for nourishment. Tipper's blood work shows traces of Dolophine. Could have gotten it from his mother, but I think minuscule doses started several days before the delivery and caused the early birth."

"Sounds like a close call for both mother and baby." Duffy sighed.

"I'll start high doses of antibiotics and vitamins and check on them daily, so don't worry."

Duffy jumped to his feet. "Oh sweet Jesus!"

"What?"

"Russell's conversation."

"Who is Russell?"

"I met an old friend for lunch, trust me he's reputable. His Dad, Martin, and I were MP's in the Marines. Afterwards, ol' Marty went to the police academy, and I found my niche in the horse world. Russell's background is in law enforcement. I thought the boy wanted to visit, but our talk bothered me."

"How does this tie into our problems?" Joe Paul leaned against the desk.

"Well, the other morning, in a little coffee shop downtown, he overheard a conversation. Two characters in the booth behind him mentioned Bulldog."

"Russell knows Bulldog?"

"No, he's contract security for Isabella's wedding. Anyway, he heard the two guys say 'nothing is detected yet'. Russell checked out their license plate, and it's registered to Silks and Saddles."

"Can he find out who they are?"

"His description fits Lee Helms, our racing manager, and Jess Owens, a new jockey apprentice. Russell needs to know about the test results." Duffy rubbed his forehead.

"I've met Lee, but not Jess. We are both concerned, but don't overreact. You agreed this information would stay right here. We have to work together.

Scent of Double Deception

"You're right, Doc." He nodded.

"I'll put my trusted ranch hands on twenty-four hour watch over here."

"Won't it look suspicious?"

"If anyone asks, say its Isabella's orders. My greatest fear is it might go deeper than horse sabotage. I'm worried about Isabella. The media already swarm like hornets in the summer for a glimpse of the bride."

"Yeah, she's like a daughter to me, too. All right, I won't contact Russell, unless something else happens." His knuckles whitened as he gripped the edge of the desk.

Joe Paul stuck out his hand. "I'll contact you daily."

****

Clair swept her long, chestnut hair up, smoothed the mauve linen skirt, and studied the reflection in the mirror. Rested and ready to go, briefcase in hand, she left for the appointment. The Riley limo waited by the hotel entrance. *How thoughtful of Isabella. I hate to drive in unfamiliar traffic.*

An early morning fog receded, and the horizon came into full view. Lush meadows encased the enormous ranch of Silks and Saddles. She breathed in the crisp air.

The gray-haired butler, Colonel, opened the front door. "Good mornin' to ya, Ms. Matthews. Mistah Riley and Ms. Isabella is out on the veranda. I'll show ya the way."

"Thank you, Colonel."

They walked through the large, marbled foyer to a glassed-in veranda. An arrangement of primrose and heather graced the center of a long buffet table. Baskets

Scent of Double Deception

of biscuits, bagels, and fresh fruit in crystal bowls tickled her senses.

"Ms. Matthews." Bulldog kissed her hand.

"Please, call me Clair, Mr. Riley."

"Clair." He bowed and pulled out a chair. "Only if you call me Bulldog."

"Bulldog." She smiled.

"Isabella got a phone call, she will be here soon. I'm sorry for this little inconvenience. Naturally, we value your opinion."

"Certainly."

The patio door slid open, and Isabella burst into the room. "Oh, Clair, it's so good of you to come. I hope Daddy didn't bore you. Where's Kelley?"

"On a little emergency for another client, but she sends regrets."

"She is still a part of my plans, right? I hired both of you."

"Yes, she'll be back in a couple of days, the downfall of being your own boss. I'm sure your father can attest.

"Absolutely, it's smart business to have a partner. You can spread yourself too thin sometimes. It will all be fine, dear," Bulldog said.

"I am sure you're right. So, you'll double-check the measurements so I can have a second pavilion tent?"

"Let's go now," Clair said.

"We might need to move the reception after all," Bulldog added.

As they started to leave, Isabella pulled back from the open limo door. "Oh wait, Daddy. I want to check on the horses before we leave. Can we drive down to the barn?"

"Sure sweetheart," he replied.

Scent of Double Deception

Clair donned dark glasses against the bright sunshine and followed the bride. "The whitewashed fences, and red barn backdrop behind the stables, could be a vacation advertisement for Tennessee or Kentucky. It's so picturesque."

"Most people don't appreciate the beauty of this country. Glad you do," Bulldog remarked.

"Come on, Clair, join me in the stables," Isabella urged.

She stared in disbelief. "In heels?"

"The walkways are all concrete, you'll be fine. I want to show you my baby." Isabella explained the pony's heritage.

Clair sneezed. "Oh excuse me. It's the dust from the hay."

"Listen to me go on. Hope I haven't bored you."

"Oh no, your horses are exquisite. I need to remember to bring my boots and jeans next time."

Isabella smiled. "You and Kelley are more like friends. I appreciate the closeness, and hope we keep in touch after the wedding."

"Of course. Are you ready to tackle those measurements now?" She slid inside the limo. A tall man beside the ranch office door caught Clair's attention. A white Stetson shadowed his face. He touched the brim in acknowledgement, and an uneasy flutter churned in her stomach. *I'm jumpy from the night at the casino. I don't know him, yet he does look familiar.*

****

The morning light beamed off the waxed Riley limo, and Joe Paul adjusted his hat from the glare. Isabella and an attractive brunette got inside. *Well now, who are you? Something about the color of your hair, the shape of your profile...take off those sunglasses, little lady, let's get a good look.* The visitor turned to face him. Hidden in the shadows, he watched them drive away. Puffs of dust trailed the sleek vehicle.

The office door creaked opened, two men approached. The older man asked, "Uh, got any idea where the foreman might be?"

"Duffy ran an errand. I'm Joe Paul Farrell, can I help?"

"Yeah, Lee Helms, I met you before. I'll check back later. Come on, Jess."

Joe Paul made sure they left before he checked on the mare and foal. Tipper lay on the golden straw next to his mother. She shook her head and snorted, eyes glassy. He took her blood pressure, 317/185. Fear rippled through him. Earlier, it registered a healthy 143/94. *What changed?* "Whoa honey, it's gonna be okay." He injected a small dose of chloral hydrate then took another blood sample. *Is this something medical or more sabotage? Where are my ranch hands?* He glanced at his watch. *Shift change...they better overlap from now on. This can't happen again. Duffy, it's time to give your friend Russell a call.*

Eight
Unwanted Arrival

Trepidation crept into Celeste Vandergriff's heart. She hesitated before the telephone settled into the cradle, lost in the secrets kept from her precious Clair. *These episodes will stop, my darling, and too soon, the façade revealed.*

The thick, brocade curtain rustled as an aged hand pushed it aside. She studied the peaceful tree-lined street through the picture window of her grand Victorian home on Moongate Hill. The house, built in 1889, of old money, boasted generations spoiled by the prosperity of the first settlers of the township. Side by side, noble mansions showcased long years of careful floriculture. Emerald waterfalls of greenery cascaded down their walls into pools of efflorescent brilliance. Townspeople paid the price for such lush foliage and rich gardens—an ever-present rain. Nevertheless, she enjoyed Seattle.

A faint sigh escaped. She turned toward the kitchen while visions of Clair's childhood played through her mind. Unlike most of the houses on this street, it sported a wrap-around porch. The memory of a feisty three-year-old, who gave chase at the prospect of a bath, brought a smile. She remembered the time when she, Clair's mother, and younger sister, romped together on the same veranda. Good times, bad, happy, and sad…this house saw it all.

In winter, birds migrate to warmer environments, and so did Clair, but not to live in the family home.

Celeste knew the moment the scholarship was awarded from SMU, her niece would never come back. Clair found a niche in Dallas, a career, and business partner—far from family. Celeste missed her quick smile and doeskin eyes, which could flash anger as well as laughter. The protection she tried to bestow dwindled across the great distance, but she could never stand in the way. Texas made Clair happy, and Kelley and Russell's friendship provided peace of mind.

The warm bouquet of homemade cocoa filled the kitchen. Steam rose from the pot, and she held her face over the aromatic brew to revel in its comfort. Simmered to perfection, she poured it into a favorite old mug; one Clair gave her many years ago. It announced *World's Best Mother* on the side. She cherished the sentiment, the most prized possession, Clair's deepest love revealed in one gesture.

"Well, it doesn't do much good to wallow in self-pity Celeste Vandergriff. Clair does not live here anymore, but is coming for a visit, so gather yourself old woman." She glanced at the calendar. "Goodness, only a few weeks left to prepare for the party. I'd better get energized."

From the drawer, she retrieved a notebook and prepared a list. Prideful of her organizational skills, lists drove her, became a mainstay. Items on paper niggled until every one disappeared under the eraser. The roster included eligible bachelors, invitations, important townspeople, the Black Forest cake recipe, hors d'oeuvres, a new dress, and wait staff. The phone interrupted. "Yes, hello, who is it?"

"No need to snap at me, Celeste Vandergriff. I'm the last person you want to piss off."

She dropped the pen. "Linford, I'm sorry. I am in the middle of something. I didn't expect your call."

"Never mind, I called to let you know I'm on my way to the States. The flight leaves at 7:00 AM our time and should arrive 3:00 PM your time. Have a car at the airport. Highgrove will call with the particulars. See you tomorrow."

The phone clicked in her ear as she protested. "Stubborn old coot, how dare he dictate to me. I have a good mind to let him rot at the airport." She threw the pen and pad inside the drawer and slammed it shut. The evening ruined, she decided to go to bed. *I must keep him away from Clair.*

****

The next afternoon, as promised, the hired car pulled into the circular drive, and like the gloom of the overcast Seattle sky, delivered a grumpy Linford Thurlow.

"Uncle, it's nice to see you," Celeste said.

"Save the pleasantries. You know as well as I, we hate each other. Show me my room and bring refreshment. I need rest before we get down to business." He hobbled up the stairs, his cane thumped on each step. Out of breath, he cursed his hostess for the second-level room. "You did it on purpose. You could have put me on the ground floor."

"Why Uncle Linford, I don't know what you mean. I gave you the best room in the house. If I'd prepared a room on the first floor, you would have accused me of treating you like an invalid. There is no pleasing you."

"Bring me tea and crumpets, or whatever you Americans call refreshment," he barked. A hint of a smile crossed his face. *Oh, how she wants to tell me off. It must choke her to hold it in. Let's see the reaction to the news about the plans for Clair.*

An hour later, rested, he stood at the top of the stairs and stamped the old, wooden cane.

Celeste appeared at the bottom landing. "Yes?"

"I am not coming down there. You need to come up to hear my decision." Satisfaction spread like a warm blanket through his being as he watched her climb. *I still have the power here. She will not soon forget it when I am through.*

Settled in the only chair in the room, he laid out the reasons for a trip to the States. "It is time to act. Enough tomfoolery, the waiting game is over. Now is the time to tell Clair. I need a replacement for my perfume industry, and since you made the bargain in her infancy, I expect action. If your sisters had backbone, any sense of family commitment, this would not be necessary. They bolted like two spineless deer, abandoned their children, and created havoc. You promised to give me Clair to take over the business. I have heard all your excuses, and now it is time. I want to speak to her in person. I won't take no for an answer." He watched Celeste squirm on the edge of the large poster bed. *Uncomfortable in her own house.* He almost laughed aloud at his power.

"Linford, I have a solution. Please give me a few more weeks. Clair is in the middle of a large wedding right now. After it is over, she is coming for a visit. Can't you wait to break the news?"

"A few weeks? You want me to stay here for a few weeks? Absolutely not!"

"No, it's not necessary for you to stay — send Mr. Highgrove. He can handle the business. I promise you, we will tell Clair together."

"Highgrove? Well, I don't know. I've waited long enough."

"Uncle, you know as well as I, your gruff demeanor might scare Clair off. Mr. Highgrove's diplomacy is impeccable, he'll convince her."

Linford stroked a wiry, gray beard, stared out the window, took a puff from the worn cherry-wood pipe, and looked back at his niece. "You are right, but I don't like it. She needs to train, learn the ropes. We must begin. There's no one else to do it."

Celeste stood and walked toward him. "Yes, I know, Linford. You'll get your wish very soon."

He jerked his hand away as she bent to pat the gnarled appendage. "Don't coddle me, Celeste. I may be old, but my brain is fine. Your condescension won't work on me."

"You're tired. I am only trying to reassure you. Dinner is at 5:00. You may come down to dine, or I will bring a tray up. Instead of stamping your cane, there's an intercom by the end table."

She turned to go, and he said to her rigid back, "I'll come down for dinner. See you at 5:00."

"Lovely."

He smiled, triumphant. *She may think she won the first round, but I am not finished. Clair and Highgrove's immediate departure will take everyone by surprise.*

Nine
An Unexpected Encounter

Clair unzipped the daily planner and ran a finger across the day's activities. *Ah, no clients today, time for me.* She made a mental note to stop by the bank after her nail appointment.

At Extreme Nails, she talked to Dixie, the owner, about manicures for the Riley wedding party.

"Girl, how can I ever thank you? I'll call Miss Riley today and work out the details," Dixie said.

****

In line at the bank, Clair mused over Dixie's exuberance and did not pay attention to the male voice behind her. A slight touch on one shoulder, and the word 'Natasha', caused her to turn around. *Oh my God, those green eyes.*

"It's you! Don't you remember me? Joe Paul Farrell — Adams Rib, on Christmas Eve?"

Natasha? Okay, stay calm, take a breath, and get into character again. "Mr. Farrell, of course, how are you?"

"Please, call me Joe Paul. What are you doing here?"

"Why, I declare, what a question."

"I'm sorry. I really meant to ask about Olivia," he stammered. "I mean, I thought I'd hear from her. I've gone back to the restaurant, but . . ."

"She's away." Clair walked to the teller and lingered at the counter. Out of the corner of her eye, she noticed his impatient expression. *Take your time. Make him sweat.* She finished the transaction, thanked the teller, waved, and hastened toward the door. "Bye Joe Paul, good to see you."

"Please wait, Natasha. Can we talk?"

She shook her head. "I really don't have much time. I need to be somewhere."

"Okay, how about dinner? Can I buy you dinner? We're friends, please won't you consider it?"

Guess I'll stop the torture, although, it's fun to watch you squirm, Mr. Farrell. "I suppose we could."

"Good, I will pick you up. Where are you staying?"

"I'll meet you. Where are we going?"

"Darn it woman, I don't bite."

"Another time then." She bit her lip to stifle a grin. *This is my game, my rules, mister.* She exited the bank, Farrell a few steps behind.

"Wait, forgive me. We can meet at any restaurant. You call the shots, Natasha. What about Copeland's?"

"Okay, I'll meet you there at 7:00 PM," she said.

"Thanks, 7:00 it is," he called out in the parking lot.

The car door ajar, Clair slowly slid a leg inside. *Ah, I'm such a naughty girl. I've never played Natasha alone. Oh Kelley, this is priceless.*

****

At 6:30 PM, Clair stepped through the elevator doors and asked the valet for the car. Excitement surged as she maneuvered through the light traffic.

The concierge at Copeland's did a double take, and she smiled, confident in the role of Natasha. The night's conquest stood in the foyer preoccupied by the maître d'. She cleared her throat.

Joe Paul turned, eyes wide. "My God, you're beautiful."

Hair in a French twist, she stood in an elegant, black strapless dress, no adornment, the only accessory, a pair of diamond stud earrings. A matching crepe shawl rested around slim elbows and revealed bare shoulders. The drape of the dress outlined her curvaceous figure.

"Pardon me, good evening, Natasha."

"Hello, Mr. Farrell." The hem of the skirt danced around her slim ankles and accentuated red, open-toed stilettos. In a fluid movement, she stepped toward him.

He touched her elbow as the Hostess led the way to a cozy table behind an ivy-covered trellis. "Would the gorgeous lady like to choose a wine?"

"Lovely, a Pinot Blanc would be perfect."

She studied him, dapper in a dark brown jacket, slacks, and open-collared shirt. *Your admirer is so debonair tonight, Kelley. I can't wait until he works up the courage to interrogate me about you.*

"Natasha, have you ever been to Copeland's?"

She opened the menu. "Yes, many times. I can't resist the Blackened Redfish. I love the Cajun spices they use."

"Good choice." He grinned.

The waiter appeared with the wine. "Good to see you again, Mr. Farrell. Would you like an appetizer?"

"We'll have whatever the lady desires."

"Yes, the Bayou Broccoli and LeCheese Toast are wonderful." She closed the menu.

"I've never tried it, but sounds great." Joe Paul handed the menus to the waiter. "Two orders, please. Now, I'd like to apologize for my rudeness this afternoon, Natasha. You surprised me. On a normal basis, I'm very dashing, if you recall Christmas Eve." He laughed.

"I thought it quite endearing, although a bit brazen," she replied.

"May I ask if your visit in Shreveport is a pleasure stay?"

"It's always a pleasure to come to the Shreveport/Bossier area." *Go ahead Mr. Dashing; get to the real reason behind your list of questions. I won't make it easy for you.*

"This is small talk, but you're so secretive. Do you and Olivia work for the CIA or something?"

A mischievous smile played at the corner of her mouth. "Now, we get to the crux of things—Olivia."

The waiter placed the appetizers on the table. "Are you ready to order, madam?"

"The Blackened Redfish, the Cajun Popcorn Salad, and Vegetables Toot Toot, I adore the steamed vegetables."

"I'll have the Seafood Platter, Red Hot Potatoes, no salad," he said.

"Joe Paul, you really should eat your vegetables."

He sat back in the chair, arms crossed. "I think I need to be straightforward. Maybe you would respect me more. It's no secret I'm interested in Olivia, but I also consider you a friend. I want to get to know you both."

"Tell you what, eat one of these Bayou Broccoli appetizers, and I'll try to let down my guard a little." She speared a tree-shaped floret.

"Bring on the broccoli." He let out a hearty laugh, removed the morsel in question, and popped it in his mouth. "This is good."

"I admire a man who accepts a challenge."

Scent of Double Deception

"You mean I passed your test?"

"No test, I'm a cautious woman. It goes with the territory." She shrugged.

"Understandable, but can't we be friends? I believe we're on the same side." He raised his glass. "Truce?"

"I suppose."

"Is it too presumptuous to inquire about your friend? I'd like to talk to her again. How can I find her? Can't you tell me anything? I don't even know your last names."

She heard the sincerity in his voice. "I'm aware our friendship isn't the paramount topic for this dinner date," her tone softened. "However, I admit you sparked Olivia's interest, and who knows, it could work in your favor. If you behave, I'll put in a good word."

"Thanks," he said. "It's a beginning."

They continued the meal in silence while strains of contemporary music filled the air.

The waiter returned and filled their water goblets.

"What about you, pretty lady? Do you have someone special?"

"I married, divorced, and have two grown sons. Not much to tell."

"You're stunning, even a bit mysterious, but I see the wall you've built. I'm sure it's valid. You should relax though and enjoy life." He paused. "If you're interested, I married and divorced, too. I have a grown daughter I haven't seen in several years. Her mother took her away at the age of eight to live abroad.

She saw a muscle quiver in his jaw, his mouth twisted. "What's her name?"

"Emma, but I always called her Princess when she was little. The distance made it hard to stay close." He let out a long breath.

"Can't you try to develop a relationship now?"

He threw the linen napkin on the table. "Oh, you're good."

"Excuse me?"

"This is about you, not me."

She raised an eyebrow. "No, it's about Olivia. I didn't change the subject. She has two grown sons, also, and understands the pain."

He ran a finger around the rim of his glass. "I want to know her, Natasha. When can I see her?"

"Do you have a cell phone? I'll tell her to call you."

"Fair enough, in case she lost my card, here's another."

She studied the information. "You're a registered vet?"

"Yeah, it pays the bills." He signed the credit card receipt and handed it to the waiter. "How about an after dinner drink? The Blue Crawfish is a couple blocks away, and they have a great jazz band."

"Some other time, I enjoyed the evening." She slid the shawl around her shoulders. "I need to get back." She watched the sparkle in his eyes vanish. *Game over.*

****

In the shadows of the restaurant, Spencer Walker could not deny a despondent heart. The vision in the black evening gown provided the glow in the room, and emotion swept him in an adrenaline rush. He recognized the Natasha mode, and loved the character, and yes, he loved the woman. The difficulty of what he must do engulfed him like raging ocean swells. His job, his whole world, rotated around Clair Matthews. He ran a hand through thick, dark hair and closed his eyes in an attempt to erase her image. *Natasha, Clair, whoever you choose to be, my heart belongs to you. This assignment is impossible now. It is time, Celeste Vandergriff. I have to call you tonight. We can't wait any longer.* He turned to leave and noticed Clair glance in his direction. *Damn! Gotta get out of here before you see my face. I've taken too many chances lately.*

Ten
Clair's Blunder

A persistent alarm coaxed Clair's eyes open. *Oh crap, morning already? Lots to do today, better get at it.*

The glassed-in shower turned into a sauna, steam curled around her body while hot water soothed tight muscles, and she succumbed to the pleasure. Too soon, the relentless clamor of the phone interrupted the daybreak delight. She wrapped her hair in a towel and hurried to quell the intrusion. "Good morning."

"Clair? Is that you?"

"Yes DeLinda, you're up early already. Something wrong?"

"Well, I'm not sure. I think I've caused a little upset."

"Don't worry, Kelley is in Hawaii. You'll get the right fabric."

"It doesn't involve the fabric—it's the cake," she said.

"The cake? It's taken care of, remember? You chose the Layers of Grandeur at Cake Celebrations, Chef LaRue's specialty."

"See, I helped my girlfriend pick out her cake at another shop. I'm afraid I found something I like better."

Clair moved the phone to the other ear and wiggled into her robe. "Really, which shop?"

"Sweet Connections."

Oh no, Chef LaRue's bitter rival. "DeLinda, please tell me you didn't call Chef LaRue and cancel or tell him where you went. You signed a contract at Cake Celebrations."

"I did, and he reminded me in language I've never heard before. I had no idea it would cause such a stir."

Clair jerked the damp towel off her head. "Do you have a picture of the other cake?"

"Yes, and it's so beautiful."

"Fax it to me. I have an idea." Her client reassured, she chuckled. Never mind, we thrive on a good challenge. She could visualize Chef LaRue's fiery red face at Delinda's news. *He needs a careful touch.*

****

White puffy clouds against a blue sky restored Clair's good mood on the drive to the scheduled appointment. She found a parking space at June's Flower Shop and killed the motor. The picture DeLinda sent revealed one simple difference from Chef LaRue's design. She dialed the baker's number. "Monsieur LaRue, how's my favorite chef today?"

"I am not well at all, Miss Clair," his distinct French accent roared. "The client of yours, that arrogant, insensitive — what *is* her name? She has…"

"Now Jacque, I spoke to DeLinda. I think I can solve the problem. Will you listen?"

"Yes, yes of course, Miss Clair, anything for you. Although, I will tell you right now, I won't stand still for this defection to my most hated rival."

"I saw the picture of the cake she chose, and frankly, I think you can outdo it. No, let me retract that statement, I know you can. The only real differences are the roses and a winding staircase. I am sure you can alter the design to accommodate our client and put one over on your adversary. What do you say? Can I fax the picture to you? Wouldn't you like to beat them at their own game?"

"I suppose I can compromise. I am known for my designs, and I won't copy someone else's work. If I put my mind to it, I can add what she wants and make it my own creation. She will love it. Fax it right away, I'll begin immediately."

"You're a wonder. I will do it right now. I knew I could count on you." *I adore this part of the job. Delinda will have no choice but to agree.*

She entered the shop and inhaled the sweet perfume of fresh flowers. "Hello Ms. Greer, how's my favorite florist today?

"Good morning, my dear. I have a couple of FTD orders to call in. Can you hang on a second?"

"Sure, may I borrow your fax machine?"

"Go right ahead, it's in the corner."

Moments later, the ladies sat down and discussed the details of Isabella Riley's upcoming event. The two worked well together and understood the wishes of their mutual client. Clair left satisfied, one more task accomplished.

****

Two athletic-looking women dressed in sweats walked past Clair in the hotel lobby.

"What a good idea, exercise is a perfect way to top off my day. I've got thirty minutes to kill before Kelley calls."

Excited, she hurried to the room, changed quickly, and sprinted back to the gym to find it empty. "Where did they go? Oh well, I'll workout alone." Headphones in place, she stepped on the treadmill, and began her mile run. *Whew, I'll sleep well tonight.* She grabbed a towel to blot the sweat off her face and looked up in time to see the locker room door swing shut. "Hello?"

No one responded.

The hair on the back of her neck stood on end. "Great, I almost forgot about these little episodes. Shreveport, Louisiana makes my imagination work overtime." She turned to retrieve her bag. A shadow crossed the glass door to the lobby, and her heart skipped a beat. "Am I hallucinating?" She gripped the cold handle of the transparent door, shivered, and forced it open. The hall looked empty, but just ahead, the courtyard door closed slowly. "Okay, I'm too jumpy. People come in and out of a hotel all the time, nothing strange about it."

Safe in her room, she tried to relax under a hot shower. *Where is Kelley when I need her? She's on a tropical island, and I'm here, paranoid and alone.*

Her warm, fuzzy robe did little to assuage any apprehension. The walls closed in, and anxiety and anger rivaled each other for control. Why hasn't Kelley called? The more she tried to sort it out, the faster she paced. *Hawaii must be irresistible. That's it. Kelley convinced Russell to stay longer, and why not? I'm here taking care of business.* One fist slammed into the other palm. *They haven't called because they don't want to hear me rant and rave. Are they on a flight or still over there? Am I supposed to sit here and twiddle my thumbs? Be the humble little twit, let them have all the fun?* She stamped a foot and threw her cell phone on the bed. "Damn it. I want to go to Bud's tonight. I don't need Russell, I'm grown. My mind is made up, I'm going."

She put on a tan, corduroy jacket, blue jeans, red pumps, and studied the reflection in the mirror. "Not bad. I'll go for a few minutes and scout it out. Not sure what I expect to see anyway. It's just a common name written on an ordinary business card."

****

The pungent odor of stale cigarettes and free-flowing alcohol invaded Clair's senses at the entrance of the seedy bar. The noise overpowered her, instinct said to turn around and leave. "Maybe I should have listened to Russell, after all."

Indecision proved a mistake.

"Howdy little lady, come on in." The deep, gravel-like voice resonated from the bar. The bartender used a dingy apron to clean a spot on the worn, wooden counter, and gestured for her to sit.

She straightened her collar, accepted the offer, and sat on the barstool, one foot still on the floor.

"What's your fancy?" He leaned over the sticky counter.

"I'll…uh, I'll have a Zima, thank you."

The overweight bartender tossed back his baldhead and rolled out a loud guffaw. He caught his breath and said, "We don't serve those fancy beverages, honey. This here's a beer joint."

Horrified, she stared in disbelief at the rude barkeep. "Well, give me a Coors Lite." *Should I leave? I'm out of my element.*

Snickers, and other derisive laughter, broke out in the background.

The plan to lay low dissolved in an instant. She fought to regain composure even though heat rose in both cheeks. Back stiff and face forward, she decided to wait out the mockery.

Before long, the normal clamor of the bar returned.

The tavern keeper slid a bottle toward her. "Need a glass, honey?"

She stood up and placed money on the counter. "No thanks."

A small, unoccupied table in the corner of the room caught her eye. She made her way toward it, defiant. *They aren't going to chase me out of here. I can hold my own.* Back against the wall, she sipped the beer and glanced around. The jukebox played a loud, rowdy song. She relaxed and scanned the faces of the crowd. Most of the men looked right at her, but levelheaded, she stared back. *Would I recognize anyone in a place like this?* A small finger of fear crept up her spine as she adjusted to the smoky room. *I'm the only woman in here. Why didn't I listen to Russell? If I leave now, someone might follow me.* She considered the circumstances. Even the bartender watched and chuckled. *Fool, all because of a business card. If I reach for my cell phone, it will translate as panic.* Beer bottle to her lips, Russell's warning echoed once more. *No consolation, he's out of town. I need a plan.*

One table over, two men, hunched together in conversation, caught her attention. The older man pointed a finger at his buddy, who resembled a popular country singer; the only difference was brown hair and no Stetson. Nerves calmed a bit, she decided to concentrate on the twosome and leaned closer.

"I tell you Lee, I don't like it. We can't be ready by February 14th." He sat back and scratched his head. "We need more time. If it's not planned right, we'll blow it. Besides, I think the foreman is a little suspicious."

Scent of Double Deception

"Jess, all I know is it has to take place at the wedding." He smacked a fist against the table. "There's no other opportunity."

Her hand tightened around the beer, surprised at the words February 14th and wedding. Even though the name Riley hadn't come up, it produced a chill. *Valentine's Day is a popular wedding date.* She tried to convince herself it meant nothing.

The table shook, she looked up.

A man pulled out the opposite chair and sat down. "What brings a pretty thing like you to a joint like this? Lookin' for some fun tonight?"

Uh oh, trouble.

A product of too much alcohol, his thick southern drawl slurred, and his breath affirmed it.

She didn't blink, but looked him straight in the eye. "If I wanted fun, this isn't the place. I'm a reporter on a story, and you're blowing my cover. Please leave."

"Why, honey, I ain't goin' nowhere 'til we get to know each other better." He leaned the chair back on two legs, beer in hand, and winked. "A reporter, huh? From around here? What paper?"

His smirk irritated her, and under the table, she balled a fist. "Look, I asked you nicely to leave. Don't make me get ugly. I'm on the clock here." She hoped the force in her tone made its point.

The room quieted. Once again, she became the center of attention.

"I'll go as soon as you tell me which paper you write for. Play nice missy, or I might find myself in a bad temper. You wouldn't want that now, would you?" His mouth twisted into a scowl. He used a beer bottle to push up the brim of the cowboy hat and waited.

Scent of Double Deception

"It's called Asshole Incorporated—not a newspaper, a magazine." Both hands flat on the table, she met his menacing stare. "I think I just found my centerfold."

Laughter erupted across the room.

His beefy face turned crimson. In a slow, deliberate movement, he let the chair scrape the floor, pushed it back, and stood.

"Hey Ralph, leave the lady to herself. She ain't hurtin' no one." The bartender stood behind the big man, baseball bat secured in his large hand.

"Mind your own damn business, Joe. This little uppity slut can't talk to me that way. You go back to pourin' drinks. I'll handle this."

"Look, I don't want no trouble outta you is all I'm sayin', okay? It's only been two weeks since I got the last repairs done." Before he finished the sentence, the intoxicated goon turned around and punched him in the face. The barkeep crumpled in a heap.

An ominous hush filled the bar, and everyone's attention riveted on the drunk.

Clair's throat tightened, and her body stiffened. She realized the calamity of her decision, but kept eyes locked on him, resolved not to succumb to fear. The only apparent ally lay sprawled, unconscious on the gritty barroom floor. The fact he resembled an overgrown gorilla caused a slight smile to form.

"Oh, I see. So you like it rough, don't you, baby?" He grabbed her arm and jerked her up.

His hand encircled her forearm so tight she thought he'd squeeze it in half. In a split second, the blood rushed back into her body, and a familiar voice boomed.

"No asshole, *I'm* the one that likes it rough."

The scenery dimmed. The muffled sound of wood breaking, the scuffle of feet, and the snap of broken bones reverberated in Clair's ears. A piquant smell of blood filled the air. The jukebox blared, tables toppled, and chairs flew across the room. Consciousness tried to elude her, vision faded, and both knees buckled. Two men gyrated in front of her. The stranger looked familiar by his size. *Who is my defender?* Someone groaned followed by a loud thud.

A soft hand cupped her cheek. "Clair, Clair, please open your eyes. Are you okay? Please, answer me, please." A voice called out.

Kelley? She struggled to open her eyes. In a flash, strong masculine arms swept up her limp body. *Who is the white knight? Everything is blurred. Did I hit my head? Wait a minute, I know these arms.*

Russell gently placed Clair inside the SUV, head on Kelley's lap. Kelley dabbed at the cut on Clair's forehead.

"Damn it, that hurts."

"Hold still, you're bleeding."

She tried to brush the hand away. "It's nothing, leave it alone."

"You bumped your head, there's a knot forming. I'm going to doctor you whether you like it or not."

"I'd say she's okay if she's fussing at you already." Russell chuckled.

"Keep it down. Why are you laughing?" Clair groaned.

"They just tossed the ignorant redneck out on his ass," Russell said. "He's sprawled all over the pavement like yesterday's trash."

Eleven
Undercover Bodyguard

Clair returned to consciousness as light filtered through the parted drapes. *It's dawn. Guess I slept through the night.* The adventure at Bud's forced its' way into her brain. She sat up, touched her forehead, and winced. "Crap, it wasn't a dream."

A quick glance around the room confirmed it. *Kelley is here. I remember a cup of hot chocolate. I washed my hair, and let's see, what happened next? I held the hairbrush...* "She's done it again. Her two secret lives, an aroma therapist and alter ego, Olivia, crossed paths." Clair's voice muffled as she pulled a turtleneck over her head. "She's gotta tell me about this fragrance thingy. Damn these tight boots, I have no patience this morning." She gave up the struggle for a moment and let her mind wander.

The dream of a fast-paced, high-profile career held her heart, and yet, the comfortable apartment in Dallas beckoned—an irresistible force. Months of consultations, stacks of catalogs, and endless emporiums culminated into her Shangri-La. "I need my quiet garden veranda, the trickle of the water fountain, music to soothe my soul." The boot went on with a pop. The rasp of the zipper on her suitcase reverberated in the quiet room.

Kelley moaned.

"Rise and shine sleepyhead, time's a-wastin'."

"What time is it?" Kelley's eyes remained closed.

"Seven o'clock, half the day is gone. I'm ready to get back to Dallas."

Kelley sat up, waffled her feet into fluffy slippers, and yawned. "Easy for you to say, 'Miss Passed Out with Your Hairbrush in Your Hand'. I had to tuck you into bed last night. What's the big hurry?"

The telephone interrupted their morning chat.

"Hello?" Clair answered.

"Yes, someone told me there's a woman in room 232 who can single-handedly take out redneck thugs. My neighbor is a troublemaker, and I'd like to hire her. Is she available?" replied the voice on the other end of the phone.

"Very funny, Russell, you're a barrel of laughs."

"How are you this morning? Did Kelley's brew do its magic?"

"I'm great, ready to get on the road. By the way, did I ever thank you for the knight-in-shining-armor act? I guess I should say thank you, although I did have everything under control."

"Actually, you didn't thank me, but you could buy me breakfast before I head to New Orleans. Why don't you and Kelley meet me downstairs in about twenty minutes?"

"New Orleans? What's in New Orleans?"

"Didn't you hear about Kitty?"

"No, who's Kitty?"

"Tell ya what, I'll let Kelley explain. See ya downstairs."

Clair hung up the phone and crossed her arms. "What have I missed? What's goin' on? Who the hell is Kitty?"

Scent of Double Deception

"Oh Clair, we have a lot to talk about. We need to sit down for one of our little gabfests. There's so much to tell."

"It'll have to wait. Russell wants us downstairs in twenty minutes for breakfast, so you better move it, girl."

****

The Lexus merged west onto the Interstate, and Clair glanced at Kelley. "Such fun, Russell in love."

"You should have seen him. His whole demeanor changed each time he looked at Kitty," Kelley said.

"I, for one, am glad. We take up too much of his time. He needs to have a life."

"Now, what's up besides trying to get yourself killed?"

Clair took a sip of the latte and grinned. "I could make you guess, but we only have two hours of driving left, so here's a hint. Olivia made a huge impression on a certain individual. I would liken his fascination to a Great Dane puppy starved for affection. The puppy lopes forward in anticipation of attention—his large, round eyes alight and trips over his own feet," she teased.

"What in Heaven's name, Clair? Did you buy a dog, a Great Dane, of all things?"

"No, but think back to Christmas Eve...a certain club...a fascinating man...a night of magic."

Kelley's eyes widened. "Joe Paul? Did you see him or talk to him? When, where? What did he say?"

"I did more than see him. He took me to dinner," she announced.

"Dinner? Oh my God, spill it, Clair! How did it happen? Did he ask about me? Did you give away our real identities?"

"Slow down, Kel. Let me start at the beginning. While in line at the bank, a voice behind me called my name, not Clair, but Natasha. It didn't sink in until he touched my arm and said it again. I turned around and big as life stood Joe Paul Farrell. Since he used Natasha I had to play along." The car handled like a dream as she moved back and forth through traffic. They enjoyed lighthearted laughter as she revealed the details of the entire encounter.

"Oh Clair, you're so bad. I can't believe you played Natasha alone. I can envision your grand entrance at Copeland's. You may not believe this, the only time my true self comes out is in the character of Olivia. What about you?" Kelley asked.

"I never thought about it, you're right. Natasha comes so natural. Wonder why? Maybe in another life we were rich and famous."

Kelley's voice softened, "Well maybe…"

"It's a joke, all in fun, a stress reliever, pure and simple. So, are you going to call Mr. Wonderful?"

"I want to, but should I?"

****

Celeste Vandergriff listened to Spencer turn in his resignation on the phone. Self-control evaporated. "Spencer, I know you love Clair, and it was a close call at that horrible bar. How could you imagine she would go alone to such a place? Thank God for Russell, but I'm sorry to say I cannot accept your resignation right now. We have all invested time and money in this project. Get a grip on yourself and act professional. She needs you now more than ever. Linford Thurlow is *here*, Spencer. Don't cross him. He'll never let you rest."

Celeste accepted his promise and sighed, relieved.

****

Spencer Walker, personal bodyguard to a woman unaware of his existence for ten years, and she has no clue. A stupid night of temptation at a nightclub where I held her soft curves against me, my body ached, desire blazed. The hotel lobby, the drink in the restaurant, what was I thinking? When she was in danger, and needed me most, I failed. She deserves better. He reclined on the bed, eyes closed. The alarm clock ticked by the seconds. Ten minutes later, he sat up, and stared at the image in the mirror. A day's growth of beard, and the panic on his face, reminded him of a psychopath in a 'B' movie. He got up, ran one hand over his stubble, and walked to the shower door. While the soapy foam cascaded over his muscled body, a plan formed. *I have to finish this job before my emotions unravel, and Clair gets hurt.*

Once again, in front of the mirror, clean-shaven, he straightened the starched white collar and addressed his reflection, "I'm getting out, out of this business, and out of Clair's life." Jaw set, he left the room resolved to regain his professional disposition.

****

Clair watched Kelley dial the cell phone. The glow on her friend's face told the story. "Put it on speaker," she whispered.

"Excuse me, is this Joe Paul Farrell? It's me, Olivia. Have I called at a bad time?"

"Certainly not, is it really you? After all this time, I didn't think I'd ever hear your voice again," he said. "Are you here in Shreveport?"

Scent of Double Deception

"Well, we're on our way to Dallas, and Natasha told me about your dinner date. I realized I hadn't called you."

Clair flinched at the mention of Dallas.

"Dallas, do you live there?" he asked.

"Our corporate office is in North Richland Hills. We will only be home a few days because we have business in San Antonio. Shreveport is on the schedule in a couple of weeks."

"Oh my gosh, my best buddy lives outside San Antonio," he said.

"Really, a friend in San Antonio? Well, maybe if the time is good for you, we might meet there."

Clair raised an eyebrow in mock surprise and suppressed laughter at the obvious tease.

Kelley winked and gave thumbs up.

Clair drove along in silence, her thoughts wandered to the night at Adams Rib and the mystery man.

"Where did you drift off to Clair, Clair?"

"Oh, were you talking to me? I have a lot on my mind, I guess. Did you talk Joe Paul into San Antonio?"

"You're not mad?"

"Of course not, you deserve a little fun. Enjoy his visit, but guard your heart."

"You're right. However, there's more. Hey, I see a Stuckey's up ahead." Kelley pointed. "I'm starved. Let's stop. I'll explain while we eat."

Clair eased into the lot. In the rearview mirror, she noticed a dark-haired man in a silver convertible.

"Something wrong, girl?"

"No, nothing, let's go eat. I want a window table, Kel. It's such a nice day." Once seated, she said, "Okay *Olivia*, what's up?"

Scent of Double Deception

"Let's order first. I'll tell you in a second." Kelley grabbed a menu.

Clair leaned forward and snatched the menu away. "You'll tell me now," her voice raised.

The restaurant bustled, and people began to stare.

"All right, all right, hold your horses. Joe Paul had a suggestion…"

"Kelley Malone?"

"Please, Clair, just consider it. I don't want to leave you alone in San Antonio while I'm with Joe Paul."

"It's a blind date, right? No, absolutely not."

"He assured me the friend is an old college roommate, a fellow rancher, and a perfect gentleman."

"You know blind dates are not acceptable, Kelley. I don't do them. Are you so smitten you would consider compromising our friendship, change the rules to get what you want? I'm a big girl. I can take care of myself."

"For your information, Miss Ice Princess, this started on a level playing field, consider it a continuation. You played Natasha without me. This evens the score."

A young waitress stood next to the table, pad and pen poised.

"I'm not hungry anymore. You order, Kelley." She threw the napkin on the table, stomped toward the ladies room, and elbowed through the crowd at the register.

A man stopped her. "Hey, you can't cut in line."

"Bug off mister," she barked.

"Leave the lady alone, buddy," a male voice interrupted.

That voice…I know that voice. She turned. "It's you."

"Just helpin' out a lady, miss. Sorry if I interfered."

"No, I mean, it's *you*, the man in Shreveport, the club. We danced, don't you remember?"

"Nope, never been to Shreveport, you're mistaken, only doing a good deed."

Her face flamed. "Oh, sorry, I thought…"

The man stepped aside, and she ran into the restroom to splash cold water on her face. "God, what is wrong with me? Have I lost it? He must think I'm crazy and desperate. On second thought, he looks nothing like the guy in Shreveport. How long will I have to wait in here for him to leave?" She opened the door and peeked out, but saw no sign of him. Another quick check of the crowd confirmed he left, and she hurried to the table.

"Get it to go, Kel. We have to leave."

"What happened? I'm hungry."

"I said get it to go—I'll explain in the car."

The waitress brought the order, and they left the eatery.

"You better start talking, Clair. I don't want to argue, but this is out of hand."

"Look, do whatever you want about the blind date, Kelley, I'll go along. I need to get home, get some rest in my own bed, and have a little peace and quiet."

"I think the bump on your head affected you. Listen, I'll set up the date, if you don't like him, you can walk away, no questions asked. I'm sorry, Clair. Our friendship means more to me than a man."

"Thanks, Kel, now let's…"

The good Samaritan from the restaurant rushed forward and stopped in front of her. "Miss, please, I want to explain."

"Look, it doesn't matter. I don't know what your game is, but I want no part of it. Please get out of my way."

"What's going on? You look like the man who danced with Clair at Adams Rib. What are you doing here?"

The stranger glanced over Clair's shoulder. "I want to apologize, and by the way, I don't play games."

She followed his gaze. "What are you looking at?"

A lone man in a black business suit stood a few feet away, arms at his sides. He gripped a leather briefcase in one hand, a fierce stare locked on the threesome.

Clair faced him, and he took a step forward. "Who's that, and what does he want?"

"Ladies, there's an ice-cream joint down the road. Let me buy you a cup of coffee or a latte. I want to explain."

"Hell no, we're out of here. Come on, Kelley."

The girls hastened to the Lexus, anxious to get as far away as possible. In her mirror, she saw the stranger approach the man in the suit. "I don't know what happened there, Kelley. Do you?"

"He looked like the man in Shreveport, I'm sure of it. It *was*, Clair, but the guy in the suit, who is he? Are they following us?"

"I don't know." She gunned the accelerator. "We won't make it easy for them."

Twelve
The Con

On top of the antique étagère, an old photo album sat undisturbed, covered in a film of dust.

The young maid retrieved the book and wiped it clean. "Ma'am, is this the one you wanted?"

"Yes, now leave and don't bother me." Katherine Forche crisscrossed the thin robe around her slender figure.

"Yes, Miss Kitty."

The door closed softly, the room silent once more.

Kitty sat down by an open window, the book clutched to her chest, hesitant to release the memories. Outside, the gentle breeze teased the Spanish moss, prisoner to the southern Louisiana humidity. Reveries danced in her head of a sassy little girl, long, ebony curls askew, tamed by a pink satin bow. A ragged teddy bear, and beautiful china doll, sat at a miniature round table, ready for lunch. Everyone drank make-believe tea in tiny porcelain cups, an idyllic time.

On the first page, aged photos captured the good and the bad. Each snapshot appeared conventional, even orthodox in nature. The façade before her brought a wave of nausea. The intense hunger for acceptance and love from her family resurfaced and snuffed out any pretense of a happy childhood.

She skimmed past several pages. "There it is." A finger traced over the old picture. A couple and two children, a boy about twelve and a girl around eight, huddled together—each presented a cheerful smile.

The young boy gripped the little girl's hand in a guardian position. On the next page, a young man rested his hands on the swollen belly of a dark-haired woman; his face glowed. A twinge of jealousy bubbled. A frown crossed Kitty's face at the sight of the next photo...a baby asleep in a pink bassinet. *Oh how unjaded I was by the world and innocent of my future.* A shiver ran across her back like a wayward snake. She slammed the book shut.

The knock on the door shattered the moment. "Excuse me ma'am, there's a Mr. Gibson on the phone, are you available?"

She nodded, placed the album aside, and picked up the extension. "Hello Russell, this is a pleasant surprise. What can I do for you?" She tried to suppress her amusement. "Indeed, I did enjoy our little rendezvous in Hawaii. Hmm, nice to know I've preoccupied your subconscious. This weekend? Of course, I would love you to come. Fountain Rue is my plantation in Chalmette outside New Orleans. I look forward to your arrival."

All previous envy dissolved. A tingle surged, her mouth pursed, and a euphoric smile formed. One accidental kismet meeting and Russell Gibson opened an untouchable door from the darkest craters of her mind. *Karma – such a glorious weapon.*

She took a deep breath and let her fingertips travel down her throat past plump, brown breasts. The sheer black robe fell open, and she let her warm palm rest inside her bare thighs. Erotic pleasure fanned a hot flame at the mere thought of the visitor. "Mr. Gibson, this time I might indulge myself, as well. I guarantee you will long remember this weekend...or forget.

"Yvette!"

"Ma'am?"

"Mr. Gibson plans to come for the weekend. Call my mentor."

The maid nodded and scurried away.

Sinister laughter filled the room, and hatred over the photo of her brother and his expectant wife faded. Today, disgust disappeared and no longer shadowed her heart.

****

Russell adjusted the seat in the truck for the second time and popped in another CD. Usually, driving relaxed him, but not today. He could not concentrate. *My heartbeat is like a metronome in my chest. What the hell is wrong? Perhaps it's the first sign of a cold. Maybe it's anxiety for Clair and Kelley's safety while I'm gone.* He bit his lip. *Those are stupid excuses. I'm the epitome of a solitary man and like to flaunt it, but Katherine Forche could challenge my bachelorhood.* He turned up the volume on the radio. Common sense screamed not to get involved.

Chalky pastel shades of dusk transformed the sky, and the sun floated on the horizon.

Crap, it's late. I didn't mean to talk so long to Duffy at lunch. He exited off the road to a hotel. Inside the room, he checked voice mail messages and the GPS device to track the girls' bracelets. Everything appeared normal.

The constant hum of traffic outside provided a palliative lullaby. He shed his clothes and climbed under the covers. Bare flesh slid across the sheets, the crisp coolness of the fabric invited sleep. *Gotta look my best for the lady.*

Wrapped in Kitty's embrace, his mouth traveled her body like a road map. A low moan escaped, and she pulled him on top of her smooth naked body. He nuzzled the firmness of her bosom. Bright red nails dug into the flesh of his buttocks. The sting aroused him more. Narrow hips and long, supple thighs writhed and wrapped around his muscular frame. He captured her mouth's sweetness while their bodies melted into ecstasy.

The slam of a car door brought him out of the intense dream. He sat up, and ran his fingers through coarse golden-red hair. "Whew, I hope that's a small intro of things to come."

The hot steamy spray of the shower peppered his skin like tiny fingers, stimulated his body, his mind locked on details of the dream.

Back on the road, pumped and excited, every song on the radio spoke to his heart while he crooned to the music. Near Chalmette, he dialed Kitty's number. "Kitty? This is Russell."

"Good morning, love. How long before you'll be here?"

"About an hour."

"Ah, I'd better put on some clothes."

"Clothes are optional, you know."

"You tease. I can't wait to see you," she whispered.

The cell phone snapped shut, his smiled widened, hungry, and lustful.

At the huge florid gate scripted, Fountain Rue, an electronic speaker stood guard. He cleared his throat to speak, a bit nervous.

"Mr. Gibson, please drive through," a voice blared from the square box.

Startled, he followed the long driveway to a large antebellum house. Majestic demeanor, regal old oaks, and Spanish moss welcomed his arrival. Two concrete cherubs, suspended on tiptoe, splashed in a mammoth water fountain. A balcony framed the entire face of the old house supported by Greek columns and ornate dormer windows. Massive rows of azalea bushes hugged the long porch.

Before he reached the antique door, it swung open.

A young woman, skin the color of caramel, and eyes like two golden coins, curtsied. "I'm Yvette. Please come in, Mr. Gibson."

"Thank you," he said.

She took a step to the side and closed the door. He watched her click the latch to the locked position.

"Miss Kitty will join you soon. Wait in the courtyard."

Outside, lush greenery surrounded wrought iron tables and chairs, an impression of seclusion. Such close quarters might give way to apprehension in another setting, but today he embraced the privacy.

Yvette brought a tray and offered a large glass of iced tea, a sprig of mint teetered on the rim.

Man, my body is hot, inside and out, maybe this will help. "Thank you, ma'am." He leaned back in a chair and stretched out his legs. A couple of deep gulps, and the cool liquid disappeared.

"Russell?"

He scrambled to his feet, his eyes swept her body — amber skin glowed against pale yellow shorts and a low-cut peasant blouse. Engulfed by desire, he kissed her extended hand, leaned forward, and pulled her close.

Scent of Double Deception

Wet lips nipped at his neck. Kitty explored his body, and he could not deny a firm response. His hands ran across the smoothness of bare shoulders, and she guided them to the swell of her breasts. He cupped her hard nipples. His kiss, slow and thoughtful, coaxed her tongue farther inside his mouth.

Wrapped in muscular arms, her back arched, and their torrid kisses continued.

Snippets of the vivid dream flashed through his mind, sweat dotted his brow. The patter of footsteps broke his concentration.

Yvette stood rigid, two glasses of tea on a tray.

Kitty continued to devour him and never acknowledged the intrusion.

Caught off guard, he tried to regroup. "Thanks for the tea, ma'am."

"Put it on the table and leave, Yvette," Kitty snipped.

The young woman quickly obeyed.

He watched a stony mask form on Kitty's face and eyes narrow to small slits. His hands settled around her small waist, and he pulled her closer. "I'm glad to see you again, sweet lady."

The glare disappeared, and her countenance brightened. Warmth returned to her voice, "Oh, I feel certain the pleasure is all mine."

"We'll see." He grinned.

"How long can you stay?"

"Only the weekend—work responsibilities interfere."

"So, let's make the most of our time together. I promise you something special. Now, tell me, what do you think of Fountain Rue?"

He leaned into the honeysuckle-laden trellis and inhaled the sweet fragrance. "It's gorgeous. How long have you lived here?"

"A while," Kitty sighed. "Yes, I suppose it's nice, although, it can't compare to some. It suits me for now. Why don't I show you around?"

They held hands and strolled through bountiful gardens, under huge oaks. Kitty narrated the romantic history of Fountain Rue. He watched her black eyes sparkle. She took him back in time where silk-shirted carpetbaggers, priests and pirates, southern belles and gamblers, renegades and rogues, roamed the territory. The tour ended at the foot of the porch steps.

Kitty rested against the carved handrail. "Would you like to hear a fable about Fountain Rue? Some in the parish believe it's a myth. I think the legend is true."

"Sure." He put his hands on her shoulders and focused on her full, luscious lips.

"The Battle of New Orleans took place in 1815. A desperate black slave of French descent, Xavier LeFlore, jumped ship to escape torturous bondage. Hours later, his exhausted body washed ashore. Fearful, though spent, he headed toward the forest to take refuge for the night. Days later, starved and delirious, he came upon this plantation."

"The owner of Fountain Rue, Gerard Dotier, a prominent statesman, left to fight in the war. Lia, his young bride begged him not to leave. Before his departure, they made love in the gazebo, and he promised one day he'd march victorious over the marshland, through the forest, and reclaim her."

"Uh, can we visit the gazebo?" Russell's hands slid to the fullness of her blouse.

Scent of Double Deception

She pushed him back. "Listen to the rest of the tale, you rascal. Each day, Lia donned her wedding gown, picked fresh roses from the garden, and rehearsed the marriage waltz in the gazebo. Xavier observed the ritual from the bough of a huge Oak tree until lust overtook him. The beautiful Lia continued to dance — unaware of the evil in the forest. The depraved trespasser drew close and waged a savage attack. The brutal rape killed her, and she died in his arms."

Russell balled his fist. "What a jerk."

"Do you scare easily, Russell?" Kitty raised an eyebrow.

"I'm not afraid of anything, sweetheart."

"The villagers maintain the ghost of Dotier still roams the grounds in search of his truelove, sword held high, ready to behead LeFlore."

"Sounds pretty damn macho to me."

"Macho? I prefer gallant...a man like you, Mr. Gibson." Gathered in his arms, she buried her hands in his thick hair.

The caress of her lips seared a path to his soul, teased, and invited a fiery ecstasy.

"Would the hot tub and a glass of wine interest you, perchance?" she offered.

"Sounds good."

She looped a finger in the band of his jeans and tugged. "Get rid of those and meet me in the parlor."

He craved her touch; an ache gripped his body. He savored the generous sway of her hips, the graceful movement of each step, as she vanished into the cavernous mansion.

"Russell?" Her voice dissolved into the void.

Two steps at a time brought him to the front door. "Right behind you." Instead of Kitty, he found the irksome maid in the middle of the foyer.

Yvette gestured for him to follow. Shoulders square, back rigid, she ascended the spiral, mahogany staircase to a room at the end of the hall. "Here's your key, Mr. Gibson. Your bags are in your suite, and your clothes for the hot tub are on the chair. Don't take too long."

He opened the door and turned to thank her, but faced an empty hallway. *Damn, where'd she go? Does everyone disappear into thin air around here?*

Inside the room, a canopied bed beckoned relaxation, a crystal chandelier hung from a ceiling fresco, and outside on the large balcony, marble statuaries stood vigil.

A thick, white terrycloth robe lay across the back of a chair. He picked it up. "What, no swimsuit?" He looked on the floor and under the chair. A slow, expectant grin spread across his face. "Wonder if she'll wear her birthday suit, too."

The wooden stairs creaked beneath his bare feet. Dressed in only the robe, a capacious smile masked any thread of embarrassment. In the parlor, a massive bookcase covered one wall. He browsed various books before he noticed a section on thoroughbred horses. *She's interested in thoroughbreds? What a coincidence.* "Knock it off, Gibson. Put your investigator mode on hold. So, the lady likes horses, there's nothing to connect her to the Rileys. You're here to have a good time, not arrest someone," he mumbled.

Several volumes of Louisiana legendry, Cajun facts and fiction, arcane and the ethereal, sparked his

Scent of Double Deception

attention. He started to read the first few pages of "The Voodoo Priestess, Marie Laveau."

"Mr. Gibson, those books are valuable editions and not to be disturbed. Follow me. Miss Kitty hates to wait."

"Yvette, you surprised me. I'm sorry...the bookcase is so unusual. What type wood is this?"

"Anyone knows its Bolivian rosewood. Are you coming?"

He replaced the book, tightened the belt on the robe, and followed.

At the solarium, Yvette opened the door. Dark curtains covered opaque glass walls. Soft music played, and copious candles provided streams of sallow light. Exotic greenery surrounded the large hot tub, and a serene waterfall trickled over steps at one end.

An icy wind blew open his robe. Hideous laughter shrieked from above, and the room went black. He shivered and crouched, blind in the inky darkness. A thunderous sound roared through the room. He couldn't deny the unwelcome knot in his gut.

One by one, numerous candles glowed to a flicker. He grabbed a bamboo chair and sat down. Thick jaundiced steam circled and swirled from the water. He tried to adjust to the cloudy lighting while the vaporous mist rose higher and snaked around his body. A caustic odor filled his nostrils. He choked, coughed, and the pungent strains sucked the air from his lungs. His eyes burned, itched, and he reached for the belt of the robe to wipe them. *What the hell? Where's my robe? I'm naked!*

The hot tub provided instant protection. He twirled around in the water to scan the room. On the tub's edge stood a dark figure covered in sheer black lace, a voluptuous body revealed through the thin material. Long raven hair shielded a woman's face. A low voice chanted. The soft music choreographed each rhythmic movement of her arms. Metallic-colored pouches glistened in each hand. She slipped inside the tub and undulated closer, closer to him.

I...I can't move. Rooted in place, his body threatened to respond. Tawny skin smoldered through the lace as she united against him. Sharp black fingernails dug into the thickness of his back, shoulders, and around to his sculpted chest until the skin tore. The pouches ripped open and glitter-like contents sprinkled onto his clammy skin. Each particle stung, burned in the open wounds. He released a low groan. The tinsel dregs sparked, sizzled, and dissolved in the water.

"Kitty?" he slurred. The tranquil warm water, the odors, the singsong ritual, lulled him deeper into oblivion. His leg muscles quivered like jelly. The trill grew louder and higher. It pierced his ears, and then...silence.

Thirteen
The Black Box

Slivers of topaz sunlight filtered into the room. Buried deep in fluffy covers, Russell batted open his eyes. On the dresser sat a tray, two cups, and a silver carafe. A familiar aroma beckoned. *Man, I'm tired, drained. I need strong, black coffee.*

As he stretched to release the tension, his hand touched something soft, warm. He bolted straight up. Kitty curled beside him, her breath slow and deep. *Did I imagine everything or have I lost my mind?* He searched his body for scratches or scrapes. *Another erotic dream?*

Wisps of short, dark hair revealed the nape of her neck.

He couldn't resist, leaned over, and kissed it.

She opened her eyes and turned to him. "Good morning, Mr. Gibson. Did you rest well?"

"Uh, I think so." A knifelike pain pierced his head, he slumped against the pillows.

Skin to skin, she nuzzled close, fingering the hair on his chest.

Does she know what happened last night? Why do I have this horrendous headache? The thoughts clamored in his mind.

Kitty threw back the covers and climbed onto his defenseless body. Firm breasts skimmed his chest. She grabbed a small crystal decanter from the nightstand, straddled his waist, tightened her thighs against his ribs, and poured something into a little cup. A hot hand slithered behind his neck and forced the cool liquid between his lips. She slid off him, and he watched her canvass each exposed inch of his body. Paralyzed, he saw her dark, chocolate eyes turn scarlet red before she blew a kiss and drifted like a vapor out of the room, nude. He wanted to call her name, ravish her body. Instead, he succumbed to the toxic potion…powerless, his eyes closed.

Eight baleful chimes tolled through the room. He opened his eyes again, refreshed and invigorated, the headache gone. He looked at the undisturbed covers on the opposite side of the bed. Bits of memory flashed like a strobe light—black lace, cold wind, sparkles. *A naked woman. Kitty? What happened?* "I need a hot shower."

He rubbed the thick towel through damp hair.

Fruit and pastries filled a wicker basket on a small cart. "Bagels? Where did breakfast come from? Good, I'm starved."

Before he finished the last swallow of coffee, someone knocked on the door. "Come in."

"My sweet Russell, are you ready to see New Orleans?" Kitty asked.

"Whatever the lady wishes," he replied.

****

The limo delivered them to the heart of the French Quarter. They strolled past St. Louis Cathedral and the statue of General Andrew Jackson. Mimes and clowns in Jackson Square used their trickery to entertain the throng of people. Talented artists sketched tourists, and tealeaf readers called to the crowd for a glimpse into the future.

"Let's have our fortunes told," Kitty begged.

"Sure." Russell laughed.

She paused in front of a palmist with a black lace mantilla on her head.

"Ugh," he grunted and cupped his forehead.

"Sweetheart, what is it?"

"My head...the pain is awful."

"Here, let's sit down on this bench and rest." Kitty cradled him in her arms.

Moments later, he opened his eyes, the pain gone, and the palmist, too. Fear gripped his heart. *What's wrong with me?*

Kitty stroked the back of his head. "Better?"

"Yeah, its okay, I'm fine."

"Do you feel up to a buggy ride?"

The carriage lumbered through narrow cobblestone streets. The horses' hooves echoed, and he tried to relax to the methodic clip-clop. Mystique shuttered doorways, and hidden courtyards, blues bars and cafés, led them to Bourbon Street. The ride ended in front of a curio shop.

"Would you like to buy some souvenirs?" Kitty asked.

"Great idea." Toward the back corner of the store, he inspected bright-colored Mardi Gras doubloons.

A woman in a black lace blouse bumped into him.

"Excuse me," she replied.

White-knuckled, he gripped the edge of the counter, the intense pain returned. Micro images, like tiny picture frames, pulsed through his head, his chest pounded. He tried to take deep breaths, block out the pain. "Sure," he muttered and looked up.

The girl disappeared, vanished, and the headache stopped.

"Did you find anything?" Kitty asked. "There are so many unusual items here, don't you think?"

"Yeah, a couple things, are you ready to leave? I'm hungry," he replied. *I can't ruin our day. Maybe I'll mention the headaches later.*

The couple dined on Oysters Rockefeller and enjoyed burgundy Sangria at Antoine's. Kitty laughed at his attempt to eat the powdery white beignets. Jazzy blues rocked the night at the Shim Sham Club, and the twosome danced for hours.

Cuddled together on the drive home, Kitty fell asleep against his shoulder until the limo stopped in front of the old mansion.

Yvette threw open the front door. "This way," she demanded.

In one strong swoop, he lifted Kitty's small frame. "Yes ma'am." He followed the stern maid up the staircase to the end of the hall.

"Do I smell wine? She drank tonight, didn't she?" Yvette spat.

"Well, yes we did have a little bit to drink."

"Never mind—put her down. I'll dress her for bed, you've done enough. Good night, Mr. Gibson."

He lingered in the hallway then ambled down the corridor. A cold breeze wafted through his room. He sat down on the bed, unbuttoned his shirt, and slid off his pants. A roller coaster of fantasies and decisions plagued his emotions. *What a bizarre weekend. I hope I don't have another hellish headache.*

****

Russell yawned, kicked back the covers, and glanced at his watch on the side table. *Morning already? I need to check on Kitty.* He scrambled into his clothes and ran down the stairs.

"Hello, Mr. Gibson." Yvette stood in the foyer. "Miss Kitty would like to see you on the lanai. I'll serve your breakfast there." She smiled.

"Thanks, you're in a good mood today."

She curtsied. "Thank you, sir."

He followed the spring scent of lavender where Kitty waited.

"Good morning," she said. "I'm so sorry I fell asleep last night."

He leaned over and kissed her forehead. "Don't worry about it. Guess I wore you out on the dance floor."

"You and the wine. Can you forgive my rudeness?"

"Does it mean you're indebted to me?"

"You scoundrel, what shall I do about you?"

"Well, I need a date for the Riley wedding," he said.

Her eyes brightened. "I accept."

"Great. Now, where's Yvette? I'm starved."

After breakfast, they strolled through the gardens, down a path where shards of sunlight glinted on a clear blue pond.

"Time passed so fast, I wanted to visit the fabled gazebo." He grinned.

The couple's laughter drifted through the dew-covered terrain.

He touched her cheek to memorize the beauty of her face.

She grasped his hand as they approached the front door. "Another time perhaps. Wait here, I have a surprise."

He forced a smile and sat down on the marbled step.

She reappeared, arm outstretched. "This is for you."

"A gift?" He reached for a small box tied in black ribbon.

"Promise me you won't open it until bedtime."

"Absolutely."

Warm, sweet lips met his kiss, slow and savage—he needed more.

****

The chauffeur pulled to the curb in front of a shuttered pub and opened the door. A woman in a black hat, face hid behind a veil, entered the tavern. Cigarette smoke hovered low and thick like an angry cloud. The glow from neon signs offered little light, but Katherine Forche made her way to the back of the club. A black gentleman, saxophone in hand, tipped his hat as she disappeared through a red door.

Incense permeated the air in the small room. Concoctions of herbs and spices, showcased in colored glass bottles, lined multiple shelves. Strands of rainbow-colored beads covered a small, dark passageway. Boney fingers snaked through the makeshift doorway, and the beads clinked and parted.

A hand, cloaked in a black-lace gauntlet glove, gripped her shoulder. "I trust you're satisfied?" a woman's voice hissed.

"Yes, Madame Moulin, everything went perfect to your plan." Kitty kept her eyes lowered. "I came to thank you in person."

"Did he accept the gift? It's essential, you know."

"Oh yes. I understand the significance. He promised to open it before he goes to bed tonight."

"And you believe he will follow your instructions?"

Scent of Double Deception

"Yes, Madame Moulin. *Love* fills the hollow canals of his heart."

The image moved like a wispy blur around the table. "Did he complain of anything?"

"Not a word, such a strong man."

"You mean...stubborn?" The figure extended a gnarled hand, a finger pointed. "The rest is up to you, my little fledgling." Throaty cynical laughter echoed throughout the tomb-like chamber.

****

Mile marker after mile marker whizzed by in a hurried haze. Russell cataloged each scene, each situation, while the animation played like an old black and white movie. A few memory lapses presented an uncomfortable void. He rubbed his forehead, confused. *I have to put the pieces of the puzzle together. Regardless of the outcome, I can't wait to see her, touch her again.*

Darkness filtered down on the Dallas skyline as he exited off the freeway. *Stupid, stupid, I haven't checked Clair and Kelley's bracelet monitors since I left the hotel. My first responsibility is their safety.* In the driveway of his townhouse, he punched in the number to the tele-page system. Everything registered normal.

He dropped the suitcase on the garage floor to lock the truck, reached for his jacket, and noticed the box wrapped in black ribbon.

Inside the bedroom, he held the inexplicable package at arms' length. One quick tug, the black satin ribbon fell limp, the lid imprisoned the contents. Anticipation mounted. *Oh hell, I can't wait until tonight. I'm gonna open it now.*

The sudden ring of his cell delayed all curiosity. "Hello?"

Scent of Double Deception

"Hey guy, how was your weekend?" Kelley asked.

"Oh fine, you know, the usual." He tried to sound nonchalant.

"The usual?"

"Kelley Malone, you know what I mean," he huffed.

"Hmm, nope, I'm sure I don't. Why don't you tell me?"

"What the heck do you want? Did ya'll have a good trip home? What is our schedule for next week? Are you and Clair together? Does she need to talk to me, too? So what's up?" He rambled to change the subject.

"Whoa, slow down. I got your page, so I called. However, I'm a little concerned about Clair."

"What's the problem?"

"I left her apartment fifteen minutes ago. Can I swing by your place so we can talk?"

"Sure."

"Great, I'm on my way."

He flipped the phone shut. *Kelley overreacts sometimes, but I sense alarm in her voice.* "I need to unpack before she gets here, but I think I'll open Kitty's gift first."

****

The sleek, white Corvette pulled into the driveway and growled to a halt. Kelley walked through the open garage. "Russell? You left the driver's door open on your truck," she called out. "Oh well, can't let the battery run down and give him an excuse to show up late for work."

She noticed luggage in the hallway. "Russ, where are you? Don't dare jump out and scare me," she warned. "What's that horrendous smell?" At the corner of the master bedroom, she froze. A thick fog-like mist hovered. The peppery odor stung her eyes, burned her

Scent of Double Deception

lungs, she gagged on the pungent fumes. Uncontrollable tears streamed her cheeks.

Across the bed sprawled a lifeless body.

"Russell!" She shook his shoulders, confused. "Wake up, wake up!" Her fingers pressed against his neck for a pulse. "Oh dear God, thank goodness you're not dead." She managed to prop his head on a pillow to check his airway. His breaths were slow and deep, almost comatose.

"Russell, talk to me. Did you take any medication? What's this nasty haze?"

She crawled to a window and opened it wide enough to let the acrid vapors escape. "Where's the light switch? I need a ceiling fan. Hell, why didn't I think of this sooner?" she screamed and ran outside.

The locks on the attaché case clicked open. "Ah, there it is." She removed the small bottle and grabbed her cell phone. "Hello? Clair, I need you to come to Russell's house immediately."

"Kelley? Are you okay? What's going on?"

"I don't know, I mean, he's got a pulse, but I need you."

"I'm on my way," Clair said.

The haze in the bedroom made her light-headed, dizzy. She dropped to her knees beside Russell.

"Who…who are you?" he groaned. "Geeze, my head hurts. What did you give me? Kelley?"

"Shhh, its okay." She stroked his forehead. "Oh Russell, you scared me. I thought you were dead; your face was so pale. What happened? I waved one of my vials for fainting brides under your nose. You mumbled something about black lace and a box. Where did the smoke and smell come from?"

Russell looked toward the nightstand. "Don't touch it, but look in the little box," he whispered.

"What? What box?"

"There...on the floor." He pointed.

She sniffed the sooty substance inside. "Russell Gibson, where did you get this?"

"A gift, from Kitty."

"What? You mean to tell me *she* is responsible for this near disaster? That bitch! Wait till I get my hands around her neck."

"Kel, don't go ballistic on me. It's a gag, good grief, and please lower your voice, there's a bass drum in my head."

"What in the world are you two doing?" a familiar voice demanded.

"I'm so glad you're here, Clair." Kelley stood, ran a hand through her tousled hair, and described the dreadful scene.

Clair listened, arms crossed, brow furrowed. Russell forced his body upright against the headboard and smiled.

"I'm gonna slap that grin off your face, Russell Gibson, and I'll let Clair hold you down. I don't see a damn thing funny here. You scared me to death, you and your weird girlfriend."

"You two are worse than sisters, all the drama; hands flying. You almost hit Clair. Besides, knock it off about Kitty."

Clair intervened. "All right buddy, tell us your side of the story."

"There's nothing to tell, really. Look, y'all harp on me to get a life. I had a great weekend, although there were a few odd moments."

"Clarify!"

"Please Kel, speak a little softer," Russell begged.

"I'll try," she mocked a whisper.

"Take your time, we have all night," Clair added.

"First off, I asked her to be my date at the Riley wedding, I had a couple bad headaches, and as far as the gift goes, a stupid prank. End of story."

"Russell, you know chemicals and oils are my specialty. I recognize the residue on the box."

"We're all aware you are the resident chemist, Kelley," he mumbled. "This fuss isn't necessary." He slumped down onto the pillows.

"I also rifled through your suitcase."

"What?"

"More like, what did you find, Kel?" Clair interjected.

"Oh, a pair of black lace panties I tossed in the trash, but it doesn't take a rocket scientist to detect the smell of pesticide," she said.

He crossed his arms over his chest and smiled. "Damn, how stupid. I forgot they exterminated the townhouse this weekend."

"You're a liar, Russell." Kelley pointed a finger. "A heavy dose can cause memory loss. You didn't even recognize me."

Silence fractured the conversation.

"I think you need some hot soup. Let's go to the kitchen," Clair ordered.

He eased himself off the bed and took her outstretched hand.

"I'll clean up in here," Kelley said.

****

Russell watched them drive away. His carefree goodbye wave masked an inner turmoil. Humiliation fired a white-hot anger deep inside his bones. Fists clenched, his eyes glared like dark storm clouds. He approached the trashcan and eyed the discarded lacey undergarment. "Hmm, no headache, you stupid bastard."

Fourteen
Compromise Reached

"Excuse me, Mr. Highgrove, please give me a second, I must answer the phone." Celeste Vandergriff found it difficult to hide extreme agitation at the presence of the man in the living room. The dread of this moment, held deep inside her heart for thirty years, still managed to prompt surprise. A curt nod was all she could muster.

Thankful for the interruption, she closed the study door and tried to make sense of the conflict inside her head. How could she convince him, this isn't the right time? Her voice stayed low. "Hello?"

"Celeste? Are you okay? You sound funny. I need to talk to you."

"Spencer, you're too late, Mr. Highgrove is here and told me the whole story." Her body relaxed at the sound of his voice. She always trusted and relied on him.

"He's there? They really *are* serious. Look, I can't continue this lie. I must tell Clair first. I owe her that much. She'll probably never forgive me—it's the chance I have to take."

"No, that's unacceptable. You know it would invalidate the Will. Sit tight for a while, maybe I can buy some time. I'll call when he leaves." She listened for his affirmation. It didn't come. "I mean it, Spencer. Remember, you work for me, too. If you tip your hand to Clair before I have a chance to manipulate Highgrove, you'll regret it."

"Celeste, I'll respect your wishes for now, but can't guarantee how long. I'm too distracted."

She swept into the living room, sat down, smiled, and reached for a favorite china teapot. "More tea, Mr. Highgrove? I apologize for the interruption."

Twenty years experience on the Board of the Art Museum taught a quiet voice and a sweet smile could get the point across easier. Spencer's call infused new energy into her soul.

The tight-lipped man waved off the tea offer. "You have a lovely home, Ms. Vandergriff. I can see the care you put into each item. Clair must have enjoyed her early days here. I assume those pictures on the bureau are of her in various stages of childhood."

"Why thank you, Mr. Highgrove, how kind of you to notice." *Did I see a shadow of doubt cross his mind? Could he actually have a heart?* She watched, fascinated at the transformation. His look softened, he leaned forward — a slight smile on his face.

"Celeste…may I call you by your first name?" At her nod, he continued, "You and I have talked for thirty years, but never face-to-face, only through telephone lines. I must say, I'm enchanted. You are a warm and lovely lady. Outside of the responsibility Mr. Thurlow placed on me, I could see us spending time together."

Her eyes lowered, flattered at his obvious interest.

"Forgive me, I'm off subject. Your beauty distracts me. Let me get to the point. Clair turned forty this past December, the agreed time of fulfillment. I would like to know your thoughts now. You've raised her as your own daughter, you *do* have a say in this."

Scent of Double Deception

His sudden generosity pleased her. *My heart is doing double time. It's been years since I used flirtation to get what I want. Will he give me more time or set me up?*

She set the fragile teapot into its cradle and remained calm. The delicate design on the porcelain held her attention, allowing time to play the game. The tender outline of pale, yellow rose petals, lacy garlands of ivy, and angel's trumpets, soothed the jumbled thoughts. This particular fine piece of china belonged to Grandmother Vandergriff. An antique cupboard in the formal dining room showcased the entire set, a tribute to the past. Family meant the world to her, and the teapot symbolized the struggles endured over the years.

More relaxed, her heart regained its normal beat, and she knew natural charm bought more time. She continued to study the dainty vessel.

"Celeste, did you hear what I said?"

"Of course, I heard you, Mr. Highgrove. Your gallantry is unparalleled. Do you really mean to give me a voice? Do you have the power to postpone this phase of the operation? After all, there *is* the matter of the Will."

One hand dropped to his briefcase. "Yes, yes, certainly the Will has its place in this little drama, but I have a deeper concern. Is Clair ready for the event?"

"My dear man, how in the world can she be ready? She knows absolutely nothing of what will transpire. Clair carved out a wonderful career. There are friends; she travels. In other words, her life is fulfilled. You waltz in here and pompously ask if she is ready for life to be turned upside down. There is also the matter of the episode in the restaurant parking lot. Is this how

Scent of Double Deception

your associate planned to spring it on her? I must say, that little fiasco leaves me doubtful. Please tell me there are procedures in place to ease her into this." Her voice remained cool.

Edgar Highgrove squirmed. "Rest assured a confrontation would never have happened. Mr. Walker almost blew his cover. We wonder if he is too close to the situation. His intensity showed when he talked to Clair."

Celeste reveled in his obvious discomfort. Now she needed to steer him away from Spencer and focus on the goal. "Nevertheless *Edgar*, might I call you Edgar?"

"Lovely lady, please do. This will only work if our charge is ready and inclined to undertake the responsibility, but please continue."

"If I've a choice, I'd like more time to prepare my niece. She doesn't know the true story of her parents or their deaths. The shock could prove too much. I've gone over in my mind how I'd tell her for years. Are you giving me the chance? I'm afraid to even entertain the thought, but it appears that is your offer." She watched for a reaction. His interest became apparent, and she planned to use it to her advantage. "If you would indulge me, I've a plan to make this easier. Would you care to hear it, Edgar?" *Ah, he wants me to call him by his first name. I believe he'd dance a jig on the coffee table if I asked.*

She used her most gentle voice, "My niece is involved in a high profile wedding in Shreveport, Louisiana right now. She and Kelley will be here for a little party I've planned in celebration. I would like to use the few days of their visit to unravel some of the mysteries for her. In recent days, Clair asked some questions, and extra time would be so appreciated."

Highgrove didn't hesitate to acquiesce, and she marveled how a woman's charm won the day.

After they came to a mutual agreement, he rose and stopped at the doorway. "May I?" He touched her hand.

She offered it and received a farewell kiss. He took his leave, and she watched him, certain they would meet again.

****

Edgar Highgrove smiled, satisfied. The fiery snap in Celeste's bright blue eyes amused him, her anger evident at his arrival. The lady exuded class and composure in the face of adversity, and he admired the obvious breeding. The charge Linford Thurlow bestowed on him consumed his entire life and left no time for other interests. Celeste's feisty, yet controlled temperament, awakened the loneliness which haunted him time and again. He would retire after this assignment. For a brief moment, he imagined Celeste at his side in their golden years. *Could a woman of such refinement find me attractive? I am her adversary, a source of fear and hatred. Oh yes, her uncle fueled the fire, but I brought the bad news. Will she see past the unpleasantness after all these years? Can she finally accept me as a man, not the mouthpiece?* For once in his long career, he'd taken a chance, made his own choice, and defied his boss. The difficult decision left him content, a different mood, indeed. He knew she would honor their long-standing agreement.

The seat belt clicked into place, and he caught a glimpse of her in the window watching. The transformation in her eyes, the gentleness of her touch, allowed him to fancy a glimmer of hope, the possibility of a relationship. Reality would hit soon enough, in the meantime, he could dream.

****

The ceaseless chirp of crickets penetrated Celeste's consciousness. The lights across the street burned bright. Shadows depicted movements of a family through the gossamer curtains of the living room. Afraid of accusations of voyeurism, she wheeled away from the window. Edgar Highgrove stirred long-forgotten warmth in her soul, an ache for the attention of a man. *Time for that later. I have to face the trunk in the attic. Clair deserves a thorough rendition of how we came to this end.*

The antique grandfather clock in the hall chimed 9:00 PM. She looked up the long staircase and sighed. *I suppose it's a bit too late to tackle those steps.* She headed for the kitchen and an evening cup of warm cocoa. The attic, and its secrets, would have to wait until morning.

Fifteen
A Mysterious Bottle

Scattered mail decorated the floor, fallen victims of the postal slot in the door. Clair retrieved the motley group of correspondence and threw the keys on the hall table. She fingered through the bills and advertisements until interest waned. Kelley's departure made her anxious, ready for the oasis of the high-rise apartment to cleanse the uneasiness of her mind after the scene at the restaurant. *Why did that guy deny we'd met? The strange man in the black suit...why would he approach our car? Coincidence or my imagination?*

The hair on the back of her neck prickled once again. *Something ominous transpired, something baneful was circumvented, and Kelley didn't catch it. She chattered about the man in the red car, and I let her. No reason for alarm before the trip to San Antonio.*

She tossed the unopened mail and debated whether to retreat to the lush garden, and a cup of cocoa, or the Jacuzzi and aromatherapy. The garden won.

A red, Japanese-style silk robe caressed naked skin, and she sighed, contented. "Now, some of Aunt CeeCee's recipe," she murmured. The hot cup snuggled into her hand. She waltzed through the French doors and into the garden, a world of serenity and peace. Verdant greenery surrounded every nook and cranny. Exotic splashes of color entertained the eye, and in the center of the garden stood a four-tiered musical fountain cut from white marble. Unicorns, cherubs, and mythological birds adorned each tier in a fanciful array to create an illusion of another place in time.

She settled into a chaise lounge to enjoy the harmonious retreat. The cheerful music, and seductive sound of water, trickled through each level. The rich cocoa slid down her throat, and soon, concerns of the world melted away. Out of the corner of her eye, a disturbance niggled at her euphoric mind. Small flashes of light danced off an object behind the bubbling reservoir near the bougainvillea, and she sat up, distracted. The waterfall distorted the view. She blinked, and returned her gaze to the spectacle. Rainbow colors continued to sparkle. She rose from the chaise, fascinated, until curiosity took over, and approached the fountain. A peek behind the cascade of water caused a ripple of shock. On the stone ledge sat an exquisite glass bottle.

"What in the world?" She stood in front of the fragile cruet, dazzled. "A perfume bottle?"

The decanter, fashioned in the manner of an antique atomizer, popular in her grandmother's day, struck a chord, a lost memory. The bulbous pump, attached to a glass bottle, stood regal, yet exuded femininity and grace. Deep cut curves wound through the entire shape, and reflected the light.

She breathed deep. *I'm seeing things.* Her eyes focused closer on the mysterious vessel. A single word, written in script across the front, stood out. One word, one unbelievable word. **Clair.** Timid, she reached to retrieve it. Her hand drew back, and she glanced around the garden. There it sat, next to a favorite rosebush—a box, shiny and silver, no bow, no wrapping. Inside, no possible clue, nothing. Intense fear engulfed her. *Someone has invaded the sanctuary. Let's see, maybe Susie will know.*

A loyal employee with stellar recommendations, she trusted Susie like no other. A close bond developed between them when she relocated from France.

Clair ran to the phone, and a sleepy voice answered.

"Hello?"

"Susie?"

"Yes ma'am, Ms. Clair? Is something wrong, mademoiselle?"

Clair explained the perfume bottle.

"Oh no, Ms. Clair, no one entered. I promise I would not allow a stranger in your beautiful apartment."

"I know, Susie. Maybe a delivery person?"

"No ma'am, no delivery, nothing, no one. I am sure."

"Okay, I'm sorry to bother you. I bet Kelley did it. You know how she likes to play jokes sometimes. Please don't worry."

"Oh yes, Ms. Clair…Ms. Kelley."

"I'll call her now, Susie. Go back to sleep." In her heart, she knew Kelley didn't do it. The concern was evident in Susie's voice. *One more look at the bottle, something will trigger my memory.*

She swung open the doors, took a deep breath, and walked to the fountain. *Should I call the police? Whoever left the decanter knew what they were doing. Not one trace of evidence or proof of invasion is visible.*

In search of advice, she called Celeste. "Did you hear me? What should I make of this? My name is on it. What does it mean? Hello, are you still there?"

"Yes, I'm here, darling," Celeste said. "I don't think it's anything to worry about. Someone fancies you, that's all. Listen, I think it is time for a visit. I haven't been to Dallas in a long time. When is the Riley wedding? I'd love to see your work, and you said it's the most prominent wedding you girls have arranged in a while. Besides, I want to see the two of you in action. What do you think?"

"Oh yes, how wonderful. I'd love for you to see our success. The Riley wedding is in Shreveport, and you haven't seen my garden since I finished it. Yes, I think I need you down here. Please come."

Sixteen
A Successful Invitation

The Riley wedding details kept Clair busy even though worries of the perfume bottle slithered through her mind. The option not to tell Kelley started to unravel, and she reassessed the decision. Her friend's vivid imagination often created uncontrollable situations. She flipped the page of the steno pad and moved to the next rationale. *If it is Kelley, what is the motive?* Russell came to mind...maybe they conspired together. She shook her head, dismissed the idea, mulled over the doubts, and decided to keep the incident quiet for now.

A new client called yesterday, and they scheduled a meeting. Purse in hand, she beeped Kelley.

The drive provided a few minutes to reflect on the scene they'd encountered at Russell's. Kitty bothered her, even triggered alarm. Clair could not quite put a finger on the emotion invoked at the thought of the woman who enamored her other best friend. Russell smiled more, laughed, teased, and acted happier since this romantic dalliance. Warning him to slow things down might encourage a more vigorous pursuit. He could dole out watchdog guidance to each of them, although, he took none of their advice. *We need to discuss how to handle Russell's latest amour on the way. He can't know our involvement...discretion is the name of the game.*

Halfway to Kelley's house, she decided to call him.

"Good morning, my love," he answered.

His jolly hello surprised her. "How is my sexy bodyguard this morning? You sound no worse for the wear. Headache better—any other aftereffects from Kitty's little *gift*?"

"You know Clair, the more I think about it, I believe it was just a practical joke. She's full of surprises and intrigues me like no other woman. In fact, I think I'll call her today and thank her."

"Well, it's one hell of a practical joke, Russ, and I'm not sure I find it so funny. Watch how you deal with this woman. Don't forget, Kel and I worry about you, too." *I sound more and more like Kelley. What a mother hen I have become.*

****

"Fountain Rue, Yvette speaking. She's on the terrace, one moment please." The young maid handed the phone to her employer. "It's Madame Moulin, Miss Kitty."

"Thank you, Yvette. Madame Moulin, what a nice surprise. Why yes, the plan worked to perfection. I feel certain he won't remember anything. However, I'll contact him today to see for myself. Your talent is invaluable, I'm satisfied each time I use your services." She ended the conversation.

Twisted thoughts of the helpless captive invaded her sanity. Heat rose off her skin as she dialed the number. "Good morning, darling. I trust you slept well."

"If you mean after your little prank, the answer is yes, my dear."

She chuckled at his confirmation. *Ah, it worked.* "Hmm, my little prank? Detective Gibson, forgive me, but I needed an excuse to hear your voice again."

"Very funny, you didn't need to go to such great lengths, though. Now you owe me."

"There's no place I'd rather be than in your debt."

"Okay, the trip to Maui revolved around business, a wedding. The big event is February 14th. I would consider it an honor if you'd accompany me. Is your schedule open?"

"Let me see, Mr. Gibson, did you just ask me for a date?"

"Yes, Ms. Forche, I did."

"My goodness, how could a girl refuse?"

"I'll make all the arrangements," he said.

She drew a deep breath to contain the merriment. "Until we meet again, ma Cherie." *Madame Moulin will take great pleasure at how well the scheme fell into place.*

****

I did it, I asked her! Goosebumps prickled Russell's skin at the final click in his ear. His mind fluttered, half in anticipation to see Kitty, half at how Clair and Kelley might react. *You'd think I'm sixteen again, my first time to ask a girl out. Hell, I'm a grown man. I'll see this woman if I want. So what if her sense of humor appears bizarre? The girls will have to get over it.*

In the bathroom, he splashed cold water on his face and stared into the mirror. "Damn it Gibson, fess up — did you sleep the time away at Fountain Rue? Perhaps the wine took more of a toll, it sure packed a punch." One hand raked through thick hair.

Cobwebs spread a blanket of confusion. "Who am I kidding? Too much wine ain't no excuse. I can hold my liquor." Scenes of the previous night exploded in his mind. "Why didn't I demand to know more about the stupid prank? Maybe I really don't want to know. I've never met a more charismatic woman. A cloud of mystery surrounds her, as if from another time, another place. God, I want her so much." He jerked a towel from the cabinet. "Russell, you're a damn coward."

The phone rang and brought him back to earth. "Damn, couldn't wait to talk to me again, huh?" He stifled a laugh. "Excuse me, oh, hey Kelley."

"My, you sound cheery. Did you expect someone else?"

"No, no, what's going on?"

"I called to check on you."

"No need to worry, you know I always land on my feet, girl."

"Yeah, well last night you landed on your **butt**, and if I ever get my hands on her…"

"Whoa, little lady, don't pop a gasket. I spoke to Kitty this morning."

"Did she call to see if you were still alive or to gloat?"

"She did inquire as to my well being, but our conversation centered on the Riley wedding," he confessed. "Kelley…Kelley are you still there?"

"The Rileys, why on earth did you discuss the wedding?"

"I invited her as my date. Remember? I ran it by you both, and I'm elated she accepted."

"Whatever. Listen, I've got to run, I'll call you later."

He flinched at the click in his ear.

****

Clair focused on the two mysteries she faced, the bottle and the box, but first things first. She pulled into Kelley's driveway, sure of their ability to work this out together.

The new client sparked excitement, though it lacked the formal status of their usual events. Since the Bohemian theme shouted 'anything goes', they could expand their imaginations.

"Kelley, I have some good news."

"I already know. I spoke to Russell. We both had the same idea. I called him, too. Sleep proved no friend last night, and if he thinks we're going to forget this, he's nuts," Kelley said.

"Slow down—I agree we need to dig a bit deeper. Russell could face real danger, and we need a plan of action. My news has nothing to do with him, however."

"What are you talking about?"

"Aunt CeeCee called last night, and she wants to come for the Shreveport wedding, and see us in action. Won't it be a hoot?" Clair watched Kelley's expression change.

"Are you serious, she would get on an airplane? How wonderful, what an opportunity to showcase our talents."

"Yes, she'll fly down after we return from San Antonio. I'm excited, too. I miss her so much, and you never know, maybe Russell will listen to *her*."

"Yeah, we'll use the big gun on him. He can't blow her off like he does us. He'll listen, or Aunt CeeCee will know the reason why." Kelley laughed.

****

Clair opened the louvered blind of their high-rise Dallas office to scan the checkered skyline, content. Her thoughts drifted. *I need to find out about Kelley and the perfume bottle. Catch her by surprise, but how?*

"Don't you think wooden jewelry for the bridesmaids will fit the Bohemian theme, Clair? Did you hear me? What's your idea?" Kelley snapped her fingers.

"Jewelry? Oh, sure, great." A light went off in Clair's head. "Do you have any plans this afternoon?"

"Nope, why? I take it we're not talking about jewelry anymore?"

"The soirée in Seattle. We have our dresses and shoes, but no accessories. Want to go shopping?" *I've got her now. Kelley cannot resist a good bargain.*

"Jewelry? Shopping? My two favorite words. When and where?"

"Do you still have the baby blue dress you bought in New York last year, Kel?"

"Yes, I haven't worn it yet. What have you got up your sleeve?"

"To try on jewelry, we need to dress up a bit, and blue is your color."

"Say no more, what time?" Kelley closed the laptop.

I can't believe she fell for it. "Pick you up in an hour."

Clair rushed home, scrambled into her dress, and headed out, hand on the doorknob as the phone rang. "Hey Russ, glad you called. What are your plans tonight? Would you like to take two beautiful women to dinner? Great, meet us at the ZaZa Hotel Restaurant at 8:00 PM."

****

Clair watched Kelley catch the eye of a well-dressed gentleman near the main counter of Josef Raybourne Jewelers.

He hurried toward them. "May I help you ladies?"

"We need something to wear to a soirée," Clair began. "My dress is crimson red, and hers is emerald green."

"We get right to the point, don't we ma'am? Let me introduce myself, I'm Josef, the proprietor. Right this way, ladies." The slight-built man, with a pencil thin mustache, directed them to a posh room embellished by red velvet chairs, mirrors on all sides, and deep plush carpet. One by one, he brought out several resplendent pieces of jewelry.

A particular necklace captured Clair's fancy — a diamond strand. The teardrop setting displayed a brilliant ruby stone. "I like this, Kelley. Do you think it will compliment my dress?"

The view in the mirror revealed Josef behind her. His hand brushed across the back of her neck and lingered a moment too long. "I've never seen anything so stunning on anyone. May I ask your name, Mademoiselle?"

Annoyed by the inappropriate touch, instinct kicked in. *A perfect setup for our role-play.* "Natasha, if it's any of your business."

Kelley stammered, "Natasha? Oh yes, of course, and I'm Olivia."

Clair smiled as Kelley fell into the part at once and entered the game.

His demeanor changed. "My apologies, ladies, this store caters to old money, and, may I say, the women of that genre can't hold a candle to the two of you. Please, let me present one more item I think you might like." He exited through a narrow, blue door in the corner of the room.

"What's up, Clair? We're Natasha and Olivia now?"

"Why not, Kelley? It'll be fun to tease a little. He's smitten." She struck her famous Natasha pose.

Kelley burst into laughter. "You're on."

Josef returned, a velvet case in hand. "I *know* this one will work for your dress, Olivia. Am I correct? It is Olivia, right?"

The beautiful emerald necklace refracted the light of the chandeliers, and Clair saw Kelley gasp. *Will she stay in character?*

"It is beautiful, but I don't know." Kelley ran a finger over the multi-faceted stone.

Clair saw a chance. "Oh Olivia, it's perfect and reminds me of the perfume bottle the way it sparkles."

"Perfume bottle? What perfume bottle?" Kelley's brow wrinkled, but she continued to stare at the necklace.

"Yes, the one in my garden." She watched Kelley's reaction.

"In your garden? There's a perfume bottle in your garden? Why?" Kelley's interest remained on the necklace.

"Never mind, it's not important. Are you going to buy the necklace?" *Mark her off the list.*

They haggled over the price, settled on an amount, and agreed to have the pieces delivered by courier the next day.

Josef stopped them before they reached the door. "I'm done for the day. Could I interest you in a cup of coffee, ladies?"

"Another time, perhaps," Clair responded in Natasha's voice. "We have an appointment."

Scent of Double Deception

Kelley gave the man a curt nod and followed her friend. "Poor man, I bet he's not use to rejection. By the way, what did you mean by an appointment?"

"The spa," Clair replied.

****

Clair tossed the car keys to the valet, and they entered the lavish oasis, ready for royal treatment.

A young Asian woman led the way to a private room. Exotic fragrances filled the air.

"Mmmm Clair, Saigon cinnamon and French sea salt," Kelley whispered, eyes closed.

"What?"

"Yes, also Freesia and Hypericum berries." Kelley kept her eyes shut.

"Is this one of your trivia quizzes? Because if it is, I'm not…"

"Clair, aren't you intoxicated by it, too?"

"I'm sorry, you have to remember I don't have your *gift*". Please continue. Tell me, what else?"

The masseuse leaned close to Kelley. "Tupelo honey."

"What did she say?"

"She told me it's Tupelo honey, you know from Tupelo gum tree blossoms. They use it for bikini waxing."

"Well, I pass on any pain and torture today."

They followed the attendant down a long hallway and chose the Free Woman package.

Smooth, warm stones penetrated Clair's bare back, and she let out a low groan.

"So Russell is going to meet us when we're through, right? Kelley murmured.

"I'm so relaxed; I think I told him the Dragonfly Restaurant at eight o'clock."

"Ooh, at the ZaZa Hotel, good choice, girlfriend."

****

Clair followed Kelley into the Dragonfly.

"Mr. King? Mr. S. King. Table for 3 ready now," the maître d' announced into the microphone.

A man emerged from the shadows, a lop-sided grin on his face.

"Russ?" Clair blinked.

"S. King?" Kelley grinned. "Stephen King, per chance?"

"Two can play your game, ladies." He laughed. "Let 'em wonder."

After they placed their orders, Clair steered the conversation. "You should see what we bought today, *Mr*. King."

"Uh, something shiny and expensive?" Russell rubbed his chin.

"How'd you guess?"

"Remember, I helped design your so-called terrace. I know a little about your taste."

"Still got my extra key?"

"I have a collection of ladies' keys. Never can tell if I'll need one."

It's him. He put the bottle there.

Seventeen
The Blind Date

"Excited this morning, Kel? You're never ready on the first beep," Clair teased.

"You bet, what took so long?" Kelley pulled down the visor. "I hope Joe Paul is as handsome as I remember. The weatherman predicted a perfect forecast for San Antonio. The Fiesta Trade Fair is in full swing, and there are two men who can't wait until we arrive."

"I'm only interested in the convention, my dear. The opportunity to see new products and trends, maybe some old friends and competitors, are first on my agenda." She cocked an eyebrow. "I am not thrilled you engineered this blind date, and may I remind you, I'll ditch the guy if I don't like him."

"Yes, yes, and I've seen you do it before, but don't judge the man yet. Enjoy the prospect of a little time off from the fast pace of the last two months. Who knows, your Mr. Right might live in San Antonio."

"For me, the trade expo is *fun*, and while I appreciate you want to see Joe Paul again, I won't sacrifice my whole trip to indulge you," she huffed.

Kelley patted Clair on the shoulder. "Hey, I'm there for you if we need to execute the plan."

****

Kelley stood on tiptoe to scan the crowded airport. Behind her, a familiar baritone voice spoke.

"Olivia?"

Scent of Double Deception

She whirled around, but Clair grabbed her arm. The intense expression on her face reined in any eagerness. Olivia emerged in full control, completed the circle, and faced the man she encountered Christmas Eve. "Joe Paul, good to see you again."

Moss-green eyes caressed her face, and his muscled body moved closer. He removed his hat and smiled. "Olivia, I can't believe it is you."

A strong, yet gentle grasp, raised her hand for a kiss. She stifled the urge to rake her fingers through his thick hair, shower kisses on his face and neck, and melt into those powerful arms.

"Mr. Farrell, you're alone," Clair intervened. "I'm sure you'd never use *me* for a chance to see Olivia. Where is my so-called blind date? Did you fabricate the man? Let me guess—he couldn't make it." She stepped in front of Kelley.

"Natasha, I'd never resort to such behavior. I thought we established a friendship after our dinner in Shreveport. You will meet my friend at the hotel. He didn't want to impinge on our reunion."

"Well, let's make our way there." Clair walked away.

Kelley tried to maintain a reserve and not give in to elation. "She's a bit miffed at me, don't take it to heart."

"I've learned enough about your friend to expect as much. Besides, Natasha isn't the one that concerns my heart. However, I promise my friend is a true gentleman." Joe Paul winked.

"Well, for his sake, he better be," Kelley warned.

****

Marcus Wellborn sat at the bar in Pete's Pub of the St. Antonia Hotel, one ostrich-skinned boot propped on a

Scent of Double Deception

nearby stool. His college buddy gave an in-depth description of a lady named Olivia, but revealed few details about the woman he would soon meet. Confident in Joe Paul's connoisseur eye for women, no doubt she would be beautiful. He chuckled. He also couldn't deny the two old pals relished a good prank now and again. "Another cold draught," he said to the bartender and moved to a table by the window.

Halfway through the drink, something caught his eye outside. The valet held the door while a trio exited an SUV. It afforded Marcus little time to assess the impending date. "Well, damn."

Marcus swallowed the last of the brew in time to see the threesome enter the noisy bar. Joe Paul's eyes never left the beautiful blonde on his arm. *I understand now why you were so anxious to see Olivia.* His eyes darted to the brunette. *Gorgeous.*

****

Clair steeled herself through the introductions. *Marcus Wellborn, huh? Not a bad name, but strike one — you're a cowboy. Wonder what strike two will be? It won't be his looks; tall, rawboned, a refined confident composure.* Clair gave a curt nod. "Mr. Wellborn, I'm Natasha."

The man removed his Stetson and pulled out her chair. "Natasha what?"

"Natasha will do just fine, Mr. Wellborn."

"Okay, Natasha, if you'll call me Marcus."

Joe Paul described Patchwork Plateau, the expansive ranch Marcus owned on the edge of the city.

"Odd name for a farm," Clair said.

"The ranch belonged to my parents originally. My mother made quilts from odd pieces of material and sold them at the old marketplace in town. Dad coined the name for their property because of Mother's creative talent. What about your families, ladies?"

Kelley grasped Clair's hand. "Gotta go...have to see our investors. We'll meet you guys back here at 2:00. Duty calls."

****

Joe Paul's gaze dissolved into empty space.

"Investors? Hey man, where are they going? Shouldn't we follow them? Or is this going to turn into a stag date?" Irritation hung in Marcus' voice.

"No! Not a good idea, Marcus. I guess they appear a bit elusive, and in some ways are, but be patient. I didn't wait all this time, or come this far, to screw up an opportunity to see the most exquisite woman I've ever met."

"Hell, I've never seen this side of you pal. If I didn't know better, I might think you've fallen for this girl." Marcus rubbed his jaw.

"What? I mean, well...let's use the time to catch up on things. Is a Silver Bullet still your choice of poison?" Joe Paul slapped him on the shoulder, and the two friends walked over to the bar.

Eighteen
A Second Bottle

Rows of vendors lined the enormous convention hall. One of the largest merchandise marts displayed new apparel, photography, floral, lighting, and gourmet products. In a crushing crowd, the two business partners talked to fellow competitors and past clients.

Kelley inspected a male mannequin dressed in a tux and tails. "He's cute, don't you think?"

Clair shook her head. "A bit too plastic for my taste."

"I meant Marcus Wellborn, silly." Kelley laughed.

"He's nosy," Clair stated.

"Nosy? Why, because he asked your last name? At some point the question is inevitable, even from Joe Paul."

"Well, he's a cowboy." Clair picked up several pamphlets, one on calligraphy, and another on chocolate fountains.

Kelley cocked her head. "Um, do you recall our little rendezvous at the Weston in Houston, and a certain suitor who caught *your* attention?"

"The cattle baron? Humph, a far cry from a plain ol' cowboy."

Kelley ignored the explanation and continued her resolve. "Won't you at least give Marcus a chance? A simple date, nothing more."

Clair shoved a folded paper in Kelley's face. "Look at this, Scrapbooking for Weddings, what a neat idea."

Kelley snatched the paper away. "You spent 20 minutes around the man. Invest a little time before you pass judgment, is all I ask." Visions of silhouetted couples on the Hawaiian shores, and a twinge of jealousy, lingered in her head. *Oh Clair, I need this date tonight. Don't take away my opportunity to learn more about Joe Paul. What makes him so different? Why do I get all jittery at his touch, yet comfortable and peaceful in his presence? The man stole a piece of my heart at Adams Rib. I won't walk away so fast this time.* "Please?" She bit her lip.

A smile formed at the corners of Clair's mouth. "For my best friend...I'll lighten up a tad, but don't expect there to ever be a double wedding," Clair said.

"Deal."

The two hugged.

"Goodness, it's almost 2:00." Kelley checked her watch. "I think I've seen enough. Let's go freshen up and meet the guys."

****

At the entrance to Pete's Pub, Clair brushed back a stray curl, and collected her thoughts. *Mr. Wellborn, Marcus...what do you think of the icy Natasha? Don't believe for a second you can tame her like a wild Mustang.*

"Hey, wanna hit on the two hunks at the bar?" Kelley whispered.

"Not really."

"Oh come on, let's sneak up and surprise them." Kelley tugged at her reluctant friend's arm and pulled her to the bar in time to hear their dates' conversation.

"Remember, what I said." Joe Paul placed a hand on Wellborn's back. "Natasha is very protective of Olivia, like a sister. After our dinner date, I gained a new appreciation for their friendship. Yeah, she's a little arctic on the outside, but consider her more of a radiant rose."

"Hey, it ain't my first rodeo, buddy," Marcus replied. "Don't worry, we'll be fine."

The overheard comments accentuated Clair's discontent. "Did he warn you to watch out for my thorns?" Clair interrupted.

The men scrambled to stand, a surprised look on their faces. "Good evening," they said in unison

"Don't you love Natasha's quick wit?" Kelley wrinkled her nose.

"Olivia, there's a new little restaurant on the River Walk. Can we try it?" Joe Paul stepped forward and took her hand.

"Sounds great. Natasha, do you and Marcus mind?"

Before Clair could reply, Marcus spoke up. "I'm sure Natasha and I can find something to fill our time. Go ahead."

I should walk right out of here, Kelley Malone. The plan is to stay together. You know how it goes! The gleam in Kelley's eyes reminded Clair of a child ready to rip into a pile of birthday presents. How could she deny her friend a few hours? Clair cleared her throat. "Of course, have fun. We'll see you two later."

The couple hurried away.

"Mr. Wellborn, guess we're on our own. Any suggestions?" *If I cast out the line, will you take the bait?*

"I'm in your hands, Natasha. Anything particular in mind?"

Yes...to make you squirm. I want to shop. Think you can hang? "Well, I love the antique stores. Wanna go, or is that too girly for you?"

"No ma'am. My ranch has several rustic antiques. Lead the way."

At the Old Tymes Curios and Antiques, Clair searched through the pieces of Depression glass. Above a display of perfume bottles from the 18th century hung an old mirror. Curious, she stole a glance at Marcus. His chestnut-brown hair complimented dark ebony eyes. He stood tall, straight, and commanded an air of self-confidence.

Hmm, if you're bored it doesn't show. You are nice — patient and polite. Couldn't hurt to be friends. I ought to explain about my quest. "My aunt in Washington collects old perfume bottles. I'm looking for a particular one she can't find," Clair offered.

He pushed aside a heart-shaped hatbox and picked up an unusual container. "Perhaps similar to this?"

Clair caught her breath. Perched in Marcus' hand sat a twin to the perfume bottle found in the garden. Etched across the front, the word *Julia* blazed. The brilliant cut glass sparkled, reminiscent of a tiny chandelier.

He presented the newfound treasure.

Delicate in her hand, its ambience pierced her soul, and she trembled.

On another aisle, the owner tagged several pieces of brass from a large box.

Clair rushed to him. "Sir ... where did you get this?"

The man scratched his thin beard. "This was my grandfather's; can't tell you. I just know the thing is old."

"Can we ask your grandfather?"

"Nope, he died a couple of years ago," the owner replied.

Scent of Double Deception

"I'm sorry, but you must have records or logs of authenticity for these items, right?" Clair insisted.

"Might be somewhere, but this place is full of glass bottles. It'd take months to track it down."

"Sir, I want this bottle. Please try to find some information on its origin. Call me anytime. Do you understand?" Clair fished out a business card.

Marcus appeared beside her. "Need any help?"

Oh great — what timing. I can't let him see my personal information.

The owner wrapped the bottle.

Clair tucked the cherished find deep inside her tote bag. "Nope, got it. Is this enough?"

The owner took the hundred-dollar bill.

"Sir, I believe you owe my friend some change," Marcus said.

"Uh, what?" The old man's eyes widened.

"The sign says 50% off, and the tag on the bottle is marked $25. The lady would appreciate $87.50 and a receipt." Marcus crossed his arms and smiled at Clair.

"Oh yeah," the man behind the counter handed over the change.

"I'm dying of thirst. Can we go somewhere and enjoy a cool drink?" Clair grabbed Marcus' arm.

"Yes ma'am." He grinned.

****

Across the street, in a plain blue sedan, Spencer Walker watched the couple get into a vehicle and leave. *God you're beautiful, Clair. It's so damn difficult to see other men fall at your feet.*

He pulled into the traffic to follow his charge. *Odd though, I've never seen you go to an antique shop. I know your likes, dislikes, and your style. I even know your favorite color...red. Did your new flame drag you in there; try to impress you with an expensive gift?*

At the next corner, he turned the car around and went back to the shop. The little doorbell jingled to announce his arrival.

"Hello, can I help you?"

"Yeah, hi...uh, I'm looking for my sister — tall brunette, slender build. She called me on her cell, said she and her boyfriend would meet me here."

"A woman just left that fits your description."

"Wonder why she didn't wait for me? She loves to collect certain pieces. Did she find anything?" Spencer opened the top of a small cedar chest and peered inside.

"Yup, sure did, an old perfume bottle with some name on it...Julia, I think. Paid cash, too."

The lid to the chest banged shut. Spencer spun around and felt the blood drain from his face.

"You okay young fellow? You're a bit pale."

"No, no, I'm okay. Thanks."

Oblivious to the traffic, a car honked as Spencer zigzagged across the street and retreated to the car. *It can't be. She found it. What are the odds? I must tell Celeste.*

Nineteen
An Enchanted Day

Sidewalk cafes, quaint shops, and galleries provided a people-watcher's paradise on the River Walk. A silver shimmer of sunlight glinted across the slow ripple from a river taxi. Atop the cross-bridge, Joe Paul slid an arm around Kelley's shoulder and pulled her close. She didn't resist. A little girl on the barge below waved at the cozy twosome.

"Isn't it a gorgeous day?" Kelley waved back.

Joe Paul kissed the top of her head. "Yes, yet nothing compares to my date."

She peered into his deep green eyes and returned a sensuous smile. "Want to take the tour?"

"I'd love it."

In the crush of tourists, he took her hand to board the barge. "Paseo del Rio."

"Excuse me?"

"It's the Spanish term for River Walk. This old town is encased in history."

They chose a seat near the front.

"Did you know a small group of strong-willed women, similar to you and Natasha, saved the fate of this river?"

Impressed by his cool appraisal she said, "Hardheaded might be a better description, but nice choice of words. What happened?"

"Around 1921, a major flood killed over 50 people. Millions in property damage overwhelmed the community. The outraged public wanted the river concreted over to avoid any future catastrophes. However, a few ladies formed the nucleus of the Conservation Society to fight the proposal. They put on a puppet show as a means to preserve the river."

"A puppet show? Don't tease me."

"Ever heard of 'The Goose that Laid the Golden Egg'?

"Well, yes, it…"

"At each performance, masses of people gathered. They donated the profits from the success of their ingenious idea which led to the river's restoration."

Her voice rose in surprise, "Goodness Mr. Farrell, you're quite the historian."

"Only trivia, my sweet, only trivia. I do find it fascinating, much like the beautiful woman next to me."

Kelley tilted her head back and let the afternoon wind ruffle her long hair. "Glad you recognize my assets."

"Oh, I noticed your assets the second I saw you." He squeezed her hand.

A tingle surged, and a smile parted her lips. She squinted toward the topaz sun as it peeked through the thick tree line.

The casual ride on the river barge ended, and people clamored off in different directions.

"What would the lady wish to do next?"

"A trip to the zoo, maybe?"

"San Antonio Zoo—next stop," Joe Paul mimicked a train conductor.

She liked this light, witty side, and it made him more desirable.

A nearby bus carried them to their destination. Crowds swelled the pathways throughout the zoo. In the slow pace of a lazy afternoon, Joe Paul and Kelley chatted, fed the animals, and laughed the hours away.

This is how I wanted our date, relaxed and comfortable together. Focused on the defined lines of his rugged profile, she stumbled on the uneven pavement. He reached to catch her, but she regained her balance, and sprinted away. Behind a large tree, near a small wooden bench, she held her breath.

"Gotcha," he said.

She jumped at the sound of his voice, and their laughter echoed.

In one quick swoop, he swept her up, and sat down on the bench.

Cradled in his arms, Kelley's heart thumped an erratic rhythm, a giddy sense of pleasure skyrocketed. "Joe Paul, I…"

"Shhh, don't say anything." He placed a finger to her mouth. "You might break the magical spell."

Familiar emerald eyes beckoned, tender lips claimed hers, and Kelley wilted. The fervent kiss kindled emotions from Christmas Eve. A welcomed series of slow, soft kisses channeled euphoria. Locked in a persuasive embrace, blissful contentment spiraled into peaceful anxiety.

Tender hands cupped her face, and sweet, warm breath fanned the flame higher. Her eyes opened. Their lips melded together, hot, and urgent.

"My balloon, my balloon," a child wailed.

Reality plunged into the surreal moment. Kelley snapped her attention to the impatient child, his arms stretched toward the runaway toy. She let out a slow breath and managed a slight, tentative smile.

"You know, that's my favorite distraction?"

"What do you mean?" Kelley slid off his lap to the bench.

"Your smile," Joe Paul replied.

Despite the warm afternoon, she shivered from a chilly breeze.

He wrapped both arms around her.

Cuddled together, a dewy haze diffused the sunlight through the trees.

"I hope our time together meant something to you Olivia," he whispered.

"Joe Paul, don't..."

"Wait. Listen to me. Of course, I'm curious, I can't deny it, but won't pressure you. Let me tell you about myself. If you'd like to ask questions, feel free. Okay?"

Kelley fought the urge to scream the truth of her identity.

"Natasha and I discussed some of my background on our dinner date. Maybe she mentioned it, but I'd like to tell you myself."

Lost in those jade eyes, she replied, "Please, go ahead."

"I'm a veterinarian. Live and work at the ranch I grew up on, love horses, sports, and the company of good friends." He paused. "And lately, one lady in particular."

Kelley watched his expressive face soften.

"I'm divorced, have one daughter, Emma. I called her my little princess, but she is grown and lives abroad now.

Kelley tried to concentrate as questions bounced in her head like a pinball machine. *Why couldn't you meet Kelley Malone instead of this stupid façade, Olivia? Kelley is a great girl. She wants to find Mr. Right, fall in love again, and live happily ever after.*

"I don't believe in fate, and I don't open my heart to many; however, I am to you," his voice broke.

Kelley jerked away.

"What's wrong?"

They both stood.

"You, you're the perfect gentleman—always."

"And?"

"It's difficult to explain. Men like you don't exist." Kelley stared at the ground.

"Hey, I'm not special. I'm just me, and I like you because you're **you**."

Oh yeah, I'm me, right down to my fake name. Suddenly, the thought of Kelley and Clair's double exposure lost all appeal.

"Listen, why don't we head back to the hotel, Olivia? I want to give you enough time to get ready for dinner."

Strong arms enveloped her like a warm blanket.

"I suppose we should."

His eyes narrowed, a muscle in his jaw twitched. "Can I ask one question first?"

Adrenaline blasted through her veins, icy fear twisted around her heart. For a brief instant, an impulse for truthfulness flared. *Should I end this ludicrous pretense, be honest, tell you who I really am? There is no Olivia, only Kelley...Kelley Malone, and my alter ego.* "What?" She choked on the word.

"Do you think a piece of world-renowned cheesecake from Wallaby Square would spoil your appetite?"

"Excuse me? Where?"

"Wallaby Square, one of the best restaurants along the River Walk. It's on our way. What do you think?"

"How'd you know cheesecake is my weakness?" she swooned.

****

Under a large patio umbrella, Clair and Marcus sipped raspberry lemonade.

"Well Natasha, this hit the spot for me."

Clair adjusted her sunglasses. "Yes it did, and uh, thanks for going on my little shopping spree."

"A little culture never hurt anyone, besides there's more to me than just cowboy. You might be surprised." He looked at his watch. "We do need to make our way back to St. Antonia's. I'm excited about our dinner date."

****

Clair ran a finger across the word *Julia*, dazzled at the sight of each cut and angle of the new treasure. *I can't wait to tell Celeste. What an exquisite find.* The unexpected click of the door startled her. She tucked the glass bottle into the tote and hid it behind the pillows.

Kelley bounced into the hotel room, whirled around, and collapsed across the bed. "Clair, Clair, Clair."

"My goodness, aren't *we* in a good mood?"

"Tell me the truth, give me your honest opinion," Kelley insisted.

"Did I ever not give you my honest opinion?" Clair teased.

"I know, and sometimes I haven't always liked it. So, what do you really think of him?"

"Him? Him who?" Clair baited.

"Joe Paul, of course."

"Well, I believe Joe Paul Farrell is an attractive man who has manners and obvious good taste in women." Clair raised an eyebrow. "Now as far as my best friend goes, I think she deserves a doting, adorable suitor."

Kelley breathed a big sigh. "Ah, you approve."

"I didn't say *approve*. Look, enjoy the weekend and let the time ahead happen. Don't rush things."

Kelley bolted upright and sat cross-legged.

"You asked my opinion. The Kelley Malone I love like a sister sometimes doesn't listen, but usually lands on her feet." Clair sat down on the bed and placed an arm around her friend. "And of course, I'll be there to catch her if she doesn't."

****

Slow and graceful, the women descended the long staircase of St. Antonia's and approached the elegant archway of the restaurant door.

Clair touched Kelley's arm. "Ready, *Olivia*?"

"Ready, *Natasha*."

Immersed in their double exposure roles, confident once more in their alter egos, they entered the Madrid Room.

Twenty
Attic Secrets

This particular visit to the attic proved the most difficult for Celeste Vandergriff after the conversation with Mr. Highgrove. Linford's administrator agreed a trip to see Clair would present the perfect time to reveal the secreted facts. Mementos, packed away in the old trunk, would see the light of day and tell the story hidden for so many years.

The strong, dark brown, leather trunk stood guardian over the keepsakes. She ran a hand over the dusty top, a 'thank you' to an old friend for confidences she entrusted to its depths. The latch squeaked, and the lid opened in slow motion. One by one, she took each item from the safety of the chest and spoke to them aloud.

A faded, worn picture of three laughing girls greeted her first. Familiar features left no doubt their relationship as sisters. The older girl, adorable in golden tresses, the other boasted tousled curls of brown, and the youngest child, about 18 months old, somewhere between. Arms entwined around one another, they posed in a sweet embrace.

"Hello darlings. So nice to see you once again," Celeste crooned to the fragile picture. She placed the photograph into a large, legal envelope and reached for the next item, a tattered manila folder. It followed the picture, unacknowledged. Pieces of lace and crochet held her attention for a moment. From the looks of them, a child's hand began the simple pattern, but never finished the project. To Celeste, they remained precious. She placed them into the paper pouch, her weatherworn hand lingered, a tender affirmation. Ten ribbon-bound letters rested on top of a picture. Unable to bear to read the written words, she moved them to one side. These trips back in time raised long-controlled emotion, and she leaned back to rest against the wall. "After all these years, it's time."

A few moments passed, strength returned, and she continued the task. The tin type of two men dressed in the fashion of the day looked stiff and inflexible. Celeste shuddered at the austere photograph and placed it in the envelope — out of sight.

A framed certificate, handwritten in French, surfaced next. *This parchment changed so many lives...and not for the better.* Toward the bottom lay items of jewelry, valuable period pieces, and family heirlooms. She opened the silver clasp of a heart-shaped locket. "These are insignificant to me, but what impact will they have on Clair?"

A tarnished, gold gift box ended the search. A bedraggled, red bow slipped off easily to reveal an antique perfume bottle. Across the front, in beautiful script, radiated a single name...*Tasha*.

****

Clair couldn't remember the last time she enjoyed a meal like this one. Her comment on the sumptuous fare halted in mid-sentence. Sparks between Joe Paul and Kelley were palpable. Neither touched the food on their plates. Kelley's admirer monitored her every move, and Clair could tell she loved it.

Kelley leaned over, her voice sensuous. "Joe Paul, the food doesn't interest you?"

His tone matched hers, "I'd be a fool to spend time eating when I can feast on your beauty.

Clair nearly choked on the porterhouse steak. *Oh please, give me a break.*

Her thoughts wandered during the conversation of how Marcus and Joe Paul met. The perfume bottle in the hotel room niggled at her mind. She wanted to withdraw to the suite and examine the find. Marcus would make a good friend, nothing more, which made it difficult to concentrate. She hadn't heard a word he said in the last 15 minutes. "Please, excuse me, Marcus. I must find the powder room."

The gentlemen stood, and Kelley jumped up.

"No Olivia, finish your dinner. I'll be right back." Before Clair drifted out of earshot, she heard Joe Paul say, "Is she upset?" Her steps slowed as she heard Kelley's reply. "Why don't you forget Clair and focus on me? Marcus is her date tonight."

The small musical ensemble struck up a soft-rock tune, and Clair stole a glimpse back to watch the couple drift out to a nearby balcony. She smiled at Kelley's ready acceptance. *Typical Kelley.*

Clair headed for the hotel room to examine the bottle one more time. *It won't take long, and I can return to dinner before anyone becomes suspicious.*

****

Spencer Walker couldn't decide where to start. In this line of business, he had all the tools of the trade to gain access to a hotel room and took the opportunity in Clair's absence to do what he did best. *I have to see the bottle. If it proves a match, everything could spin out of control.* After rummaging through the last dresser drawer, he turned toward the closet. *Maybe she put it in a pocket or a bag.*

Persistence paid off. In the bottom of a green canvas tote, he found the prize, grabbed it, and prepared to make an exit. A sound at the door stopped him in his tracks. "Damn."

****

A strange uneasiness swept over Clair. The hotel door swung open, but she didn't enter. *Something is not right.* The familiar tingle on her neck added to the anxiety. "The light is still on. I know Kelley switched it off before we left." She tried to shake the disquiet, and in a bold move, went straight to the closet. Frantic hands searched the empty bag. "Oh my God, it's gone!"

She surveyed the room. The inventory only disturbed her more...an open drawer. *My shoes are out of place. Someone went through our stuff. What should I do? They might still be here. Should I call house security, or Joe Paul and Kelley?*

"So, there you are."

She spun around. "Marcus?"

"If you didn't want to have dinner with me, you could've said so, Natasha. No need to ditch me." A wide grin showed pleasure at her indefensible dilemma.

"You startled me, and I didn't ditch you. I left something undone and wanted to make sure I took care of it before rejoining the party." She shoved the drawer shut. "There—all done. Shall we join the others?" Clair took his arm. *I can't ruin Kelley's evening. I'll have to tell her, but not now. Olivia needs to enjoy this night.*

In front of the elevator, Marcus stopped and faced Clair. "Look, let's cut out the nonsense. This isn't a relationship made in heaven. You feel it; I feel it, but can we at least be friends?"

Caught off guard, she stammered, "Why Marcus, uh, I'm sorry."

He squeezed her hand. "It's okay Natasha, if indeed that is your real name. I'm fine. Let's have some fun. No expectations. Agreed?"

Clair smiled, relieved. "You know, some men wouldn't understand. Their egos would get in the way. Thank you for your candor, Marcus. I see a great friendship forming."

"So…you really don't want to go back to dinner, do you?" He pushed the elevator button. "What would you like—a drink, maybe dancing?"

"Yes, thank you. It'd be nice to eliminate the pressure. Lay all the cards on the table." She dismissed the concern of the bottle.

"Sure, I came here to have fun, so let's go. Wanna tell the lovebirds our plans?"

"No," she replied. "I feel a little wicked tonight. Why not let them wonder? Are you up for it?"

"You *are* a little wicked, aren't you, Natasha? I love the idea. They won't miss us anyway."

The elevator door opened, and they stepped inside.

Clair's amusement heightened. *What a delightful twist to this little scenario.*

Twenty-One
The Green Horse Saloon

"Green Horse Saloon? Looks like an old building. What is this, Marcus?" The brisk evening air made Clair shiver.

Marcus handed the cab driver a twenty-dollar bill. "One of the oldest dance halls in Texas, pretty lady — a hundred and fifteen years, to be exact."

She gave a weak smile. "I don't think I'm dressed right."

"You said you were up for some fun tonight, Natasha. Does it really matter if you never see any of these people again? But if you're just plain chicken..." Marcus laughed.

Clair took the bait, irritated by his impish grin. "All right, you're on. Lead the way."

They entered the club and apprehension grew as she glanced around the room. Long tables lined one side of the large hall, and patrons sat on rustic benches to enjoy their meal. A live band played on the other side, and she recognized the peppy swing music. The drummer put on quite a show, and she noticed the name on the bass drum, *The Slipshod Shooters*.

Marcus led her to a table, pulled out a chair, and invited her to sit. A waitress appeared with a bucket of peanuts and asked for their order. After her disastrous experience at Bud's, Clair ordered a Corona Light with lime.

"Good choice. I'm impressed. I'll have a Silver Bullet."

The beer soothed her nerves.

"More comfortable now?" He flipped a peanut shell across the table.

"Nice shot. I'm fine, so when does the fun start?" she challenged.

"Your wish is my command. How about a dance?"

Her eyebrow arched. "So, you can handle swing?"

"I can hold my own, my dear." He reached out a hand.

Previous escapades on the dance floor brought a grin. *You haven't a clue.* However, Clair was the one swept off her feet. Marcus proved a very adept partner, and as they whirled around, she enjoyed the freedom of the dance.

They made their way back to the table, out of breath and laughing.

"You are good, my lady," Marcus said. He tipped his hat and drew her chair to the side.

"Thank you, sir. You left me surprised, too." His versatility impressed her, and gradually, her guard relaxed. He was a good man, a decent individual, and she believed she could trust him.

"Well, *hello* Marcus. Quite a display out there. Who's your little friend?"

They looked up to see a pretty, petite blonde dressed in jeans, boots, and a cropped western shirt. Clair noticed his obvious displeasure at the intrusion.

"Hello Nell, this is Natasha. Natasha, this is Nell."

"Hi Nell," Clair said, still flushed from the dance.

"Whatever."

The instant dismissal left no doubt the woman wanted Marcus.

Nell pulled out a chair and focused on the cowboy.

Scent of Double Deception

"You haven't called me in a long time, Marcus honey. You're a bad boy."

Marcus motioned for the waitress and told her to settle the bill. He rose from the chair and looked at Nell, face stony, hands clenched. "This kind of theatrics is exactly why. Let's go Natasha, we're done here."

Clair didn't say a word as they stepped out into the night air. Surprised, she took his arm. A sudden kinship blossomed. *Why would a woman like Nell feel the need to be so tacky?*

The annoyed cowboy unlocked a midnight blue dually.

A cowboy Cadillac. "Is this yours, Marcus? We came in a cab. How did it get here?"

"My ranch is close by. One of my ranch hands brought it."

She could see he fought hard to control his temper.

"Look, I'd like to apologize for that little scene, Natasha. I should've known one of them would show up."

"One of *them*?"

"I won't beat around the bush. Female friends are few and far between, and sometimes we cross paths. Too often, we don't part friends. The competition to get me to the altar leaves me cold and resigned to bachelorhood. I enjoy the company of a female, but when the pushing starts, I bolt like a frightened colt. Although I love a sophisticated woman, there has to be a human side, too. Romance isn't in the air for us, I get that. All I really want is your friendship. Think it's possible?"

Clair smiled. She understood the need for distance. "No problem. So what do we do now?"

"How about going for a little drive. We can talk, get to know each other better," he offered.

"Sounds good to me."

They drove in silence for a while as Marcus eased around the curves in the road.

She sat back in the comfortable leather seats and savored the total lack of pressure to make forced conversation.

The miles passed in quiet companionship, and finally, his attention turned to her once more. He glanced her way, then back at the road. "So Natasha, tell me a little about you while we drive. What were you like as a little girl? I need to hear the sound of your voice."

Calmer now, and more relaxed, Clair began the tale of her childhood.

Twenty-Two
Double Dates

The glass-wall elevator ascended to the top of the Tower of the Americas and stopped at the observation deck. Joe Paul and Kelley stepped out to a spectacular, panoramic view. An inflated moon outlined the city, and a kaleidoscope of color twinkled in the onyx night.

"What an incredible display," Kelley said. "I've visited San Antonio many times, but never took the time to experience this."

"Well, I'm glad we could share a first." Joe Paul placed a firm arm around her shoulder.

"It reminds me of the first time Natasha and I saw Paris from atop the Eiffel Tower. What an adventure."

"I imagine the two of you took Paris by storm." He chuckled.

"Yes we did, my dear man, yes we did. I must admit we like to leave permanent impressions."

"I'm sure the French are changed forever. I've traveled overseas, too." Joe Paul gazed on the city below.

"Really?"

"Is there a tone of surprise in your voice?"

"No, I mean, well…"

"Oh, I see. You didn't think this old cowboy could get involved in anything cultural?"

"I suppose I thought your enthusiasm as a horse rancher wouldn't leave much time for other interests."

"Well, I can always make time for certain things of refinement."

Kelley turned her back to the railing.

Joe Paul placed a hand on either side of her arms. "My love for horses is only one reason I travel."

"One? What's the other?"

A crooked smile played at the corner of his mouth. "Ah, now you're curious."

"No, I'm not." She crossed her arms.

"Well, if you don't want me to tell you its okay." Joe Paul kissed her forehead.

"Don't think you have me figured out Mr. Farrell, but yes, I'm curious, so tell me."

"All right, the other reason is a beautiful female."

"Another woman?"

"My daughter, Emma," he explained. "I mentioned she lives abroad."

"Of course, Emma." *How could I forget about his daughter?*

"She is a student at a prominent art school."

"An artist? You must be proud. Where is the school?"

"Brittany, France—not too far from Paris. She's lived there for several years. Her mother thought if she took my little girl out the states, we couldn't develop a decent relationship because of the obligations on the ranch. However, when Emma turned eighteen, she came for an extended visit to grill me about the divorce. I gave honest answers, and we worked through it. Our bond is strong now, and we keep in touch."

"What caused the divorce? Did you cheat on your ex-wife, whatever her name is?"

His gaze never wavered. "No Olivia, I didn't cheat on anyone, and her name is Felicia. The truth is, I came home early from a conference and caught her in bed with one of my stable boys. I threw them both out. In my rage, I never considered she would use Emma against me. Of course, in her version of the story, I'm the villain."

Kelley looked away. "I'm sorry if I sounded harsh. Forgive my rudeness."

"I told you to ask questions today. Don't apologize for curiosity," his voice calm and tender.

He stepped closer, his muscular body silhouetted against her. She slipped slender arms around his neck, and thoughts of their earlier passionate kisses whirled in her mind. The brim of the cowboy hat shadowed their faces.

****

The truck rumbled to a smooth stop in front of the hotel, and Clair unlocked the seat belt. The tale of her years in Washington State and migration to Texas simply spilled out. Marcus added comments to the animated conversation and laughter rolled between the couple. To Clair's surprise, the perfume bottle found its way into the little narrative. She needed to share the concern of its disappearance. "My goodness, I've chattered all the way back to town. I'm sorry Marcus, it is easy to talk to you."

"Nonsense, your past is still safe." He winked. "Besides, your stories amazed me. You're a strong woman, different from most, and I'm quite impressed. However, I will admit the idea of an intruder in your hotel room is worrisome. I want to help. Let me post one of my ranch hands at your door tonight. You can sleep unafraid."

"Oh Marcus, please no. I haven't even told Olivia about it. I'll be fine. Maybe someone saw me make the purchase today. Anyway, they obviously got what they wanted. I don't think they'll come back," Clair pleaded.

The look on the cowboy's face stated disbelief in the excuse, but he refrained from any further comment.

"I don't know why I told you. I suppose it was just on my mind. You needn't worry. It's nothing, really."

"We'll see, Natasha. Right now, let's get you back to your room." He opened the truck door and glanced at his watch. "It's pretty late...past the bewitching hour. Olivia might be mad at me." He grinned.

"I doubt neither your buddy, nor my friend, missed us at all. I think they both wanted to be alone," Clair said.

They exited the elevator, and Clair placed a hand on his arm. "Thanks again for a fun evening. This is the first time I've relaxed around anyone in a long time."

He took off his hat. "We did have fun, didn't we?"

"Yes, and the next time I need a swing partner, I'll know who to call." Clair slid the key card.

"Please do, however, before I leave little lady, I'm inspecting your room. Wait here."

Clair didn't argue and watched Marcus through the open doorway.

"All clear, nothing looks disturbed, even Olivia isn't in there. She'll never know how late I brought you back."

"Ah, so we got away with our little truancy?"

"Natasha, on a serious note, maybe I should stay tonight. It is possible Olivia and Joe Paul went to my guesthouse. Don't mistake my intentions; I'd sleep on the couch in my clothes."

"Marcus, you're a rare friend, and I appreciate the offer, but go home." *I don't want to play Natasha any longer. A hot bath is what I need. As tired as I am, a slip of the tongue is a possibility.*

"I wouldn't be much of a man if I didn't at least ask. Can I call later to check on you? Please give me that much. I intend to keep this friendship we've formed."

"Sure Marcus. By the time you arrive at your ranch, I should be ready to hit the pillow." She gave him a slight hug.

****

Marcus waited to hear a solid click of the bolt on the other side of the door. Reluctant to leave, he pulled out a cell phone. "Mac, get dressed and meet me at the St. Antonia Hotel in 20 minutes."

Confident the man on the other end of the phone understood the order, Marcus took the elevator to the lobby and waited outside.

"Room 703, guard it. I want a description of everyone who comes in or out of that room or even walks down the hallway. Report to me at 7:00 AM, got it?"

An older, stocky-built man nodded. "Understood, Mr. Wellborn."

Twenty-Three
A Closet Rendezvous

Clair closed the door behind Marcus and propped her back against its strength. A deep sigh escaped her lips, relieved to shed Natasha at last. Although Marcus and she ended up fast friends, the strain of role-play took its toll. The missing bottle popped in and out of her mind all night. She knew Marcus noticed the distraction, but didn't question anything. *The consummate gentleman.* One last glance through the peephole confirmed his departure. *Finally, I can finish what I started.*

Apprehension caused her heartbeat to accelerate. The closet door opened at a touch and revealed the source of anxiety. The shopping bag rested in the corner next to a pair of black dress pumps. She reached out and picked it up. *What's this? I know the bag was empty when I left.* The bottle sparkled and twinkled reflecting the light. *How did it get here? Is my mind playing tricks on me?*

Without warning, a light switch clicked, the closet went black, and a powerful, brawny hand clamped over her mouth. *A man? In our room?* A struggle ensued, and the wooden clothes rod crashed down, pain seared her forehead. She couldn't see, couldn't scream. The masculine arm held her immobile and tightened around her waist. Clair felt his warmth as it encircled her body. He continued to hold her, silent and unmoving.

Moments passed like an eternity until slowly he turned her toward him. His hand remained firm across her mouth, and her body pressed against his smoldering frame. The embrace tightened around Clair's waist again, and warm, sweet lips found hers. She went limp.

****

Damn!

Clair slipped from Spencer's grasp in a dead faint. He caught her before she collapsed on the floor. There would be only minutes to make a retreat before she regained consciousness. He lifted the slack body and placed her on the bed. She looked so beautiful lying there. He ached for want of her.

Spencer took a last look at Clair, turned the key into the adjoining door, and closed it. Back in the room, he looked through the peephole. A stranger stood outside the girls' door. *Who the hell is that? A guard? Who is this bloke? Good thing I'm here. It would have blown my cover if I'd left through her doorway.*

He knew he couldn't waste time. Kelley might be on the way to the room right now. Spencer decided to lay in wait outside the hotel, ready to take action if needed.

****

An eerie silence filled the hallway, and Mac shuffled his feet…uneasy. He'd learned the hard way not to question Marcus on the purpose of an assignment, however, he couldn't help wonder.

The intrigue in his boss's life came and went like a revolving door. Always women. He had yet to see the woman who could ensnare Marcus Wellborn.

Mac thought about the girl left in his charge, and wondered what Marcus found attractive. Thoughts scattered when the door to the next room opened, and a man emerged. Mac stood tall, arms down and clasped together, sunglasses on like Secret Service. He surveyed the man as he passed and noticed the guy gave him a sideways look. *Something's not right about this joker.*

When the stranger reached the end of the hall, he turned and stared back at Mac in an unsettling way. The look convinced him to leave his post and follow. *Why would he take the stairs and not the elevator?*

****

Spencer smiled when he saw the large man in front of Clair's door hesitate and move toward the stairs. *Perfect, it worked. Got him away from Clair.*

He sprinted down the stairs and made his way through the large front doors of the hotel. Once outside, he headed for his red convertible parked on the curb.

Settled into the leather seat, he caught sight of the slower moving man coming through the hotel entrance. Spencer watched the frantic search, amused. A belly laugh almost escaped, but he stopped short. Kelly stepped out of a taxi right in front of him. Spencer scrunched down in the seat, hoping she wouldn't notice. In the meantime, the Secret Service wanna-be paced the street. *Crap. Kelley's gotta make it back to the room before this guy gives up the search. Wait, who is the cowboy? Oh yeah, that Joe Paul fella.*

Kelley's date followed her out of the cab. They linked arms and strolled toward the hotel. Tiny patches of amber began to preface the horizon for a spectacular sunrise.

An all-nighter, eh Kelley?

Scent of Double Deception

They walked by the cars parked parallel to the curb, and Spencer sunk lower in the seat. She did a double take, and he stifled a shiver. *Oh God, does she recognize the car? Crap, why didn't I think of that?*

****

Out of breath, and more than annoyed, Mac made his way back to the assigned post. He'd lost the guy pretty quick. *Was it a ploy to get me away from the door? Man, I'm slowing down in my old age. He disappeared awful fast.*

Marcus expected him to do his job well or answer to him personally. He'd worked for Wellborn, Inc. long enough to know the consequences, but this time Marcus caught him unprepared. *I'm starvin'. The old boss man called in the middle of my midnight snack.*

He surveyed the hall, empty. On the way back up to the room, he noticed a vending machine. *I should have stopped. What the heck, it will only take a second. What could happen?* He headed down the hall, mouth watering.

****

From the deepest regions of her subconscious, Clair heard a familiar voice call her name. She struggled to open her eyes. All of a sudden, she came wide-awake.

Kelley gently jiggled her arm. "Clair? Hey girl, are you going to wake up? My goodness, did you have too much to drink last night? You're usually the early bird. I'm sorry we didn't call you, but when Marcus disappeared too, I thought you went off together."

"No, that's okay. I guess I was deep in Neverland. I'm awake now," Clair replied, sluggish. "How was your night? When did you get in? I didn't hear you." *Maybe if Kelley talks, I can get my thoughts together. Was last night a dream or did it really happen?*

Kelley began a moment-by-moment account, and Clair put her thoughts in order. *Okay, Marcus brought me home, checked out the room, and left. I went to the closet and...* Thoughts came fast and furious now, and she blushed. *The intruder, the kiss.*

"What is it, Clair? Your face is flushed. What are you thinking? Did you have a bit of a naughty night?"

"No, no. I think I must have had too much to drink, though. I really don't feel well. Let me get a glass of water while you finish your story." *I can't tell her what happened. I've got to sort through this.* She splashed cold water on her face. *I've got to look in the closet.*

Kelly went on about Joe Paul, and Clair took the opportunity to open the closet. Nothing unusual there. The clothes hung neat and the tote bag sat undisturbed. *What's sticking out of the top?* She unwrapped the paper to reveal the perfume bottle, safe and sound. *What is going on? If they didn't want the bottle, then what?*

"You've hardly heard a word I've said Clair—are you going to tell me what happened last night?"

"Nothing happened. Hey, we have to pack. We have a plane to catch. Let's get our things together and go down for breakfast. You can finish your part, and I'll tell you mine."

****

Spencer chastised himself, exasperated. "Man, you're really gonna blow this. You stupid idiot."

After examining the perfume bottle, the truth could no longer be denied. It matched the other two. He put in a call to Celeste, and she confirmed it. Three original bottles: the one in the trunk labeled *Tasha*, the one Clair found in her apartment inscribed *Clair*, and this one branded *Julia*.

"Wherever did you find it, Spencer?"

"I didn't. Clair did," he explained.

"Well, it's happened. Fate intervened. Did I tell you I'm coming to Dallas?"

He registered surprise and listened while she told him of the impending trip. "So, it's time then? Time to tell her? I knew this would come one day. I guess none of us prepared for it though."

"Spencer, I'm glad you replaced the bottle. Hopefully, Clair won't contact the police and start an investigation. I'm almost sure she'll call and tell me what happened. I'll downplay the episode until I get there and can talk to her in person."

Spencer explained how he was caught in the hotel closet. "I know how feisty she is. It threw me for a loop when she fainted."

"I hope she is okay."

Spencer reassured Celeste of Clair's well-being. Before they hung up, she gave him the details of the flight. He promised he would be there, but out of sight.

His hand rested on the phone, and his mind flew back to the episode in the closet. To actually have his arms around her slender waist, hold her sensuous body next to his, proved more than he could stand. He would savor the stolen kiss for the rest of his life. *It'll probably be all I ever have of her.*

Everything unraveled in his mind. *How can I protect her when I care so much? Love is in the way. I can't think straight. When Celeste informs her of the inheritance and my part in all of it—well, I'm on unstable ground. I need to let Celeste do her work, but will she understand my passionate love for Clair? Will the revelation kill any chance I might have?*

Twenty-Four
The Long Good-Bye

Amid sounds of surprised hellos or sad goodbyes, babies cried, children shouted, and people funneled through the crowded airport. Oblivious to the babble of a hundred tongues and thunderous footsteps, one particular couple held hands and chatted: she—a paradox in honesty; he—the paradigm admirer.

Sensual snippets from the night before toyed with Kelley's heart. Joe Paul only asked for some time alone, but the encounter became much more, an unexpected fusion of pleasure and disbelief. While he talked, she struggled to stay focused, but the depth of the cowboy's eyes manipulated any rational attention and usurped all sensibility. *I can't wait until we're together again. No, stop it stupid. It can't happen. Olivia only exists through fantasy, an innocent pretense.* She couldn't deny the magnetism, at least not last night. *Have I gone too far? Oh, why did I entangle my heart in such a compromise?*

The musical ring of the cell phone provided an uninvited irritation. "Please excuse me." Kelley turned her back to Joe Paul. "Hello? Yes, this is she. Oh Isabella, how are you? Is there a problem? I see, no I understand. I'll consult my partner and call you tomorrow."

"Everything okay, Olivia?" Clair called out.

"Nothing we can't handle. We'll discuss it on our flight back."

A protective hand touched her arm. "Olivia is something wrong?" Joe Paul asked.

"No, just work."

"Funny…I still don't know exactly what it is you and Natasha do."

"Let's not talk shop right now. My flight will leave in a few minutes."

"Well, I didn't mean to eavesdrop, but I couldn't help overhear you say the name Isabella."

A pang of fear charged in the pit of Kelley's stomach. *Did I say her name aloud?*

"I have a close friend named Isabella who lives in Shreveport. Maybe a unique coincidence, but it isn't a very common name."

Kelley slipped an arm through his and moved a couple steps away from Clair. "I believe it's more ordinary than you think. So, just how *close* is your friend, Mr. Farrell?"

A smile crossed his face. "Several years ago, this particular lady had long, skinny legs and freckles on her nose. Grown now, she's many things to me; the little sister I never had, my neighbor, and my best friend, until recently."

"So, do you have many lady friends?" Kelley put a hand on his chest.

Joe Paul wrapped his arms around her waist. "I'd hoped to trade Isabella in on a new lady friend…someone, the first time I met, belted out some fine country tunes without an ounce of intimidation."

Clair tapped him on the shoulder, and the embrace dissolved. "Well, whomever that is better make her farewell short. It's time to get on our plane. Thanks for an interesting weekend, Joe Paul." Clair picked up the carry-on bag and started toward a group of people in line to board.

He shook his head. "Never let it be said your best friend is shy."

"Yes, if only she could come out of her shell a little." Kelley faked a sigh.

He pulled her toward him again. "Olivia, thank you for this weekend. I'd like to think it's the start of something more important."

Tears threatened to spill, and she blinked hard. How could she just walk away now? A sob rose in her throat. "Joe Paul, I didn't expect things to...well, happen."

"Tell me I can see you again."

Her spirits sank even lower. Suffocated by guilt and selfishness, she looked away. The belief she would probably never see him after today brought on a surge of despair.

He touched her face, and hope warmed her soul.

"Past relationships left me vulnerable, so I vowed never again. Then, one ordinary night, I stopped for a steak at Adams Rib, and everything changed. You walked into my life."

"Things aren't always as they seem," she whispered.

"Tell me — explain. Are you married? Is there someone else?" His voice remained calm.

"No, I'm not married, and there's no particular person in my life." She glanced toward Clair.

"Is it Natasha? I know I'm not her biggest fan, but if I've done something to offend her, I'll apologize."

"No, no, it's not Natasha's fault, Joe Paul. It's me," Kelley choked.

"Olivia, let's go." Clair motioned.

He grabbed Kelley shoulders and forced her to face him. "Damn it, I've fallen for you. Can't you see it?"

Her breath caught. She stared speechless at the smoldering flame in his eyes.

What am I doing? This isn't Olivia talking, it's Kelley. Olivia would never allow any transparent sentiment. Where is my alter ego when I need her? Caught up in the conundrum, she forced herself back into character. Molded against his body, she kissed him with a hunger that belied an outward calm. With intense reserve, she picked up the shoulder bag and disappeared through the jet way alongside her business partner.

In the first-class section, Clair took the aisle seat. Kelley scooted over to the window in silence.

The enormous metal bird took flight into the vastness of blue sky and billowy white clouds.

Silence lengthened between them until Kelley kicked off her shoes. "It was different this time." She sighed.

"I noticed." Clair turned the page of her novel. "Well?"

Kelley expected a barrage of reprimands, but Clair's voice emanated concern. "Well..." she started. "I got my head back on straight, and Olivia left him at the altar."

"Excuse me?"

"No matter what happened in our game of pretense, I blew him off." Kelley crossed her arms in triumph.

"First, my dear, I never doubted you. Second, I meant the call from Isabella."

"Oh Clair, I don't have you fooled, do I?"

"Not a bit honey, and I also think I've got Joe Paul figured out. Don't misunderstand me, I don't expect you to jump into a relationship, but you might want to think twice before you brush off this particular man so hastily."

Surprised, Kelley leaned over and hugged her. "Thanks Clair. Maybe I'll give him a call after the Riley wedding."

"I heard Joe Paul's comment about his friend Isabella. So what did she want?"

"It appears they've decided to have the reception at Silks and Saddles instead of the oval track at the Downs. Bulldog says it is still too wet. You've seen more of their ranch than I, what do you think?

Lost in the details, the girls discussed the different facets involved if the original plan changed. The short flight back to DFW Airport ended, and Clair never mentioned the newest treasure.

****

Russell tossed the gym bag on the couch and checked the clock. *The girls should be back from the convention in San Antonio. Tomorrow, we need to organize our schedules for the big wedding in Shreveport.* He grabbed a small electronic device and punched in a code. *I'm glad Clair and Kelley wore the bracelets I gave them.*

The GPS chip inside each tiny **M** charm monitored their locations, and it appeared they stayed fairly close to each other. Only once, Clair distanced herself from Kelley for a brief time, but that's Clair. He made a mental note to ask her about it later.

Their trip provided him an opportunity to hit the gym. He wanted to be in good shape for his date. *The girls will see the real Kitty in action at the wedding.*

Twenty-Five
Voice of Frustration

Fifteen minutes southeast of San Antonio, Marcus Wellborn's ranch sat nestled in the quiet, Texas hill country. His father acquired the massive acreage in a high stakes poker game 36 years ago. Pump jacks pedaled up and down nonstop, and Longhorn cattle roamed the fertile pastureland.

The sun dipped low in a coral-colored sky while two caballeros rode across the verdant meadows in a deep discussion of the past and present.

"Man, I don't know about you. What happened to the old Joe Cool?" Marcus pushed up the brim of his gray Stetson.

On the crest of a hill, they stopped for their horses to graze.

Joe Paul wrapped the reins around the saddle horn. "Yeah, how ironic, the one woman I want, I can't have. The last female to entice me out of bachelorhood mothered my only child."

"Hey, if you're really serious about Olivia go after her," Marcus encouraged.

"I don't know if I should."

"Now what's that suppose to mean?"

The dark haired man sat up straighter in the saddle and let out a long sigh. "I made several attempts to track her through the phone number she gave me, but everything led to a dead end. It's as though Olivia doesn't exist."

"I can't believe you never got a last name, although, Natasha didn't give me one either. She did loosen up and talk a bit about her childhood on the way back from the Green Horse Saloon. She never mentioned Olivia though."

"Guess you got more information than I did," Joe Paul said. "Truth is, I'd like to blame Natasha."

"She's a feisty female, I have to agree." Marcus grinned.

"Even though the woman can irritate me at times, she reassured me of Olivia's interest at dinner in Shreveport," Joe Paul said."

"Ever hear the term 'player'? Maybe she thinks the mystery will lure you in."

"I think you're wrong. Remember, I walked into her life on Christmas Eve."

Marcus patted his friend on the back. "Don't forget, I've got connections in Dallas. One guy in particular owes me a favor. If she's genuine, he'll find out. Say the word, and I'll make the call."

"No thanks, Marcus, I've decided you can't make someone love you. Maybe fate will bring her back to me."

"Hell, can't believe you've mellowed over the years," he teased. "I'm not so sure about you."

They sat silent, the only sound—the rhythmic grind of the pump jacks in the background.

Joe Paul forced the cowboy hat down farther on his head. "Well, there's one thing I'm sure of."

"What's that?"

"I can still outride your butt. Beat you back to the ranch house." A quick kick of the spurs, and Joe Paul disappeared down the hill.

"Wait." Marcus jerked the horse into a heated stride.

A mixture of laughter and swearwords echoed through a trail of dust.

****

The unpredictable Seattle weather rattled Celeste's nerves. The plane lurched in the turbulence, and a small prayer escaped her lips. *Dear Lord, take me safely to see my sweet niece and keep my mind occupied on the task before me.* She leaned back in the seat and tried to gather her thoughts. *How can I prepare my precious Clair for the truth? Will she still love me, and embrace the outcome of this reality, or allow contempt to harden her heart?*

The little coffer she carried on board rested in her lap. Aged fingers smoothed the dainty ribbons tied around it. *Such deception. This small box, so ornate and beautiful on the outside, yet inside holds a magnitude of life-changing information.*

The redheaded stewardess stopped the cart in the aisle next to Celeste. "Ma'am, would you like something to drink?"

"Might I have a little red wine?" Celeste asked.

The plane leveled off, and she relaxed. Drowsiness encircled her like an old friend.

****

Inside the Dallas airport, travelers bustled toward their individual destinations.

Clair checked the marquee. *Thank goodness, Aunt CeeCee's plane is on time.* The hair on the back of her neck prickled, and a flicker of apprehension surged. She came to an abrupt stop, rapid panic gnawed through the excitement to see Celeste. *Dear God, not now.* In the throng of people, Clair thought she saw a familiar face. She blinked hard at the ever-changing wave of individuals, but it vanished.

Anxious to vacate the mass of humanity, she scanned the crowd of passengers in the jet way. The last person to exit ambled at a slow, steady pace. *There she is, elegant and timeless.* "Aunt CeeCee," Clair called.

The older woman waved...her smile reminiscent of the one Clair cherished as a child. They embraced in a joyful reunion.

"You look exhausted from the flight, Aunt CeeCee."

Celeste held on tight to Clair's arm. "Yes dear, I am, and a bit groggy, I'm afraid."

"It's called jet lag, silly. Let's find your luggage and go to my apartment."

An hour later, the two women talked and sipped hot tea in Clair's garden.

Aunt CeeCee cradled the teacup. "Where in the world is Kelley? I haven't seen her in ages. Is she going to come today?"

"Yes, of course. She wanted to give us a little time to catch up. You know her personality. She'll take over the conversation once she sees you." Clair grinned. "We agreed you'd need a chance to relax first. Besides, I want you to see the bottle. You see, I haven't mentioned it to Kelley, yet." She rose to retrieve the item.

Celeste put up a hand. "Could we talk about it later, my dear? I'm afraid the effects of the flight have overcome me."

"I'm sorry, how rude I am. Naturally, you need to rest." Clair led the way to the guestroom, pulled back the coverlet, and they hugged.

In the solarium, Clair stood next to the fountain. The water trickle soothed the anxiety from the episode at the airport. She tried to visualize the day the bottle first appeared. The jangle of the phone jarred her from the reverie.

"Is she here? How is she? Did she ask about me? What time can I come over?"

"Yes, she's here and asleep in the next room." Clair chuckled.

"How did the flight go? Does she want to go out to eat? What about Russell? He's excited to see her, too," Kelley said.

"I told Russell to show up at six o'clock and bring dinner from the little Italian bistro down the street. I decided, at least tonight, we'd eat in. Why don't you come about 5:30?"

"Wonderful, and tell Aunt CeeCee I'll bring a bottle of her favorite red wine."

****

Small puffs of dirt trailed behind the dually along the fencerow. The need to mend a couple sections of barbwire provided a welcome distraction today, an outlet for his vexation. Joe Paul opted to do the chore alone, time to think, clear his mind. *Why in the hell can't I get over her?*

He took the heavy T-post driver and pounded the metal rods deep into the soil. Over and over, the weight of each blow forced the spike further downward. Frustration bubbled inside, and the rampant beat of his heart controlled each movement. Sweat trickled down his face, and he raked a forearm across his brow.

Dewy grass sparked against an early morning sun. He leaned against the fender of the truck and stared beyond the fencerow and fluid pastures. *How did I let her slip away?*

Twenty-Six
Wedding Day

Lester McDuff walked through the stables of Silks and Saddles and drank in the aroma of fresh oats, hay, and hot coffee. He stole a look back at the big colonial house owned by Bulldog Riley, and a smile crossed his weatherworn face. *How did this happen? Little Isabella gettin' hitched. I can still see her in pigtails on her favorite steed, battin' her eyes, and beggin...Please Duffy, just around the corral, pretty please?* Uncharacteristic tears appeared. *Those days are gone for sure.* A slap on the back caused him to jump.

"Hey Duffy, how are you today, buddy?"

"Uh, I—I'm fine, Joe Paul. Got somethin' in my eye. Why aren't you up at the big house gettin' all fancied up?"

"I know you're dying to see me in the monkey suit, aren't you?" Joe Paul joked.

Duffy cleared his throat. "Well, I'm just gonna wait to see the video. I'll be stayin' down here at the barn where I belong."

"Chicken...you're afraid one of those *mature* ladies will try to latch on, you handsome stud. Stable manager...ah, women can't resist."

Duffy swung a left hook, but Joe Paul ducked.

"You're getting slow, pal."

"Didn't wanna hurt ya, JP. Besides, I'm still keepin' tabs on Ms. Tips and Tipper. They look okay, but the colt bears watchin'. Ain't no need in me takin' any chances on spoilin' the big day."

"Yeah, yeah, well, I'll have my pager on if you need me." Joe Paul waved good-bye and disappeared out the door.

****

The warm hay barn rendered the denim jacket a nuisance, and Joe Paul shed it in a hurry. He attacked the morning chore ritual at an intense pace and struggled to block thoughts of the woman who haunted them. Every pitchfork of hay recreated the image of flowing blonde hair. He stopped and imagined. Sheltered in his arms, Olivia swayed to a slow waltz. He controlled the dance, and she fell into perfect harmony. He reveled in the combination, delicate as a flower, but a resolute force, if prompted — sassy, fresh, intoxicating.

The pitchfork fell to the ground, and he plopped onto a hay bale. *I thought the weekend in San Antonio turned a corner for us, a beginning. What a fool. Damn Natasha, always right there to put the protective wall up for Olivia.*

He swiped the shirtsleeve across his dry mouth and looked toward the water cooler. *Get real Farrell; Natasha had no part in it. Sure, atop the Tower of the Americas anyone might mistake the view for magic. Olivia got caught up in the atmosphere, that's all. The chains of chemistry created an intimate closeness, and she twinkled like a star. We shared a secret that night…from the whole world.*

Anger raged, he stood and picked up the rake. The pitchfork flew, and hay scattered overhead. His arms ached. "I guess she got a dose of reality in the airport. I'll probably never see her again, never see those bright, blue eyes, and never taste her sweet kiss."

He tossed the square bales of hay on the flatbed trailer. The chambray shirt, soaked in sweat, chafed his skin. Even the crisp, morning air didn't provide relief. Soon, the shirt and leather gloves came off. Droplets of perspiration fell, and he tied a red bandanna around his forehead.

The barn door creaked, and the horses whinnied. *Who is that?* Around the corner of a stall, he ran into a slender female. Caught off guard, he grabbed her arms. "Whoa."

"Hey Rambo, it's me, Isabella."

The grip relaxed, and he pretended to give her a paddling. "Rambo, huh? You'll holler uncle when I get through."

"Hey, you're not my brother. You can't spank me." She wriggled out of reach.

"What are you doing? Shouldn't you be getting ready for the wedding?"

"I had to sneak away for a while. I knew you'd be here. This is yours and Duffy's favorite hiding place."

Joe Paul scanned her beautiful face. "Hey sweetheart, what's wrong?"

"I realized this morning I'm all grown up."

His arm draped around her shoulder, and they walked to the open barn doors. "You see the house up there? Today, there will be the most magnificent wedding, the prelude to a loving and happy marriage. Many people will come to see the pretty princess marry the deserving prince, and her daddy and I guarantee they will live happily ever after."

A tear ran down her cheek, and Isabella threw both arms around Joe Paul's neck.

He watched her run back to the house while she blew kisses as she'd done as a small girl. Thoughts of Olivia took a back seat.

"Thank you, I love you. See you in a little while," she called.

****

Poised, organized, and professional, Clair relished the role she and Kelley played at these special events. It always amazed her how they both fell into the finely tuned performance and worked in perfect harmony. Kelley took their business as serious as she did. *Couldn't have chosen a better associate. Success depends on our ability to read each other's thoughts, and we do it perfectly.*

Small, undetectable earphones kept them in constant touch. Proficient, in sleek, gray business suits, their attire blended in so they could work unnoticed. From a fainting bride, or an uncooperative ring bearer, a late arriving ice sculpture, or unpredicted weather, Memory Makers worked in well-rehearsed synchronicity.

Sounds of excitement drifted through the east pavilion as guests arrived. The huge tent resembled an enchanted forest—the focal point, a fairytale gazebo. Flowers cascaded down the outer walls, and tiny, white lights twinkled throughout to give the structure a celestial aura.

"Kelley, what's the status of the band setup?" Clair buzzed her partner.

"They've finished their sound test. The last of the tables and chairs are in place, and the floral decorators left the west pavilion. I'm going to check on the electrician about the lighting. How's our bride fairing?" Kelley adjusted the headset.

"She's fine, a little anxious. I had to intercept the groom. He thought he could sneak by me. I don't have to tell you how that went." Clair laughed.

"Yeah, I recall several other persistent grooms who thought they could get past your strict sentinel. Thanks for the visual. I needed the distraction."

Strewn clothes, eyeliner, lipstick, and a strong smell of hair spray mingled in the room full of bridal attendants as Clair entered. The excited chatter of females added to the confusion.

Isabella posed for approval from her best friend, Betsy Babineaux. "Well, what do you think?"

"I think...Troy is going to just die when he sees the most beautiful bride ever walk down the aisle," Betsy squealed.

The other bridesmaids agreed.

A knock on the door brought unexpected silence.

"Isabella, can I see you for a moment?" The request came from a familiar deep voice, the father of the bride.

"Daddy?" Isabella opened the door. "Is everything okay?"

"Sure, sure angel, I need to give you something. Excuse me ladies for the interruption, but I have a little gift for my baby girl." Preston Riley gasped when he stepped inside. "My God Isabella, you're even more beautiful than your mother on our wedding day."

"Oh Daddy, thank you. I love you so much," she said.

Big arms engulfed her small frame.

"Daddy, are you okay? You're shaking."

He placed his hands on her shoulders.

"You know I'll always be your little girl," Isabella said.

"I know sweetheart, sorry if I'm emotional. This is your special day, and I'm happy for you. It's a little hard to accept you're all grown up. The reason I asked to see you is because I wanted you to have this." He presented a delicate, lace handkerchief. "It can be your 'something old'. Patrice carried it, too—your grandmother gave it to her."

The predictable melancholy moment made Clair smile. *I've seen it a thousand times.*

"It's beautiful, Daddy. I'd love to use it. Perhaps my daughter will want to carry it at her wedding, too."

"You're getting way ahead of me talking about grandchildren, unless, you're…?"

"No Daddy, I'm not pregnant. Troy and I don't plan to make you a grandpa for a while."

Father and daughter hugged once more.

Clair opened the door, hand on hip. "Now scoot, Mr. Riley. We need to stay on schedule. The organist has already started the prelude."

Twenty-Seven
The Discovery

Behind an ivy-wrapped, stone pillar, Russell Gibson stood unnoticed, an imperative part of his job to blend into the background. He kept a watchful eye on Clair and Kelley as they choreographed the setup for the spectacular Riley wedding. The threesome each wore minuscule earphones. A clear wire attached to one of Russell's ingenious technical toys allowed them to toggle from microphones to a pager. Should they need him…a single word, or beep, and he would appear.

A check of his watch showed the countdown was on—5 minutes. Anxiety welled inside; a knot pulsed in his gut. *Man, I can't wait to see Kitty again.* He popped his knuckles to ease the tension. *You gotta show up and somehow prove to the girls what an extraordinary woman I've found.*

The organist began the introduction for the paramount moment, and the guests settled in for the gala event. Bridesmaids strolled down a red carpet runner in their practiced step-stop pace. The little flower girl randomly tossed white rose petals and giggled at the sight of her parents. The young ring bearer followed and marched up to the groom, a tight grip on a white satin pillow. Everyone waited for the familiar chords to announce the bride's entrance.

At last, the pastor raised his hands and instructed everyone to rise. Troy Maxwell's handsome looks mirrored Joe Paul's as he, and the other groomsmen, gazed toward Isabella and her father.

"Oh my God," Kelley said under her breath.

Clair adjusted the earpiece. "Kelley, what's wrong? Where are you?"

"I'm behind the first lighted trellis. I slipped in to see them exchange vows. I can't believe it, Clair. I...I must be hallucinating."

"Kelley, what's happened?"

"Him, uh or *is* it him?" Kelley stumbled.

"Who? Him who?"

"Don't you see him...right there?" Kelley pointed.

"Where? I'm engrossed in details, not people."

"Look at them, the wedding party, look at *him*."

"You mean the groom? Okay, yes, everyone is in the right place. I don't see anything wrong, and who is *him*?" Clair continued.

"Joe Paul Farrell. I think he's a groomsman." Kelley gasped.

"The one next to Troy?"

Scrambled thoughts dashed through Kelley's mind, the scene at the airport, Isabella's phone call. "Clair, did you hear me?"

"Oh my God," Clair replied.

"The airport," Kelley's voice squeaked. "It all makes sense now."

"Yes, the airport, and his comment about the call," Clair agreed.

"What should I do?"

"Now listen girl, keep a cool head. We're in the middle of a huge affair," Clair said.

"I prayed I would get to see him again, but today, of all days. You don't understand. I believe...I think I'm in love."

"Kelley, have you forgotten? He only knows Olivia, not Kelley Malone."

"I *have* to talk to him."

"Maybe you have invested your heart this time, but you can't disrupt the whole process of the Riley nuptials. Not now, at least. Think Kelley, think."

"Oh damn Clair, you're right," her voice broke. "What if he recognizes me?"

"He won't even see you. We are always behind the scenes. Besides, in a crowd this size no one will notice us. Don't worry. It's fine—I promise."

****

Celeste Vandergriff sat on the bride's side dressed in a maroon lace suit. She met the Rileys two days before, and they welcomed her into their family in an instant. *How lucky I am to witness this sweet couple pledge their love to each other, their lives become one.* She adjusted the veil of her chapeau and stared at the bridal party. *The room looks like a palace. I am so proud of Clair and Kelley, their talent and creativity is incredible.* Sentiment and pride forced a small tear down Celeste's cheek.

"I do," Isabella said.

"I do," Troy repeated.

"You may now kiss the bride," Pastor Rob announced.

The couple turned to their guests, arm in arm.

"I'm honored to present to you, Dr. and Mrs. Troy Maxwell."

Isabella blew her daddy a kiss.

Bulldog stood up. "Please everyone; join me in a huge round of applause."

Guests cheered as the bridal party rushed down the aisle amid well wishes and clapping.

After the ceremony, Bulldog ushered Celeste out on his arm to the grandeur reception. "Please sit next to me at the head table, Celeste," he insisted.

"What an honor, however, I couldn't." She pointed at a table nearby. "I'll be quite fine over here."

"Your wish is my command, young lady." He pulled out her chair. "Will you promise me a dance later?"

"Why I would love it." Celeste smiled.

A waiter brought a tray and offered a glass of champagne. "Thank you." Celeste took a quick sip.

"May I serve you a plate of prime rib?" the young man offered.

"Yes, please do."

Other guests filled the tables, and Celeste joined in the conversations. During the festivities, she caught only glimpses of Clair and Kelley. *Goodness, to the normal eye they appear as mere shadows.*

****

Kelley attempted to push away prior apprehension. She monitored the busy Chez Bazaar caterer's efforts to supply a continuous sea of people hors d'oeuvres and drinks.

The harpist played the strains of the Wedding Waltz. Preston Riley circled the dance floor, Isabella in his arms. He handed the bride to her new husband. A spotlight chased the newlywed's every step, and they whirled around a champagne fountain. Their romantic grace culminated in a seductive dip to the approval of the crowd who gave them a standing ovation. The couple bowed in appreciation, clasped hands, and strolled to the oval cake table.

Troy beamed as they held the beribboned, silver cutter. He kissed the nape of Isabella's neck, and together they sliced the monogrammed, multi-tiered cake.

Joe Paul lifted the fluted crystal glass, and his voice resonated above the crowd, "May I have your attention, please? Time for a toast."

Kelley scooted farther behind a sheer curtain.

Isabella smiled at Joe Paul.

"I've never seen you look more beautiful or happier, Isabella. Here is to true love, and I pray it never escapes you."

Kelley watched his lips touch the rim of the wineglass. Her eyes closed, heady in the memory of their kisses.

****

Joe Paul forced a bogus smile. *Troy Maxwell, you lucky bastard.* Raw grief overwhelmed him. Memories of a failed marriage, and many futile attempts to win Olivia's heart, shrouded him like steel weight. His pager vibrated and shattered the reflective thoughts. He recognized the number…Duffy. *Oh God, the colt, the mare!*

Twenty-Eight
A Silver Dagger

At the reception, a pyramid of wedding gifts covered a lace-draped table at one end of the canopy. Shiny white and silver boxes, dressed in silky, pearl ribbons, towered almost to the ceiling. Clair sighed, satisfied. *Another perfect ceremony.*

"Here they come. Don't they look happy, Clair? What a great day. We did it again," Kelley whispered into the headset.

Clair turned as the couple entered the tent, and a twinge of envy pierced her heart. *I can do it for other people...I simply can't make it happen for me.* She watched Troy take Isabella's hand, seat her in a satin covered chair, kiss her cheek, and take the other chair. The photographers waited for Clair's cue. At her nod, they took their places, ready to capture another memory for the couple.

"I don't know where to start," the bride gushed.

Bulldog stepped forward. "Might I suggest..."

A voice interrupted. They looked toward an elderly, black gentleman. "Miss Isabella, the new man who works for Mistah Duffy said this gift come special delivery—said you should open it first." He held a small box close to his chest as he approached.

"Why thank you, Colonel." Isabella reached out.

Clair shot Kelley a quick glance. *Great, the first unscripted moment of the day.*

****

Scent of Double Deception

Joe Paul jumped into a nearby motor cart, jerked the top button loose from the tuxedo shirt, and sped toward the stables. He entered the large barn and killed the engine. "Duff, Duff are you here?"

No answer.

Duffy's office door stood ajar, and he hurried forward. Papers and files lay scattered on the floor. "What's going on here?"

Before he could make sense of the mess, snorting sounds came from the horse stables. At the second stall, the ranch foreman lay in a heap on the ground, hay covered part of the sprawled body. A thick rope bound Duffy's hands behind his back.

Joe Paul pulled a kerchief from the foreman's mouth. "What in the hell happened? Are you okay?"

"Get back to that wedding," the old man demanded.

"Who did this to you?" Joe Paul untied the man and helped him stand.

"Don't worry about me," Duffy cried hoarsely.

"Who paged me? I thought you did. I'm confused."

"It's a decoy. I'll call the authorities. Go make sure Isabella is okay. Hurry!"

Joe Paul reacted to the fear in Lester McDuff's voice and bolted out the door.

****

Russell's heart stopped in total recall...a delicate, black box, a gold ribbon. Could this be coincidence or a bad dream? He watched the bride untie the ribbon and lift the lid. A pungent mist penetrated the air. Isabella's body went limp and slumped to the floor. Russell saw Troy's attempt to reach his new wife, only to succumb to the caustic smell and collapse next to her.

Chaos gave way to the dream-like scene. People shrieked and scattered to escape the horrible smell. Chairs toppled and tables overturned as panic spread.

Russell struggled to make sense of the scene before him when something caught his eye. The image of a woman dressed in white, face shrouded in a sheer gossamer scarf, appeared from behind a nearby ivy trellis. She drew out a gray-blue revolver and pointed it at the bride.

Expert training kicked in. Catlike movements put him next to the woman in a split second. In the same instant, shock rocked his world. *Kitty Forche?*

Unable to process it, he sprung forward, and threw a strong, muscular arm around her. The force of the impact knocked the gun from her hand, and it slid across the floor. They both scrambled to regain control.

"Stop," a masculine voice demanded.

Russell froze.

A large dagger gleamed from the intruder's hand. "Let her go, or you're a dead man."

"Jess, I can handle this," Kitty screamed.

"Not alone, you can't, Mother," Jess Owens replied. "Okay sis, get the gun."

Bliss Owens stepped out from behind her twin brother.

Russell's pulse quickened as the father of the bride rushed forward. "My God Kitty, what's this all about?" Preston Riley yelled.

Russell tightened his grip on Kitty. "Mr. Riley, get back."

"This is about *my* children's rightful inheritance, dear *brother*," she spat at Preston.

"But I don't understand," Bulldog said.

"Well, understand this." Jess hurled the dagger in Russell's direction.

"Gibson!" Spencer Walker appeared out of nowhere. Kitty's gun landed inches away from his feet.

Russell snapped his head up in time to see Spencer toss the piece toward him. *Oh God, too late.* Jess released the knife at the same time. Struggling to hang on to the squirming Kitty, Russell managed to catch the gun in mid air.

The long, silver weapon hit its mark, and crimson drops of blood spilled onto the floor.

****

Joe Paul couldn't tell whether fear or pure adrenaline made him breathless. He rushed into the frenzied reception area, stepped from behind a large column, and prayed Isabella was safe. Instantly, everything went black. In slow motion, he felt himself float above the floor and then fall…spiraling down, down. *What happened?* Somewhere in the distance, he heard his name. Emma? Isabella? He tried to open his eyes wider to escape the darkness. An angelic-like vision hovered over him. It beckoned him back. The presence gave him peace. He strained to see details, but a hazy aura of light blurred his sight. He tried to speak, to answer the plea, but a piercing, burning pain in his chest forced him to shut his eyes.

****

Confident Russell had the gun in his hand, Spencer turned his attention to Clair. She stood frozen in mid-stride, a look of horror on her face. He grabbed her waist and pulled her to the floor, caring little if she recognized him or not.

"Please, my aunt. Where's my Aunt CeeCee?" she cried.

"I'll see to her, just stay down." Spencer wheeled around, dropped to a crouch, and sprinted for Celeste, trapped by a chair and table. The terror etched on Celeste's face broke his heart. To see such fear crushed him. Tangled by a tablecloth, she struggled until he freed her. "Everything is okay, Celeste. Don't worry," he crooned.

After a minute or so, her shaking subsided, and he raised his head to check on Clair. Someone fell victim to the flying dagger, but who? He searched for a glimpse of Clair and assessed the scene. Russell had Kitty subdued, but Jess, frantic and devoid of a weapon, worked to pull something from his pocket. *Another knife; perhaps a gun?* Spencer knew he had only a few precious seconds. He slithered through the tables as Jess freed the object and sprang from the floor to tackle him to the ground.

A pair of handcuffs appeared, and he looked up at Russell's lop-sided grin. A quick survey assured him Kitty wore a pair, too. Bliss made a swift retreat out the door.

The police arrived to find Kitty and Jess in handcuffs, a man with a knife in his chest, and a bride and groom unconscious on the floor. An officer spoke tersely to the crowd in general. "Who'd like to tell me what happened?"

Several guests stepped up to take the spotlight.

****

Clair, glad to avoid an interrogation, sought out her aunt and best friend. She found CeeCee safe in a chair surrounded by staff and looked around for Kelley. It didn't take long to find her. Kelley knelt beside Joe Paul, blood on her hands, tears streaming down her face. A few of Troy's medical colleagues worked on the fallen man. She heard Kelley repeat the words, Joe Paul, Joe Paul. "Please, we must go, sweetie. He can't see you here. We'll check on him later." She placed both hands on Kelley's shoulders.

"No…no…no," Kelley mumbled.

"He's breathing, and doctors are here. Please, don't give away our identities, let's go."

Kelley stumbled to stand, and they started toward the main house. Clair looked back. Preston was talking to the police, and Russell tended to Aunt CeeCee. *Who is the man who pulled me to the floor? He's gone.* The hair on her neck prickled.

Twenty-Nine
The Motive

"Wedding for Daughter of Local Casino Mogul, Attempted Murder Scene," Clair read aloud.

Russell drove west on Interstate 20 toward Dallas. "Didn't I always say you girls would make headlines one day," he teased.

"Well, thank goodness our names aren't mentioned in the article." Clair shuffled the newspaper. "That kind of publicity we don't need. The mayhem—our vulnerability, it gives me goose bumps."

Kelley sat next to Clair and watched the landscape pass in a blur as they sped toward home.

"Kel, are you okay?"

Clair's hand on her shoulder made her jump. "What?"

"I asked if you're okay," Clair repeated.

"Sure." She returned her attention to the scenery.

"Listen, I saw the hollow look in your eyes. Talk to me," Clair urged.

Kelley fidgeted with the seat belt. "Okay, since you asked, I'm still upset you hurried me away from Joe Paul while he was unconscious."

"Perhaps my actions appeared a bit brash at the time, but we almost exposed our alter egos," Clair reminded. "Anyway, I believe Olivia left a piece of her heart in Louisiana, and that bothers you the most. Before, we never let our little charade follow the path to romance. How did you expect things to play out?"

Scent of Double Deception

"Clair, I read the article too, and it said a close family friend suffered a near *fatal* wound." She crossed her arms. "To answer your question, somehow, I thought I could walk away from Joe Paul Farrell until…"

"Honey, please calm down," Russell broke in. "Let me tell you something. Before we left Shreveport, I went to the hospital to see him."

"What? Didn't he question who you were?" Kelley sat upright.

"Yes, and I explained I was contract security for the wedding. I also apologized about his injury. The knife was aimed at me, not him. He laughed, and thanked me, but said he would get over it, not to worry."

"You actually saw him, and you're positive he's okay?" Kelley's voice quivered.

"It'll take some time for the wound to heal, but darling, trust me, everything will work out fine."

Kelley saw a smile on his face through the rearview mirror. She leaned forward and squeezed his huge shoulders. "You're a good friend, Russell. Thanks."

"Still mad at me?" Clair piped in.

Kelley relaxed. "No, I love you like a sister, Clair. You did the right thing. It's my own fault. I have to move on and accept I'll never see him again."

"Let's change the subject, I have more information." Russell adjusted the mirror. "Ever hear of Freeman and Zella Riley?"

"What kind of name is Zella, Russell?" Kelley shook her head.

"Snooping again? Old habits die hard don't they, Mr. Detective?" Clair added.

"They are Preston's parents which makes Kitty his half-sister. Intrigued?"

Scent of Double Deception

"You know I love gossip. Tell us more."

"A stable boy, a dark barn, an irresistible Cajun Venus. Innocent and unaware of his primal impulse, she entered the dimly lit stable to say goodnight to a favorite steed." Traffic bottlenecked in the narrow construction area, and Russell slowed down.

Clair leaned forward. "What? What happened next?"

"He forced himself on Zella, raped her in the hay. Nine months later, a baby girl came into the world."

"Kitty?" the girls asked in unison.

"Hold on, don't get ahead of the story. Freeman's passionate love for his wife allowed him to force the incident aside, but he passed the seed of resentment to Kitty. The unassuming little girl grew up happy, never aware Freeman couldn't accept her as his own child."

"How sad," Clair muttered.

"Sad? You *liked* that voodoo woman," Kelley huffed.

"I think it was sad because Zella tried to shield her daughter from the truth." The traffic fanned out, and Russell accelerated into the fast lane. "You're not gonna believe what happened next."

"Cut it out and get on with the story," Clair said.

"Preston and Katherine's lives changed forever. Tragedy struck, and both parents died in a car wreck. Despite his wife's wishes, Freeman designed their last Will and Testament for Preston to receive all the family wealth, primarily the casino empire," Russell continued.

"Regardless of the fact I don't like her, that's cold," Clair interjected.

"It gets worse. Freeman's last request included a harsh stipulation. He banned Katherine and all of her heirs from Preston's life. However, Bulldog refused to leave his little sister penniless. He divided his dynasty and gave Katherine the lower parishes of Louisiana."

"So, why did she turn on Preston?" Clair said.

"Embarrassed and humiliated, Kitty vowed to settle the score. Even though she married several times and produced children of her own, the twins, vengeance consumed her. She never found true happiness...not even with me," he sighed.

"Thus, the irony of our trip to Hawaii," Kelley joined the conversation.

"Good grief Russell, you offered this madwoman a golden key to the door of opportunity. Plus, she manipulated Jess and Bliss for inside help in her malicious scheme," Clair said.

"Well, before the cops hauled Kitty off, I asked her how she knew of Isabella's big wedding."

"She actually told you?"

"Hell Kelley, I needed some answers." Russell pounded the steering wheel. "Amid phony sobs and pleas to help her, she admitted she read the announcement in *USA Today*, but hadn't figured out how to get there. Thick-headed, gullible Russell fell into the trap heart first," growled the driver.

"My dear, you were a pawn in her vicious hands," Clair mused.

"Russell, I'm so sorry things didn't work out. Anyway, you deserve a lot better than a voodoo witch," Kelley's voice rose in anger.

"Thanks Kel, but I don't believe I was the only one swept off their feet," he added.

Silence fell over the threesome like a heavy blanket.

Kelley leaned back and closed her eyes. *How did I think my relationship would play out? Mere chance brought*

Joe Paul into my life. Maybe it's predestined for the story to end this way.

Thirty
Honored Allegiance

Celeste Vandergriff settled into the seat on the plane and sighed in relief. Exhaustion overtook her, a last remnant of the recent drama. *Guns, daggers, and deadly gift boxes. Never in all my years can I remember such a day. I need the solemnity of my Washington home, the peace of my garden, and yet...*Dread infiltrated her nettled mind and threatened to disturb a chance to rest. The mission failed, and she knew the consequences would not be pleasant. *I'll think on it later. Right now, I need to sleep.*

The stewardess stopped and asked if she would like a pillow. She turned to answer and stopped in midsentence. Across the aisle, and back two rows, sat a man with dark hair, muscular build, and white shirt. Before she got a good look, he bent down. She accepted the pillow and glanced at him again. He sat upright, their eyes met, and he blushed. "Spencer? Is that you?"

"You got me, Celeste. Guess I've lost my touch." A sheepish grin spread across his face.

The heavyset man next to Celeste appeared annoyed and asked if she would like him to change seats with the gentleman in the back. "I need to sleep. I don't want to hear mindless chatter."

Spencer didn't hesitate. "Thanks, mister. It's mighty kind of you."

Celeste, still in mild shock, didn't answer.

He settled in the seat beside her. "This is better."

She found her voice, "Spencer, what are you *doing* here? Who is watching Clair? She is in more danger now than before. I didn't get a chance to tell her."

The private detective took her hand. "It's obvious you're distressed. Please stay calm. Clair is fine and protected. I'm worried about you. I know you never had the opportunity to tell our girl, and I didn't want you to face Mr. Highgrove, or the uncle, alone. They're ruthless, and you've had quite enough excitement."

"I can take care of myself, young man. Your duty is to see to Clair, not **me**. Who in the world is watching her? No one knows the enormity of this situation like you." Celeste slapped the armrest.

"Remember the man I threw the gun to, the one who stopped Kitty?"

"Yes, yes, of course—Russell. What does he have to do with this? How much does he know?"

"You know him?" Spencer's eyes widened.

"Of course, I do. He is like a part of the family. How much does he know, Spencer?"

"Only that I've kept an eye on Clair because she's about to come into an inheritance. I told him I needed his confidence, and she would find out about it once they arrived in Seattle. He assured me he wouldn't let the girls out of his sight. He works for them...they'll be safe." Spencer patted her hand.

"I am so tired. I have no choice but to trust you did the right thing. Maybe I don't need to face those merciless men alone. You will be there, won't you? Do you promise?" For the first time, she needed to lean on someone, and Spencer fit the bill.

"Yes Celeste, I'll be there for you. Now get some rest. Lord knows you need to be fresh when Thurlow interrogates you. Breathe easy, I'll stay awake and make sure all is well."

Celeste saw pure affection in his eyes and surrendered to the comfort of his presence.

Thirty-One
Reflection

The brisk, Seattle morning air revived Clair's jet lag as she padded down the creaky stairs of Aunt Celeste's palatial home. Her goal — a steaming cup of homemade cocoa. In anticipation, she turned at the bottom. From her vantage point, she saw CeeCee on the veranda in conversation with two men in black suits. Hand gestures flew back and forth in animated repartee. A silhouette through the gauzy curtain revealed another person in the shadows, but she couldn't tell the gender. *Auntie's friends call mighty early. Guess I shouldn't spy.*

She returned her attention to the cocoa, ignored the prickle on the back of her neck, and breathed in the warm, delectable steam. *This would taste much better on the lanai.*

Sun streamed across the deck chair and lessened the morning chill. The warm drink, and bright daylight, rejuvenated her travel-worn body. *What a wonderful Seattle daybreak.*

A door closed, and footsteps evaporated the daydream.

"Good morning, Clair. I didn't know you came down."

Clair noticed her aunt's startled expression. "I'm sorry, I saw you on the veranda. Anyone I know?" She tried not to appear nosy, but didn't like the look on CeeCee's face.

"No one, dear, just business. How's your cocoa?"

Scent of Double Deception

Celeste looked almost pained at the question, and she worried if something was wrong. *I suppose if she wanted me to know, she would tell me.* "Heavenly, I swear you should market this. You'd make millions."

"Oh, how you do flatter. You relax, Clair. I have a party to put together." Celeste Vandergriff made a grand exit.

****

Now is not the time to discuss the uncles. I will wait until after the soirée. Celeste shook off the pall of dread and set about the task of arranging the last details for the lavish party.

The day passed quickly, and she made sure to visit Kelley and Russell, and set them to the tasks assigned. She loved the idea of a party for Clair and Kelley—what fun. It diverted attention from the upcoming mission and kept total despair at bay.

Before she knew it, friends arrived. To Celeste's delight, sounds of laughter and conversation filled the formal living room, and the old historic Queen Anne home brightened from the gaiety. In years past, she was quite a socialite. She had not entertained on this level for many years, and it gave great elation. The celebration proved a nice reprieve from all the unpleasantness.

Russell and Kelley added to the joy—another bonus. The bodyguard's antics made her laugh.

"Aunt CeeCee, what do you call these little cakes? They're delicious." Russell stuffed another in his mouth.

"Actually, my sweet, those are trifles, and I soaked them in brandy. Maybe that's why you think they are so tasty," Celeste said.

"Leave it to you to seek out the booze," Clair teased from the doorway.

"You two…and where is our darling Kelley?" Celeste looked around.

"I'm sure she's still upstairs getting ready," Clair replied.

"Yeah, she'll make a fashionably late entrance as always." Russell reached for another hors d'oeuvre.

"I think I'll check on her. Mind you leave some goodies for our guests, Mr. Gibson." Celeste left the room.

****

Kelley sat at an antique vanity in front of the oval, beveled mirror and applied makeup. She caught the reflection, and for a moment, saw the college girl who enjoyed the fancy bed so many years ago. *I always loved this room. Where did the time go?* She slept sound in the huge, canopy bed, surrounded by sheer netting, and snuggled beneath the plush covers.

Suddenly, a nearby siren made her jump. She flew to the window, opened the shutter, and peered out. Dusk descended on Seattle, and the city lights twinkled the evening greeting. *Captivating.*

Euphoria washed over her, and she recalled the trip to the Tower of the Americas and Joe Paul. The lights over San Antonio shone just as magical. A dark cloud invaded those happy thoughts, however. Unbidden, pictures of the horrible scene at the Maxwell wedding reception interrupted the trance, and she shivered.

It had been a while since she allowed him to cross her mind. Did she feel ashamed or proud? Maybe Clair was right…she knew Clair was right. It ended the way it should have.

A light knock on the door interrupted.

"Kelley, may I come in?"

"Aunt CeeCee, yes please." She ran to open the door.

The attractive, older woman took Kelley's hand as she entered. "Come here, my dear. Sit down on the edge of the bed. You look so pretty, sweetheart. Won't you join us downstairs? I am worried. Aren't you feeling well?"

"Oh, I'm fine, Aunt CeeCee. Sorry I took so long. Of course, I'll be right down."

"Wonderful. I have so many people I want you and Clair to meet, one in particular." Celeste smiled.

"In that case, I'll hurry." Kelley reached for her lipstick, determined to make this a memorable evening.

"That's my girl." Celeste winked.

Thirty-Two
Seattle Soiree

"Good evening, Judge Hines." Celeste ushered in the stately man. "You cut a dashing figure in black tie."

"May I say your lavender dress brings out the brilliance in your eyes? We missed you at the last City Council meeting, young lady." He caressed her hand.

"It's kind of you to note my absence."

"We value your input, especially on the courthouse library renovation, not to mention there are several propositions in the works to fine tune."

They exchanged a polite, simultaneous smile.

"Do you plan to make the one next month?"

The doorbell chimed. "Most definitely...oh, excuse me, Judge."

"Perhaps we'll talk shop later," he offered and walked away.

"She nodded and opened the door. "Senator and Mrs. Henry, it's good to see you again. Please come in."

"We can never resist one of your invitations," the woman replied.

"You're so kind, Victoria." Celeste hugged the guest. "May I take your wrap, and by the way, Dr. Rutherford's wife, Amanda, asked about you earlier. She mentioned the Spring Cotillion Ball. I believe you'll find them on the veranda."

"Celeste, you still plan to chair the event, don't you?"

"I've already marked my social calendar."

A blend of conversation, merriment, and soft, classical strains floated through the old house.

This is the grandest soirée I have given in years. I can't wait to introduce my houseguests. She appreciated the enormity of her home for such affairs as tonight. The capacious guest list, which included the crème de la crème of Seattle's most elite and renowned invitees, wandered through the large rooms and socialized. A small, string quartet provided a mellow atmosphere while wait staff offered trays of canapés and drinks.

The demure hostess eyed the prestigious crowd. *Clair and Kelley don't need my help for business referrals, but my hidden agenda can't hurt. I hope the little strategy works.* She maneuvered through the partygoers to pause next to a tall gentleman.

"Madame Vandergriff, you look magnificent tonight." He blew a kiss from his fingertips.

"Why thank you, Professor Delecroix. I see you still have a smooth tongue, even for an old woman."

"Ah, woman yes, old — never, my love."

"I could listen to your French twaddle all night, but there are people I want you to meet." She slipped an arm through his.

He let out a hearty laugh and accompanied her to the next room.

"Professor Delecroix, this is my niece, Clair Matthews and her friend, Russell Gibson. They are two of my houseguests."

A brief handshake passed between the men.

"Nice to meet you, Professor." Russell nodded.

"My pleasure, and Miss Matthews." He clasped both hands around Clair's. "Yes, I can see the resemblance, Celeste. I'm honored to meet such a beautiful woman, much like your elegant aunt," his heavy French accent rolled.

"Thank you, Professor. Please call me Clair."

Their conversation continued until the Frenchman stopped in midsentence, attention riveted on the top of the stairway.

Celeste saw Russell nudge Clair. "I told you she'd be fashionably late."

"Yes, and you're not the only one who noticed." Clair winked.

"Please, tell me Madame Celeste, the gorgeous woman in green, who is she?"

Celeste could see an obvious attraction. "Ah, my other houseguest. Kelley, come here, dear."

Kelley descended the stairs and joined the group.

"Professor Cabot Delecroix this is Kelley Malone, Clair's business partner."

"Good evening, Professor. I'm delighted to meet you."

"Mademoiselle Malone, you are a vision. Please, call me Cabot." He lifted her hand to his lips.

"If you'll call me Kelley, and thank you for the compliment."

Celeste attempted to disguise a grin as Russell commented to Clair, "I don't believe we got an invitation to call him by his first name."

Clair cocked her head. "What can I say? That's our Kelley. Besides, after the Shreveport incident, she needs a distraction."

****

Kelley nudged Russell. "Look, it's time for dinner. You remember the bell, don't you?"

Scent of Double Deception

Celeste retrieved a small, china bell from a nearby shelf. The melodious jingle interrupted the festivities. "Excuse me, excuse me. May I have your attention? I am sure everyone is ready for dinner. Please follow me."

"Is the Frenchman a bit awestruck tonight?" Clair whispered to Kelley.

"Whatever do you mean?" Kelley assumed a southern drawl.

Guests made their way to the huge dining room where the menu boasted of lobster cocktail, sweet pea risotto, wild mushrooms, crabmeat tortellini, and an exquisite apricot ribbon Charlotte for dessert.

The three friends found places at the long, mahogany table, but as Russell attempted to seat the girls, someone stepped in front of him.

"Excusez-moi. May I?"

Kelley turned to find Cabot beside her, a firm hand on the chair.

"Why, thank you," she said.

"Might I also dine next to you?"

Kelley brushed back a long, blonde curl. "If you like."

The twosome engaged in conversation as they partook of the divine meal. When the topic navigated to business, she gloried in the lucrative partnership of Memory Makers and detailed their talents.

"Mademoiselle, since your expertise is in the wedding planning, have you ever considered another type venture?" Cabot refolded his napkin.

"What do you mean?"

"Please, let me explain. I am a professor of the arts, teacher, and instructor…but no longer. However, a few months ago, I acquired an art salon."

Kelley listened, entranced by his urbane accent. "Where is your gallery?"

"It is in Paris, my home place, and I am anxious to return. Today, I spoke to my curator. There are plans for a grand opening soon. You see, I am so fortunate. One of my past students consented to let me be the first to display her works. My protégé is a gifted young artist. Her style is unique. I see a great future ahead and want to help her career."

The sincerity in Cabot's voice touched Kelley's heart.

"You and your business partner could be beneficial to my plans."

"You think you might need our services?" Kelley raised an eyebrow. She saw him try to hide a slight smile.

"Oh, I'm very confident in your, uh talent, as you call it. Whatever your fees, I will match a more handsome price, as well as expenses and fares. I will accommodate in any manner you wish." He allowed his hand to rest on top of hers.

"I'll have to discuss the matter with Clair, but it's possible we can do business together."

****

Celeste reveled, satisfied in her gala's success. Everyone appeared content, happy. She observed Clair easily intermix with debutantes and dignitaries. Pride filled her heart. *Such a beautiful girl — polished and adept as a businesswoman.* She scanned the room and noticed Kelley and Cabot. *It appears Kelley has him spellbound. I can only hope he discussed the possibility of the girls going to Paris on assignment. Now, where is Russell?*

Out on the lanai, she found him talking to an attractive redhead, Nicole, Mayor Vozza's daughter.

The chatty woman stood between Russell and the doorway. The uncomfortable expression on his face made Celeste snicker. "Russell dear, might I interrupt you a moment? I need your assistance in the kitchen."

"You bet Aunt CeeCee, excuse me, gotta go." Russell didn't hesitate.

In the kitchen, Celeste laughed.

"Aunt CeeCee, it's not funny. She had me trapped. I mean, she's got the looks and all, but what a talker. She never took a breath, and I couldn't get a word in sideways. Thanks for the escape route." He chuckled.

"Are you sure?" Celeste teased. "Nicole runs in some pretty influential circles. I feel certain I can get her phone number if you like. You never can tell where it might lead."

Russell rubbed the back of his neck. "No ma'am. I've had my fill of powerful women for a while."

Thirty-Three
Secrets Revealed

Clair leaned against the porch rail and watched the last guest's tail lights disappear into the night. Her hand lingered in a wistful wave as the car turned the corner at the end of the block. *Aunt CeeCee outdid herself this time. She looked tired. It takes so much to pull it all together. I wonder how many more of these galas I will see in this old house.*

A gentle touch on the shoulder brought her out of the reverie. "Auntie, I was just...what's wrong, why so serious?"

"Could we talk before you retire?"

Clair glanced in Kelley's direction and smiled. Kelley and the Frenchman laughed together at the door, their heads close in conversation. *Ah, I'll have to wait a while for those juicy details. It looks like a long good-bye. Good luck, Cabot.* She looked back at her aunt. "Sure."

"Let's go out to the gazebo since it is such a nice evening." The older woman led the way to the garden arbor.

"You really went all out on flowers this year. I particularly love the pink roses and the star-like lights. I'm surprised Kelley didn't find a way to get Cabot Delacroix out here. He would be putty in her hands in this atmosphere, so romantic and private. We should keep an eye out. She might lure him out here, yet. They're still at the door trying to say goodnight."

"Men can't resist Kelley's charm, that's for sure."

Both women stopped to check the scene at the front door and chuckled.

Celeste reached out, took Clair's hand, and resumed the walk to the pavilion.

Clair pulled back, surprised. "Aunt CeeCee—there's someone in there," Clair whispered. "I thought all the guests were gone." She saw the outline of a man inside and looked back at her aunt. When CeeCee didn't answer, a familiar, unmistakable dread filled her bosom. "Who is it?" she demanded.

"You will see dear girl, be patient," Celeste replied.

Candlelight flickered inside the enclosure, and it took a moment for Clair's eyes to adjust. The scene developed before her like something out of an old movie, and shock replaced calmness as her focus sharpened. He stood there, white shirt illuminated by the soft light, and jarred her memory. *It's him. Shreveport, Christmas Eve, Stuckey's restaurant. He's one and the same, I knew it.* Outraged, she whirled on her aunt. "What's going on, CeeCee, and what is he doing here?"

Celeste opened her mouth to answer, but Clair circled back to the stranger. "Who are you, and what do you have to do with my Aunt Celeste?" Before either could answer, Clair blurted, "It's you! It was you…at the wedding. You shoved me down to the floor and went to aid my aunt. It never registered before, but it *was* you. Who in the hell are you? Are you following me? What's going on?" Almost in tears, emotions spun out of control.

"Please, Clair. We will explain. Sit down, and I will properly introduce you. I know there are many

Scent of Double Deception

questions. Let's take a deep breath, and I will start from the beginning."

Clair hesitated, but finally smoothed the folds of her dress, sat on a wooden bench, and waited.

Celeste Vandergriff remained standing beside the man. "This is Spencer Walker. He has followed you for many years, hired by the family to watch over you, keep you safe," she began.

Panic rose in Clair's throat. "Keep me safe from what? What are you talking about?"

****

Kelley's natural curiosity peaked as she watched Clair head away from the house and toward the garden. *What is going on with Aunt CeeCee and Clair?* She needed a distraction to get her bearings, and not let the moonlight, and Cabot's sexy accent draw her into a romantic liaison. "Huh, what?" Kelley realized she hadn't heard what he said.

"I see my words are of no consequence to a woman like you, mademoiselle. You must be shown." He leaned forward, lowered his face into her long curls, and drew a deep breath.

The night air caught his intoxicating cologne, and she felt the scruff of his fashionable nine-o'clock shadow scrape her cheek. It was a heady mixture. Unsure of his meaning, she stiffened and looked him straight in the face. "Professor?"

"Mademoiselle, please forgive me if my actions appear out of line, but I cannot stand it any longer. Your perfume—the fragrance is bold, exciting, and very…euphoric. I must know what it is; that is, if I may be so brazen."

"To be honest, Mr. Delecroix, it's one of my own potions."

"My dear lady, I do not understand, your *own*?"

Delighted at the turn of the conversation, Kelley realized she captured this man's complete attention. *I love the adventure of the hunt. This could prove a lovely cat and mouse game.* "Yes, I have a gift of sorts, at least Clair thinks so. I experiment, mix different fragrances in a form of aromatherapy. It proves helpful for some of our nervous grooms or fainting brides." She pulled her hair to one side. "I prefer to dab some of my oils on the nape of my neck, as well as behind my ear lobes. Do you like it?" Kelley taunted him, pitched him an open invitation to get close. Pleasure heightened as he accepted the flirtation. *No fool here.* His lips, hot and sensuous, touched the exposed skin. The air turned electric, and she leaned into the caress.

As if on cue, Aunt CeeCee's old grandfather clock struck midnight, and the spell dissolved. She swung around, let her hair cover the object of his desire, and for the first time, realized they were totally alone. *Just in time. I played the game too long.* "Cabot I've enjoyed our visit, but it's late."

"Oh mademoiselle, vous avez raison."

His eloquent speech raised goose bumps on her skin. "I beg your pardon?"

"I said, you are correct. I apologize for the monopolization of your time."

Kelley enjoyed playing the coquette, and she captivated Cabot as planned, but on the other hand, the French guest mystified her. "It's my pleasure, Professor," she said softly.

They approached the front door, and he turned to face her. "Pleasure is a simple word. I do not believe there is anything simple about Kelley Malone. Goodnight, my cherié."

Kelley charged upstairs, eager to talk to Clair, but no light shone through the foot of the bedroom door. *Darn it, Clair must be asleep. Oh well, she would only fire questions at me and ruin the aura of the night. Plus, I'm confused why I so enjoyed the interlude with Cabot, and yet, want Joe Paul. Clair will pin me to the wall on that one. Besides, I've already resolved the issue. I started the relationship in the character of my alter ego, Olivia. A lie. What man would trust a woman who couldn't even tell him her last name?*

In her room, she studied herself in the mirror. *The magnetism I felt for Joe Paul is the result of the charade — exactly like Cabot. I can't trust my own emotions at this point. Look how quickly I succumbed to the attraction of another man. I'll have to wait until morning to talk to Clair. She will set me straight.*

****

The next morning dawned bright and cool after a light shower. Celeste straightened the pillows on the bed and headed downstairs. She began each day in prayer, and this morning, it centered on her precious Clair. A strong faith kept sanity in check through the years. Tiny streams of sunlight filtered through the kitchen curtains and brightened her spirits. *I hope that is a good omen.*

She started to prepare breakfast and her infamous cocoa for everyone. As a child, Clair believed the smooth, dark liquid could magically fix anything and hoped her niece still felt the same today. Celeste stopped stirring the chocolate mixture and reflected on recent events. *I believe God, in His infinite wisdom, wants Clair and Kelley to know the truth. He will help them make the right decisions.*

Sitting down at the table in the breakfast nook, she escaped to the past. She chuckled at the memory of Clair's excitement to bring her college roommate home on spring break. The day Kelley walked into the grand old house, Celeste's heart almost stopped. She looked exactly like her beautiful mother. The eyes, laugh, and mannerisms were a carbon copy of the long lost sister Celeste mourned for many years. When she asked about Kelley's parents, the reply was they were deceased. Although saddened, her heart rejoiced at the realization the good Lord brought Kelley back into her life.

Celeste took a sip of the warm cocoa, both hands wrapped around the cup. To keep such cherished knowledge for so long proved difficult, but reality would soon open a new door for the girls. *I wonder how the news will affect Memory Makers?*

Thirty-Four
The Lost Room

The melt-in-your-mouth orange muffins consumed Russell's full attention. "These are delicious, Aunt CeeCee."

"Thank you sweetheart, enjoy them. I'm going to water my plants." Celeste shut the screen door.

Russell savored the last bite...slowly, like the kiss before a final good-bye. He buttered another muffin, but stopped and did a double take at the sight of Clair. She stood on the bottom step of the old wooden stairs, a blank, disoriented look on her face. Embarrassed by his oblivious fascination toward the muffin, he cleared his throat. *Geesh, those stairs creak big time, and I didn't hear a thing.* "Are you all right girl?"

"Do you *know*?" Clair turned blank eyes to him. "Did Spencer tell you?"

The muffin fell from Russell's hand. "Clair, sit down." He moved to her side and steered her toward the kitchen chair. "Yes, last night Spencer explained Aunt Celeste's revelation and his part in the deception. It's unbelievable. I tried to find you. Where'd you go? I checked your room."

"Where? Oh, I went to my secret closet."

"Your secret closet? What secret closet?" He had never seen her like this before. Clair prided herself on her strength. Everyone counted on her to maintain control. Clearly, she was nowhere near that today.

"Under the stairs, that's where I go—to my secret place." Her eyes grew large and round and one solitary tear rolled down her cheek.

"Clair, I'm here. Take it easy." He encircled an arm around her shoulders and pulled her to him. *Oh God, the sobs are coming, the breakdown. It's sure to be a terrible onslaught.* To his surprise, she brushed the tear away and straightened in the chair.

"Thank you, Russell," her voice a bit stronger.

"Do you want to talk about it? I know most of the story. Spencer told me you are an heiress, and you and Kelley are actually kin, but that's all I know. He didn't give me many details."

Clair looked up. "Do you want to see it?"

"See it? See what, Clair?"

"The room."

"Clair, I…" he started.

At that moment, Celeste entered. "Clair? Are you ill? Russell what's wrong?"

"I'm okay, Aunt CeeCee, but I need to speak to Kelley. She doesn't know." Clair walked to the stairs, mumbling.

Russell moved to follow her, but a hand on his shoulder halted him. Celeste shook her head in silence. They watched her climb the stairs. Russell asked Celeste in a soft whisper if she knew about Clair's secret hiding place.

CeeCee looked at him. "Secret place? She talked about a secret place?"

"Yes, under the stairs. She must have stayed there all night. I looked in her room, but she never showed. I finally gave up and went to bed. This morning when I asked where she'd been, she told me of the secret room beneath the stairs."

"Russell, it *does* exist, but I didn't know Clair knew about it. It was *our* place as little girls. I had it boarded up years ago after my sisters disappeared. I couldn't bear to go in there alone. How did Clair know? How did she get in?" Celeste walked toward the stairs near the kitchen door, Russell close behind. She tried the small, inconspicuous knob on the almost invisible door. It didn't budge. "Russell, it's still nailed shut. I'm really worried."

"Don't fret, Celeste, I'll check it out. That's what I do, after all, remember? Check things out. She is in shock. I've never seen her like this. I hate to think what will happen when Kelley finds out. *She* is the hysterical one. Shouldn't we be there when Clair tells her? If Clair reacted this badly, it might overwhelm Kelley."

"I think you're right, son. It's too much for either of them."

Thirty-Five
A Family Discovery

A silent, cold stairway greeted Clair, along with an occasional creak of the steps, and the faint sound of receding voices. Sheer, lace curtains billowed from a draft in the hallway and added to the ethereal atmosphere. In front of Kelley's room, awareness returned, and the smothering fog lifted. Knocked off center, the news rattled her. *I can only imagine Kelley's reaction.* White knuckled, she tapped the door.

****

Kelley stood in front of the mirror, a silver-handled brush in one hand. *Clair made a mysterious disappearance last night. Wonder where she went? I can't wait to tell her about Mr. Delacroix's offer.* Excitement heightened at a rap on the door. She raced to throw it open. "I'm so glad you're here. I have news." Both hands drew Clair into the room. Lost in exuberance, she disregarded the dark circles under Clair's sunken eyes and the trance-like movements.

"I have something I need to tell you," Clair's voice shook.

"Miss Matthews, where were you last night? I looked everywhere. I have to tell you what happened."

"Wait, I need to tell you something. Please listen." Clair pressed Kelley's hand.

"Sure, but me first."

The two women faced each other and blurted in unison. "We're going to Paris."

The room went silent. Wide-eyed, astonishment registered on their faces.

Both began again as the question tumbled out, "How did you know?"

Clair took her friend by the shoulders. "Did Aunt CeeCee tell you? Why didn't she let me?"

Kelley interrupted, "What do you mean did Aunt CeeCee tell me? How would she know about Cabot? I haven't told anyone—you're the first."

Clair shook her head. "What does Cabot have to do with this? Who is he, anyway? What are you talking about?"

"Your news doesn't have anything to do with the Professor?"

Clair breathed deep. "Sit down, this can't wait. It is life changing for both of us."

Alarm washed over her. "Hey girl, what is it? Here, sit down beside me."

The mattress springs squeaked beneath their weight.

"Kel, did you know Aunt CeeCee is the youngest of three sisters?"

"No, but she is your aunt, wonder why she never told you?"

"That's not all."

Startled, Kelley put an arm around her friend. "Okay, settle down. Obviously, you're upset."

Clair jerked away. "Linford Thurlow is CeeCee's uncle."

"Whoa, I'm lost. Who is Linford and what happened to the sisters?"

"Let me regroup," she began. "My mother, the oldest, and the middle sister fled their domineering uncles who wanted to force them back to France and take over the family business."

"Uncles, there was more than one?"

"Oh God yes, Lionel Thurlow, but thankfully, he is dead."

"Where are the sisters? I thought your parents died…Celeste raised you."

"Who knows if her sisters are alive or not? Frankly, I don't know what to believe anymore. She said something even more disturbing. They are after me, now."

The taste of fear left Kelley shaken. "You're scaring me. If you're in danger, we need to tell Russell."

"He already knows, and there's someone else involved. Spencer Walker is my bodyguard."

"What's going on? I thought Russell was our bodyguard. My head is spinning, this is a mess, explain."

"Last night, Aunt CeeCee asked to meet in the gazebo to talk. In the shadows, stood Spencer, the same mystery man at Adams Rib on Christmas Eve and at Stuckey's. He's been watching for years."

"Why, for gracious sakes?"

"Linford Thurlow is on the way to Seattle because I'm next in line. The sisters disappeared, and an agreement was made to groom me in Natasha's place."

"Natasha? That's your alter ego, silly."

"No, it's my real mother's name. One more thing…the middle sister's name is Julia."

"Clair—that's *my* mother's name. Are you saying this is not a coincidence?"

"Attending the same college was also by design. Our mothers planned it, and Celeste made the arrangements."

****

Clair stopped and waited for the full impact. *Kelley needs a little bit of solitude.* She walked to the window seat and sank onto the green, velveteen cushions. Down below, a tranquil scene unfolded. Spencer Walker, dressed in blue jogging shorts and a white tee shirt, stroked the shiny coat of a stray dog. *My guardian angel, in the body of an Adonis, how is it possible I never realized your eyes caught my every move? Christmas Eve, lost in the arms of a stranger, I never suspected you.*

He glanced up, and their eyes met.

Her heart flip-flopped, but she smiled and walked away. *The matters at hand are priority, sorting out my feelings for Spencer Walker will have to wait.*

Clair looked at Kelley and wondered if the connection was made.

"Natasha is your mother?" The color drained from Kelley's face. "And Julia...Julia is mine?"

"Yes, Kel, we're cousins."

Thirty-Six
The Canine Prophecy

Diamond droplets glistened on the grass and flowers from the light shower. Spencer's shoes squashed a rhythmic beat on the morning jog. After the events of the past twenty-four hours, he needed time to clear his mind, process the circumstances. *I knew this time would come.* "Oh, Clair."

Another jogger fell into the same tempo beside him.

"Hey man, out for a run, too? Glad to have the company."

A palomino-colored canine returned the glance.

"What a cool, leather collar. You live around here?"

English oaks, elms, and white poplar trees lined the side street to form a leafy canopy.

"I kinda need to bend your ear. Are you a good listener?" Spencer sidestepped to avoid a small puddle.

The collie glanced up in perfect stride.

"See, I've got girl trouble, buddy, and for once, I'm not sure how to proceed. You wouldn't believe this woman. She's exquisite—looks, class, and brains."

The twosome turned a corner side by side.

"Years ago, I took the job as her secret bodyguard. Can't quite tell you the day it happened, but I've loved her for years. She didn't know I existed until last night. Now, aware of my role in her life, I doubt she'll have anything to do with me." Beads of sweat dotted his forehead. "I made a mess of things because she saw my face."

The dog looked up again.

"Not smart, I know, but I had to protect her. Of course, she's distracted because a bomb sorta dropped last night, and a lifelong secret revealed. I guess...I'm the least of her problems."

Spencer slowed the pace, and the dog followed suit.

"This is my dilemma. I want to tell her I love her, but after the other shock, I'm not sure she's ready for more truth. So, good buddy, should I give her a little time or announce my personal intentions?"

The four-legged comrade panted and stopped. Spencer also halted, curious. The dog peered down a small side street and took off at a steady pace.

"What is it, partner?" They jogged in silence for a few minutes until Spencer froze in mid-stride. *The gazebo — this is the back of Celeste's property? I know there are several entrances and exits, but I never noticed this alleyway before.* He knelt down and stroked the soft coat of the friendly collie. "Is this close to your home?"

The animal let out a soft whine and continued to stare toward the window of the house. Slowly, Spencer followed the dog's gaze and gasped—Clair stood in the window of Kelley's room. *God, she is beautiful.* He took the dog's head in his hands. "Wow pal, how did you know? Are you a real dog or a figment of my imagination?"

The collie gave a sharp yap.

"What's your name?" Spencer searched the collar for an address tag. Stitched in red letters he saw the word *Destiny*. "Hey guy, I don't believe in coincidences. So is your advice not to give up? You're right. I'm going to Clair right now. Maybe there is a chance she will talk to me. I can't hold back any longer. It's time." Spencer glanced down to thank the dog, but it had disappeared.

Thirty-Seven
Kelley's Disbelief

Through the bedroom door, Celeste and Russell listened to Clair explain the situation to Kelley. The conversation went on for a few moments and then…a thud and a scream.

Russell burst through the door to find Clair kneeling beside an unconscious Kelley.

Celeste rushed in. "What happened? Is she okay?"

Russell crouched beside Clair who cradled Kelley's head in her lap.

"She fainted."

"Oh, the poor child," the older woman whispered. "I'll get a cold compress."

"Wait, I know what to do; Russell take over." Clair ran to the dresser and searched for a small decanter. She opened the glass jar and waved it under Kelley's nose. "I knew this would come in handy someday. She always carries these vials of aromatherapy concoctions, and this one is for a fainting bride."

Spencer bounded into the room as Kelley struggled to open her eyes. She screamed at the sight of him.

"Kelley, it's okay. Please stop," Clair soothed. "It's Spencer Walker—a friend, actually, a bodyguard. Let's get you off the floor, and I'll explain."

Russell lifted her limp body onto the bed. Celeste returned and applied a wet cloth to Kelley's forehead.

"Don't be frightened, it's just Spencer," Clair added.

"Maybe I should wait downstairs," he offered.

Russell nodded. "Let us get her calmed down, and then we'll all talk."

Kelley looked around the huge bedroom, dropped her head to one side, and began to weep.

"Why don't you two go with Spencer? Let me talk to her. Auntie, can you make a batch of your hot chocolate? I know I'd love some, and I bet Kelley will perk up after a sip of the magical brew."

"Yes, that's the ticket. Hot chocolate is always a good remedy," Celeste agreed.

"I'm staying right here, Clair. I know her as well as you, and I'm not leaving until I know she's okay," Russell insisted.

"Russell." Clair pointed to the door.

He lowered his head and followed Celeste into the hall.

Clair spoke softly, "Are you better, now?"

"I...I think so. What is happening, Clair? Are we really cousins? Why would Aunt CeeCee keep it from us? My head hurts. Who is this Spencer Walker, and why do we need guarding? I'm so confused and frightened. You spoke of sinister uncles and such. Is that why we need protection?"

"Shhh, you must be better, you're back to firing questions nonstop—a good sign." Clair laughed. "Let me explain Spencer to you." She told Kelley how the uncles hired Wade Walker to track Clair to insure she didn't disappear like her mother, and when he died the mantel passed to Spencer, his son.

"He looks so familiar, Clair. I know I've seen him before."

"Remember the man at Adams Rib that night? The one who asked me to dance? He broke the rules and made himself known to me. If the uncles found out, he would be fired. Does Stuckey's restaurant ring a bell? The man in the parking lot. It was him. Aunt CeeCee kept the information secret to allow us a normal life. Kelley, our normal life is over." Clair let out a long sigh.

"There's still so much I don't understand either. However, I do know our mothers are sisters, and Aunt CeeCee is the youngest. I know these uncles wanted an heir to their family perfume business, and they hired Spencer Walker to track us. Last night, I hid from everyone because I felt betrayed, abandoned, and alone. However, I'm not alone. I have you, and together we will sort this out. Now, I need you to get a grip and go downstairs. We'll figure out the rest and where we go from here. Can you do that?"

Kelley tried to sit up. "Whoa, I'm dizzy, hold on." She closed her eyes for a moment. "Yes, I can do this, Clair. I'm okay now." She stood, reached for her friend, and held on.

"Wait a minute, Clair, what did you mean about going to Paris?"

"We know your mother died in New Orleans, Kel, but nothing about what happened to my mother. I brooded over this last night and decided she might still be alive. That is why we are going to Paris, to find her. I think she's probably hiding right under his nose."

"Whose nose?"

"The remaining uncle, Linford Thurlow," Clair stated. "She's watching out for us, Kelley. I believe she knows how diabolical he is, and I'm going to find her. Are you with me?"

Thirty-Eight
A Hidden Door

Russell opened the door to the morning room. "Spence?"

A muffled voice whispered, "It's my fault." Cross-legged on the floor, Spencer lifted both hands from his face. "This mess is because of me. They are so devastated. How can they take it all in? Their lives are upside down. All this drama, intrigue, and possible danger to them…I can't protect them now."

Russell patted Spencer's shoulder. "Listen, this isn't your fault. It's the uncles. You've watched over the girls all these years, and you didn't know *I've* guarded them, too. Now we have to work together. I need your help." The detective instinct resurfaced, and curiosity niggled at his brain. "There's a secret room, and we need to find it."

Spencer looked at Russell. "Secret room? What are you talking about?"

"Last night, I looked everywhere for Clair. Her bed was empty. When I asked about it, she mentioned a secret room. Celeste came in, and interrupted. Clair went upstairs to tell Kelley, and I asked Celeste about the room. Obviously surprised, she hurried under the stairs and tried to open a door. It was still nailed shut. Spencer, there is another room even unknown to Celeste. We might uncover more answers to this mystery about the uncles. Will you help me?"

Spencer sprang to his feet. "Anything, where do we start?"

Scent of Double Deception

"The girls can't know we're skulking around. Kelley is a mess, and I'm worried about Clair, too. She never loses focus. I don't want to cause any undo alarm, so we must be sly, and start in Clair's room."

"You're addled, man. If she found out, she would go ballistic."

"I know—I need you as the lookout. If we can get the girls downstairs, we'd have time to snoop around."

A creak from the hallway made the two men jump.

"It's them." Russell held a finger to his lips. Spencer nodded and moved out of sight. After they passed, Russell showed him the transmitter device and explained the girls' bracelets to monitor their movement.

"Wow, you think of everything."

"Here, take it, and let me know if they come toward the stairs." Russell pointed. "Go."

"Now? But…"

"Now." He pushed Spencer forward. They tiptoed up the stairs.

"You look around in here, I'll take the closet," Russell instructed.

Spencer examined the paneling, the flowered wallpaper, and the paintings. "Maybe there is a hidden door.

"Good idea." Russell entered the walk-in closet. Boxes of Clair's childhood memorabilia stood in neat stacks, labeled, and sealed. A quick check of the ceiling revealed no attic door. One box sat askew, different from the rest, scooted away from the wall. "Bingo."

On closer investigation, a crack in the floor led to a door. It opened with one tug. After his eyes adjusted to the darkness, a downward spiraling staircase came into view. "Spencer, come quick," Russell called softly.

In a split second, Spencer's large frame filled the closet.

"Close the door and follow," Russell said. He pulled out a penlight, and the two descended the steep, narrow stairs into the murky darkness. At the bottom, they found a wall. Russell ran his hands over the surface, detected a small trigger latch, and tripped it. The penlight did little in the dimness of the small, airless room.

"Check the walls for a light switch," Spencer said.

"Hey, I think...damn." A loud crash accompanied Russell's expletive. He flipped the switch, and the room transformed in a soft light. A toppled, antique table proved the source of the noise. "Crap, will you look at this, Spencer?"

"It's beautiful."

An old-fashioned, chaise lounge, covered in white satin material, languished in the corner. A contemporary lamp beside the chair didn't fit the rest of the room, obviously a new addition. Old bookcases lined two walls, full of books. An overstuffed armchair, and matching footstool, adorned the center of the room. Plump, colorful pillows completed the cozy retreat.

"Is this what they call antique French design?"

"Man, I'm no interior decorator," Russell replied.

"Well, I've followed Clair long enough to know it's definitely not her style." Spencer shook his head.

A small table nestled next to the chaise held an open journal; a pen rested across the page.

"What's this? Looks like a private diary, Russell."

Scent of Double Deception

Numerous pictures placed around the room, and on the wall, caught Russell's attention. "Hey, these must be Clair's mother. She looks just like her."

"Look at the bride in this wedding picture next to the journal. There is something sticking out." Spencer opened the back of the frame.

"It's a woman and a baby—gotta be Clair and her mother. Look how worn it is. Someone handled this many times."

Russell took the photograph, and a sudden sadness came over him. "She grieved for her mother for a long time." He replaced the picture in the frame. "Where's the other door, Spence. It's here somewhere."

They scanned the walls.

Russell grabbed the shelf. "Behind the bookcase, help me move it out."

"Just like you said—nailed shut."

"Yep, obvious Celeste has no idea of the alternative opening. Wonder how Clair found it?"

"Probably by accident, Russ. Maybe she played in the closet as a kid."

"So, we know Clair came here last night—mystery solved. The girls are still in the kitchen according to your tracker. Let's go, I feel like an intruder."

"Wait, I want to see the journal," Russell replied.

"What? You can't read that. It's Clair's private diary," Spencer sounded alarmed.

"Listen, think about it. You watched Clair probably longer than I've even known her. It isn't normal for her to space out like this. She stayed down here all night. Don't *you* want to know her thoughts and plans? We can't protect her, otherwise. The spooky uncle worries me; after all, he hired a bodyguard—you."

Scent of Double Deception

Thirty-Nine
The Journal

Russell sank down in the armchair, picked up the journal, and began to read:

"Mother...Mother, I wish I remembered you. I have talked to you all my life, but somehow, it never seemed enough. Aunt CeeCee is a guardian angel, and I love her dearly, but now, they tell me you ran away, you left me. I am not mad, just so sad. I came down here to our secret room to talk to you.

"I remember the day I found out about this room. Rain pelted the windowpanes, and the day stretched in front of me, bleak and lonely. I was nine. Aunt CeeCee busied herself in the kitchen, baking. She wanted me to help, but it was not my idea of excitement. I thumbed through the books in the library, chose one, and retreated to my room to read. After I plumped my pillows, and settled in my little nest, I studied the book. I had passed it by many times, thought it looked complicated, more for an older girl. Somehow, today, it caught my interest.

"*Lost in Paris*, by Francine Antoine. I flipped it open and read the inside flap. 'My dearest daughter, Clair, you won't understand why I left you all these years, and so I'll try to explain.'

"You went on to say, you were in danger and left me in the care of Aunt Celeste, but you never identified the danger; only it was for my own good. You said you would come back someday if you could, but never did. When I questioned Aunt CeeCee, she said you died."

Russell turned to Spencer. "Wow, this must have been a shock for Clair."

"It's incredible. We shouldn't do this, but sounds like there might be some clues here. Keep reading."

"I cried for a while. The message from you shocked me to the core. You touched this book, read it, penned the message, and somehow, it brought me close to you. I thumbed through the pages and found a map in the back of the book. Your father built the room for you, a special room, a secret room for his oldest daughter. I came down here often to be near you – in our secret place."

"She knew the room existed since childhood. How in the world did she keep it from Aunt CeeCee? Her heart must have broken, not to know her mother." Russell shook his head.

"I'm here now because I need you. I have learned the truth about the danger, and I'm frightened, Mother. I don't know what to do. I think there is something you want me to know, but were afraid to speak about in the book. What is it, Mother? Please give me a sign, anything to point me in the right direction. I have to tell Kelley, and I don't know how. What should I do?"

Russell noticed Spencer staring at her picture. "Damn man, she's devastated. The pain is palpable."

Spencer's gaze drifted to Russell. "I know, I feel it, too."

Russell continued to read:

"Mother, why is my life so upside down? How can I pick up and go on? I am so confused. What were you trying to tell me? Why didn't you say it in the book, Lost in Paris? *Why did you choose that book? You knew it would be years before I found it. Wait! Is it the book? The uncles are from Paris. Is that the clue?"*

Russell stopped. "That's it...the last entry. Do you see a book around here, *Lost in Paris*?"

Spencer's brow furrowed at the picture of Clair's mother. "I know this woman, Russell. Yes, she is younger here, but I've seen her before. A book, *Lost in Paris?* No, I've not seen it."

They searched the room, but to no avail.

"So, tell me about the picture. You say you know her?" Russell turned over the last pillow.

"The picture of Clair's mother, the way she is posed. I don't know, she looks familiar."

The light of Russell's transmitter indicated the girls were on the move.

"We need to get out of here before we are caught, Russ."

The men headed for the door, and Spencer doused the light. The transmitter beeped as they bounded upstairs, two steps at a time.

"Hey, the girls went in a different direction," Spencer whispered. "Looks like the attic."

They left Clair's room and continued outside. Spencer motioned toward the gazebo. "What do you make of this, Russell? It's a whole new side of Clair."

"You're so right, Spence. This journal worries me. The side *I* know is up to something. We gotta find the Paris book."

****

Kelley agreed they must act together. The aroma of cocoa wafted up the stairs. "Something smells so good. Let's go to the kitchen."

Two steaming cups of cocoa waited on the table.

Celeste ordered them to sit. "Are you girls okay?"

"I think we'll be all right, Auntie. How about you, Kelley?"

"I'll be fine, Clair...as soon as I get some of this wonderful elixir into me."

Kelley sipped at the hot liquid and reveled in the warmth flooding her cheeks. Celeste cleared her throat. "Girls, there's more—even Clair doesn't know, yet. I want to share it with you both. Sweetheart, do you feel well enough that you could stand?"

"I think so, Aunt CeeCee," Kelley replied.

"Good, because my dear darlings, I need to finish telling you this story." She let out a long sigh. "First, we must climb the stairs to the attic." Celeste led the two women up the creaky staircase to the top floor of the grand old house.

Forty
The Old Trunk

A kaleidoscope of colors graced the old attic as the morning sun reflected through the circle-top window. Surrounded once more by treasures carefully stored away, Celeste felt a certain comfort, like visiting old friends.

Kelley and Clair entered the small garret, and their eyes displayed child-like wonder.

Clair immediately went to a faded rocking horse. She ran a fingertip over the wooden relic. "Aunt CeeCee, this is Tasha."

Celeste smiled wearily and found her way to an old wicker chair. "I know, my dear. You're beginning to understand, aren't you?"

"I don't understand *anything*," Clair stated. "Kelley, I have to tell you about this horse."

"Please girls, come over here," Celeste beckoned.

They settled on a braided rug near her feet.

Celeste unclasped a chain from around her neck to reveal a small golden key and unlocked an old trunk. "Before I begin, the reason behind all the secrecy was because you are loved so much." An arthritic hand lifted the lid and retrieved a photo of three young girls, and the rest of the truth. "You girls are not only sisters, but twins—your mother is Natasha."

"What do you mean *twins*? Last night, you said our mothers were sisters which makes us cousins." Clair stood arms akimbo.

Celeste shook her head. "No my dear, you assumed you were cousins."

"Outrageous, I'm dark-haired, and *she* is blonde." Clair pointed.

Kelley grabbed Celeste's arm. "This is too much, I'm confused."

"The answer is simple; you and Clair are fraternal twins, not identical. Clair was born first, and you, twenty-three minutes later. Ironically, you were born on the *next* day. I remember how you marveled at having such close birthdays," Celeste continued. "Through that 'twin spirit', you fought to reunite the bond God gave from birth."

"Clair, the day you came home for spring break with Kelley almost sent me to an early grave. The moment I saw her, I knew who she was. My heart sang like a meadowlark to think I could possibly have *both* my nieces once again." Tears trickled down her cheeks.

"At first, I didn't understand why Natasha and Julia fled in the middle of the night. In time, I realized it was for your safety. Natasha took Clair, and your 'Aunt Julia' took you, Kelley. It must have been devastating to separate you...our precious twins."

One hand on her chest, Kelley raised the other in protest. "So, you mean my mother was really my aunt? How could she lie to me all those years about something so important?"

"Sweetheart, please believe me when I say, the uncles would have stopped at nothing to complete their plan. Natasha sent me word to come to a nunnery in Louisiana. Of course, I expected to find all three of you. However, a letter she left, in the confidence of the nuns, explained everything—except where Natasha had gone. I learned Julia took Kelley, but I never knew where. I was so overjoyed to at least have one of you." Celeste dabbed tears with a small, lace handkerchief. "I trusted the good Lord to keep my sisters and my niece safe."

"Mother told me my father, or I guess I should say *uncle*, died in the military. Another lie, Aunt CeeCee?" Kelley's voice rose.

"I'm afraid I have no answers regarding him, my darling. He disappeared without any details." Celeste placed a hand on Kelley's shoulder.

"None of this makes sense because it's not the truth." Kelley pushed away. Before Clair or Celeste could respond, she spouted, "My mother's name was not Julia...it was *Jewell*."

"Please, please Kelley, as hard as this is to believe, I think I can fill in most of the gaps," Celeste pleaded. "I had totally given up until the spring break visit. You have so many of Julia's mannerisms; it just couldn't have been a coincidence. I called Wade Walker for help because through common conversation you gave me a starting point."

"What? How is that possible?" Clair turned to Kelley.

"She mentioned her hometown was New Orleans. What tipped me off was the description of their apartment in the French Quarter above the shop where her mother sold potions and curios. Through Wade's investigation, he discovered Julia employed an elderly woman to tend you and keep the books. I believe her name was Belle Chevalier, correct?"

Kelley stared at Celeste. "Aunt Belle?"

"Ms. Chevalier was kin to your real father and more than happy to provide a safe haven. At that time, Julia changed her name to Jewell." Pausing briefly, Celeste began again, "A bond formed after the realization your mothers were both dead. Am I right?"

Kelley nodded.

"Didn't you ever wonder how a woman who earned a very modest living could afford so many of the luxuries you had, much less college tuition?"

"But I had a scholarship to SMU," Kelley replied.

"True my dear, but from the day Natasha left you in her sister's care, she sent money to help. She knew where you were, and she knew where Clair was...always."

Clair spoke up, "You learned all this from Mr. Walker?"

"Yes, I suppose I might have been a bit cynical at first, but I trusted Wade with your secrets, so I trusted him with Kelley's, too. When his health forced him to retire, he passed this assignment on to the corporate partner, his son. Spencer Walker came into your life on a full time basis, Clair. Because of the relationship you two shared, it made it easier for him—and me." Celeste breathed a long sigh.

"This is hard to believe, Aunt CeeCee," Kelley whispered. "It's as though I'm caught in the middle of a dream and haven't woke up yet."

"I understand, but you do have to admit the closeness you've always shared is uncanny, as well as the parallels in your lives. I am sure you have many friends, but none as close as each other. Am I right? Now, you can understand why."

Clair dropped to her knees beside Kelley. They hugged and cried.

Scent of Double Deception

"You're experiencing a lot of pain, as well as joy, but the story doesn't actually have a happy ending." Celeste showed the girls a photo of the uncles. Next, she presented the framed certificate written in French. "I need to show you one last thing." Trembling hands reached for the old, gift box with the bedraggled bow. Inside was the other original glass bottle with the name *Tasha* etched on it. "This was made for Natasha to be passed on to you...Clair."

Forty-One

The Next Adventure

Celeste stared at the dusk-painted Seattle sky, a fusion of peach and blue. Vivid conversation and laughter from the parlor lifted her visage, belied her years. *Such a blessing, their light-heartedness appears to camouflage all the unpleasant concerns.* She blinked back a tear, picked up a silver tray, and left the kitchen.

"Here, let me help you," Spencer offered.

"Thank you. Please, sit it next to the small plates on the coffee table."

Russell slapped his hands together. "Boy, those look scrumptious."

"Help yourself, everyone," Celeste urged. "There are apple tarts, French meringues, and…"

"And slices of Black Forest cake. I bet I gained ten pounds in the last few days, Aunt CeeCee." Russell scooped up the goodies.

"Got any more java?" Spencer lifted the cup.

"Yes dear, there's a fresh brew in the carafe," Celeste replied.

"Will you pour me one?" Clair handed a cup to Spencer.

"Glad to." He smiled. "Black, right?"

"You should know." Clair wrapped her hands around the warm mug. "Hey Kelley, tell us about Cabot Delecroix, or would you rather we talk in private?"

"Oh, I'd love to explain our little tryst. I can't believe his proposal." Kelley flashed a wide grin.

Scent of Double Deception

"Proposal? Hold on girl, you barely know the man. Did you let his personality and panache confuse you? Remember, romance not rebound," Clair scolded.

Kelley placed an apple tart on a plate. "Romance? You're way off base this time."

Celeste settled on the couch next to Russell. *Ah yes, Cabot Delecroix. I hope Clair embraces Kelley's excitement.*

"The distinguished professor purchased a new art gallery last month. To draw renowned critics, he wants a grand opening, something outlandish." Kelley refolded the napkin. "There is a young lady he mentors, a protégé. He offered financial assistance if she would showcase her unique artistic genre."

Celeste watched an intent expression on Clair's face.

"The guest list isn't limited to the French. Statesmen, lords and ladies, governors, congressmen, even some of Hollywood's most elite, complete the register." Kelley pointed to Celeste. "Thanks to our Aunt CeeCee, Cabot requested Memory Makers for the task."

Clair gasped. "This sounds like a golden opportunity."

"Of course, it would mean…" Kelley faced her business partner.

Clair's eyes widened, and together they shouted, "We're going to Paris!"

****

Spencer pulled the heavy, front door shut, careful not to make any noise, and peered through the etched glass. The occupants inside continued their animated discussion, unaware he had left. *Goodbye my darling. I'm sorry.* Hungry eyes rested on Clair's face. Shoulders bowed, he followed the path around the house. A tight grip dug the car keys deep into his palm. A sense of loss shrouded his thoughts, jagged and painful. *Dear God, all these years I worked for unethical, manipulative people. This stupid debacle defines the whole journey of Clair's life. The night in the gazebo, resentment and disbelief burned in her eyes. Any glint of hope she would recognize my personal intentions, my deep love for her, dissolved. Well, I mailed Highgrove my resignation today. Despite Clair's impression of me, I will right all the wrongs.*

****

The repetitive page for Dr. Franklin echoed amid the shuffle and clamor of hospital traffic.

"Honey, don't doze off. I still need another blood sample," the plump nurse warned and waddled away.

Joe Paul shot her an impatient frown. His physician emphasized the need for rest, yet every time he closed his eyes, someone barged in to take vitals or puncture an arm for more blood. He tried to run a hand through his hair and not disturb the spider web of medical paraphernalia connected to an IV. *This is ridiculous; I have a ranch to run.* A light knock on the door invaded his complaints. "Come in."

"Uh-huh," a sweet voice replied. "Look Troy, Joe Paul is a lounge lizard these days." Isabella shook a finger at her friend.

"Point your finger all you want. I'm thrilled it isn't wrapped around a hypodermic needle." He grinned.

The young newlyweds laughed.

"Hey man, how do you feel? I've put everyone on notice to give you the best of care," Troy said. "I even requested the prime nurses."

"So, *you* assigned the big army nurse to hover in my room, huh?" Joe Paul teased.

"Gosh, I know the one you mean," Troy added. "I'm a little scared of her myself."

Joe Paul's attempt to laugh ended in a wince of pain.

"Bless your heart. I'm so grateful though you're better." Isabella leaned over and kissed his forehead. "Can we do anything for you? What about the ranch? Are you hungry?"

"Troy, settle your bride down. She sounds like an old mother hen. I'm fine. Anyway, I needed a chance to relax."

Troy wrapped an arm around Isabella's shoulder. "I told her you're tough."

"Stop you two, he's lucky to be alive," Isabella scolded.

Joe Paul shook his head. "I'm too mean to die. Let's change the subject—why aren't you on your honeymoon?"

"We postponed the trip. After you're released, and back at the ranch, we'll go, not a minute before," the new bride huffed.

"See how hard-headed she is Troy? It's better to give in and let this woman have her way. Make life easy on yourself."

"Thanks for the advice, I see your point." Troy grinned at his wife.

The phone rang, and Isabella said, "Don't dare strain, I'll get it." The corners of her mouth turned up in a smile. "Yes, yes of course." She handed the receiver to Joe Paul.

"Who is it?"

"I believe an admirer," Isabella replied. "You might want to take this call."

Scent of Double Deception

He pressed the dial and adjusted the bed to an upright position. *Oh my God, Olivia? How...would she know to call the hospital?* He sighed and dismissed the idea. "Hello?" Eyes closed, a large smile spread across his face. "It's Emma," he whispered. The conversation ended, and Joe Paul replied, "Do you know how long I've waited to hear from my little girl?"

"What a grand surprise." Isabella beamed.

Joe Paul rubbed a hand across his jaw. "She read about your wedding ordeal. It made international news. The article mentioned a close family member injured, and she feared the worse. You won't believe what she told me."

"Don't make us beg. What?" Isabella touched his arm.

"She said its time for us to have a ... a real relationship."

Tears filled Isabella's eyes. "Oh my goodness, how wonderful, what are your plans?"

"Well, as soon as I get out of this *jail*, I'm going for a visit. She wants me to see her newest art work."

"Oh, I think it's a grand idea. Where does she live?" Isabella asked.

"Paris!" he answered.

Made in the USA
Charleston, SC
16 March 2012